SPIDERTOUCH

Alex Thomson

**ANGRY
ROBOT**

ANGRY ROBOT
An imprint of Watkins Media Ltd

Unit 11, Shepperton House
89 Shepperton Road
London N1 3DF
UK

angryrobotbooks.com
twitter.com/angryrobotbooks
The lightest touch leaves the darkest mark

An Angry Robot paperback original, 2021

Cover and map by Kieryn Tyler
Edited by Gemma Creffield and Andrew Hook
Set in Meridien

ISBN 978 0 85766 960 5
Ebook ISBN 978 0 85766 961 2

Printed and bound in the United Kingdom by TJ Books Ltd.

9 8 7 6 5 4 3 2 1

MIX
Paper from
responsible sources
FSC® C013056

For Isaac and Seth

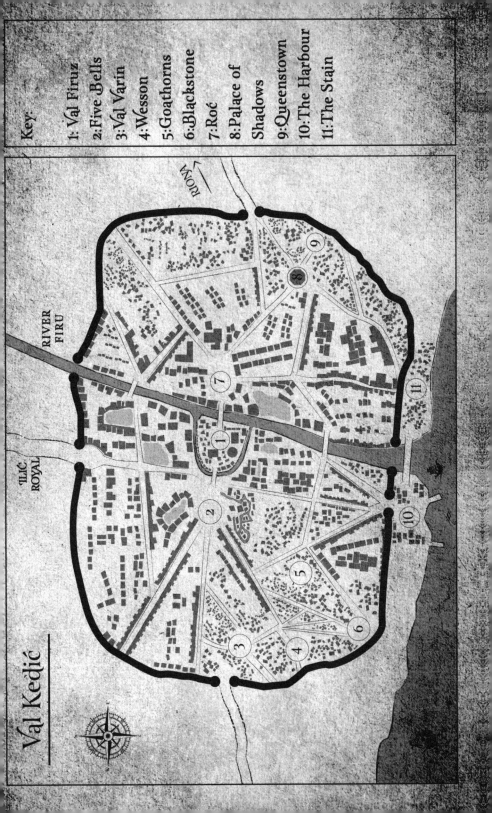

Val Kedić

RIONA

RIVER
FIRU

TLIĆ
ROYAL

Key:

1: Val Firuz
2: Five Bells
3: Val Varin
4: Wesson
5: Goathorns
6: Blackstone
7: Roć
8: Palace of
   Shadows
9: Queenstown
10: The Harbour
11: The Stain

1.

The touch for /Donkey/ is infuriatingly close to the touch for /Mother/ in fingerspeak.

For /Donkey/, the forefinger and thumb squeeze the middle band, and then the little finger taps the lower band twice, whereas /Mother/ uses the middle finger.

This is just a small example of why whoever came up with this bastard language should be thrown from Traitors' Rock into the Southern Sea.

Unlike the handful of other known languages, fingerspeak also has no permanence. You can repeat a foreign word in your head, and then mull it over until you can winkle out its meaning, but you can't repeat someone's touch to yourself, or replicate a sensation. If you had to dream up the most inconvenient language for us to learn, you would be hard pressed to improve on fingerspeak.

Which is bugger all use complaining about in my current position. I say 'current' as though it's a choice, like I'm weighing up a range of exciting career opportunities. The truth is that the elders will never let me leave; there's too few of us who can interpret fingerspeak. That fact used to make me think I was a cut above the other kids from the quarter – you could see their limited lives mapped out for them in the wrinkles of their fathers' leathery skin – but who turned out to be the fool in the end?

I stand in the High Chamber and wait my turn, watching the councillors in conversation. They all wear hooded cowls and their crimson robes denote the highest rank of the Keda. They are in pairs, each with their right hand on the other's bare left arm, fingers dancing between the three silver bands worn there.

There is one advantage of fingerspeak: it's virtually impossible for anyone to eavesdrop on your conversation. Even now, ten paces away – I'm not stupid or vulgar enough to stare at the Keda – I can see Double's fingers moving, but I don't have a clue what xe might be saying.

For over a century the Keda have ruled Val Kedić, and yet there's still so much we don't know about them. The language barrier keeps us apart, with us translating to maintain a purely functional relationship. The majority of Keda, in their blue robes, have next to no contact with citizens; it's only the councillors and Justices who matter. And the less we know of them, the greater power they have over us. Gender, for example, is a closed book. Someone introduced the pronoun "xe" to describe them a century ago, and there's been no advance ever since. Their mouths are another example: hidden by their cowls, but thanks to servants' gossip, we know they do have them – twisted and grotesque, but mouths for eating, all the same. Just not speaking.

There's only a handful of the Council I know by name – Double, because xe's the main contact for my quarter. Xe is the one who summons me to pass on instructions and information. Xer name is, by its nature, untranslatable to our tongue – being a mixture of taps and squeezes and no spoken words – but I know xer as Double because it's a repeated sequence of taps.

Then there's Giant, who I've never fingerspoken with, but xe is unusually tall for the Keda. Xe is the same height as me so xe always stands out.

The most senior member of the Council, though – they have no leader, but it is clear that xe is the top dog among them – is known to us as Eleven, because of the complicated series of eleven taps that make up xer name. At a rough guess, it means something like "xe-who-lives-by-the-eastern-something-something-tranquil-grove". But who knows. The taps all blur into one.

Then there's Chicken. Now xe, I can't stand. I mean, obviously, I hate all the Keda – they stole my son, they squeeze us dry, they've sucked the life out of our city. They are our captors. But Chicken? Xe is a real pain in the arse.

It pleases us to call xer Chicken because xer given name is not far away from the touch for /Chicken/. It also reduces xer somehow, takes away some of xer power over us. But no matter what we call xer, I can't forget the way xe looks at me.

You don't see much of a Keda beyond the bare left arm – their cowls cover most of their heads, so you can only see their flat noses and threatening eyes in the gloom of the hood. But I'll never forget that one time when we were fingerspeaking, I had to ask xer about the quotas due from our quarter. I essayed a phrase, something like:

(Question) / Number / Barrel /.

It was a simple squeeze and trill of the fingers. But the look of disgust xe gave at my clumsy accent took my breath away. The contempt blazing from xer flared nostrils and eyes felt like hard chips of marble cutting my skin. I wanted to scream at xer, "Don't blame me for not being touch-perfect in your stupid language!"

Needless to say, I sucked it up, received xer answer, and bowed before withdrawing.

Anyway. What I'm trying to say is, there are Keda and there are *Keda*. Most are anonymous; you see their robes, their piggy little eyes, you hear the occasional snuffly exhalations they make to express shock, pleasure or humour. While they're all scum, the ones I can't stand are those like Chicken, who treat us with open contempt.

I catch Ira's eye. She's standing by a column twenty paces away, waiting, as I am, for the Keda to summon her services. I raise my eyebrows a fraction, trying to convey "how boring is this?" But she studiously ignores me.

I used to do that with Borzu all the time, trying to read each other's minds and having a whole conversation with eyebrow twitches, side-eyes and grimaces. Afterwards, we'd compare notes, see how much of each other's part of the conversation we had understood. Very little, was the usual answer. But Borzu... well, it doesn't do to dwell too much on what happened to him. He is a salutary lesson as to why the best thing to do is keep your head down among the Keda and be as dull and obedient as possible, as Ira has clearly set out to be.

Astonishingly, some people act like it's a cushy number being an interpreter for the Keda. Some resent the occasional perks given to us: our interpreter's residence, and the fact that we skipped our seven-year service in Riona. It was only so that we could learn fingerspeak. But people ignore those years of study and the fact we're now on the front line, dealing with the Keda and their banal whims every day. Trained monkeys that appear at the snap of a finger. Our lives are not our own, not in the way most citizens can say, and I sometimes wonder why anyone would choose this path on purpose.

As if on cue, Double inclines xer head towards me and beckons with xer forefinger. Xe stands a foot shorter than me, but xe stands imperiously as if towering above me. I approach, bow, and xe places xer long, cadaverous fingers on my left arm. Like all the Keda, xer right-hand nails curve round like vicious scimitars, the better for fingerspeaking. Although I've been doing this a while, I can't help but swallow a grimace when I feel the nails' prickly caress on my skin.

In preparation, the rest of my body zones out and my whole attention focuses on the three bands that enclose my arm. Murky bronze, of course, unlike the delicately engraved silver ones that the Keda earn the right to wear on their thirteenth birthdays. It pays to keep ours unpolished – these small status signifiers mean a lot to the Keda, especially anything to do with fingerspeak.

I close my eyes and shut out the distant whisper of the sea, and the buzz of Val Kedić outside. I switch off everything that I don't need right now, and I feel.

Visitor / (Future) / Day /, Double says without preamble, *From / (Unclear) /*.

It's some distant land; I don't know the touch and don't need to know.

Pulse / Fish / Vegetable / Nut / Date / – xe breaks off to make a gesture with xer left hand, like "etcetera, you get the idea".

(Positive) /, I say. *Prepare / Many / Good / Food / Council /*.

Double does not react. There is no word for "thankyou" in their language. Or perhaps there is, and we've just never heard it. Then xe frowns, and grasps my upper band: *(Past) / Fish / Small / (Disgust) / Many / Bone / (Question) / Reason /*.

I ache to make a sarcastic retort, to say, "A million apologies, Excellency, our lazy fishermen must have guzzled all the plump mackerel themselves, I'll have them whipped." But I stifle my irritation and take xer bare arm to respond. It tenses, like it always does.

(Regret) / Councillor /, I say, *(Negative) / Many / Fish / Now / (Question) / More / Vegetable /*.

Double listens to me, then replies with a curt series of touches.

More / Fish /. Then, as an afterthought, xe spreads xer fingers and taps, *Girl / Send / Many / Girl /*.

It was my old teacher I have to blame. Myriam, I think her name was. I adored her, and her classroom. It was down by the beach, next to the wharf where most of us lived, where our fathers fished. The rest of Val Kedić called our quarter The Stain – a fetid blot that festered outside the city walls – but we didn't care. The shacks sprouted from each other like a fungal growth, staggering off in all directions, creating twisted alleys, and eaves that jabbed into other buildings. A reek of fish clung to the walls and our clothes. It was a dirty slum, but it was *our* dirty slum, and most of us stayed happy there, insulated from the rest of the world.

We knew little of what was going on in the city proper, still less of the Keda who rarely troubled to come out to such a distant fringe of Val Kedić. Occasionally, you might see a green-robed Justice striding down the alleys, but we were warned to keep clear of them, and they were the bogeymen in our bedtime stories.

By the time I was seven, I was helping my father unload his fish in the market each morning, and in the afternoon I would go down to the school by the beach. There we learned our numbers and letters, and, if the heat was tolerable, Myriam would take us outside to the famous black sands, and we would practise counting with shells and pebbles.

I found it all easy – couldn't understand the trouble numbers and letters caused the others – and I soon found Myriam was taking a special interest in me. At first, I noticed the lessons were increasingly directed towards me as the sole audience, while the others were allowed to play and bicker. Then, around the time of my eighth birthday, I took the first steps towards becoming an interpreter.

Myriam had sent the other children home, and sat down by me, unrolling a piece of parchment. She spread it across the table, displaying two lists of words in scratchy calligraphy.

"What's this?" I asked her.

"This is a different language," she said. "It might look funny, but just think of it as a secret code."

"Like the one they use in the market?" I said, thinking of the argot they all used to describe fish and customers – gillies for sunfish, stump for the massive lobsters that were considered a Val Kedić delicacy, dryden for outsiders who were ripe to be exploited, and so on.

"Exactly," she said. "I want you to take a look at the code, and see if you can learn it."

So I sat there, greedily drinking it up. I started to understand that I was good at this, and that not everyone could do it. Sometimes I asked her about a word from the list, checking how it sounded, but mostly I absorbed it alone. Years later, I realised she'd given me a glossary of Gerami, a creole from Mura – our nearest neighbours over the Southern Sea and a major trading partner. At the time, all I saw was the magic of language, and the realisation that the concept of bread was no longer just "bread" but had doubled in size to both "bread" and "deenah".

I learned it as best I could, allotting two names to every one of the concepts. Then she quizzed me: *"Three lemons?"* she would say in Gerami, and I, with the parchment in front of me, would have a go at understanding the message, and coming up with a suitable response. I loved it. It was a game, a good one, and my brain started creaking into life after years of fiddling around with numbers and letters.

We did that for a while, gradually getting harder, Myriam taking away the parchment, and giving me more complex constructions to decipher. I found it a challenge, and struggled to remember everything, but she didn't seem to mind.

Then, one afternoon, she took me to the beach, and told me to sit on a boulder. "There's someone who wants to meet you," she said. "He'd like to have a chat with you about what you've learned. Could you do that for me, Razvan?"

I nodded, a wary eye on the man who had emerged from behind the limestone steps that led up to the wharf. He was small, Mecunio, clean-shaven back then, a young man but already wearing the black sash of the city elders. He approached me with a bland smile on his lips, and Myriam turned away, leaving us to go back to her classroom.

"Your teacher's told me all about you, Razvan," he said in a deep, raspy voice that didn't sound right for such a small man. "She says you're a bright boy. That right?"

I didn't know what to say, so stayed silent.

"Show me," he said. "Show me what you can do." Then, in rough Gerami, *"Where do you live?"*

I recognised the words, and pointed towards the slum beyond the wharf. "The Stain," I said.

"Describe it for me. In the words you learned."

"*Small house*," I said in Gerami, "*near… fish shop*."

It was a long way from perfect, but he seemed impressed. We did a few more exercises like that, with him probing to see the extent of my knowledge, trying to trick me with some words that could easily be confused. Then he took out a baat pipe, tapped the stem, and lit it. It was an odd habit for someone his age, but I was to learn he had always been a septuagenarian, trapped in a younger man's body.

"Have you ever thought, Razvan," he said, "that languages don't just have to use sound?"

I didn't answer, so he went on. "What's that smell?" he asked, sniffing.

"The sea."

"The sea. Right. But go a hundred paces to the east, and you'll receive a different message to your nose – the stink of The Stain. The fish market."

"I suppose."

"Same with taste. I could blindfold you, give you a variety of foods, and each one would be sending you a different message. You'd be able to work out what food I was giving you, even though you couldn't see it. And touch is no different. Close your eyes."

I shut them, and he grabbed my hand and shook it twice. "What message is that?"

"What?"

"What am I saying to you with this touch, this movement? Translate it for me, just like you did with the words."

"Pleased to meet you?"

"Good. What about this?" He delivered a stinging slap to the back of my head, and I opened my eyes, and glared at him.

"Ow!"

"Translate." He raised his hand, palm open.

"I'm cross with you?"

"Right. But what if we could make it more complex than that, base the whole language on touch alone...?"

And that was how it began. Mecunio came to my father's stall with me that afternoon, and I sat by the fountain while the two of them had a long conversation in the shade of the tattered awning. At one point, my father turned to look at me, as if seeing me for the first time. Finally, they shook hands and Mecunio walked out of The Stain without another glance at me. When it was time to pack away, the two of us worked side by side, lifting the wicker baskets and putting the leftover stock in crushed ice.

"So," he said, "the man says you're clever. Says you could learn another language."

"The touch language?"

"That's it. Spidertouch, they call it. The one the Crawlers use." Nobody would risk calling the Keda "Crawlers" in public, but the market was nearly deserted, and we knew everyone who was in hearing distance.

We'd never talked about the Keda – I'd never heard of fingerspeak before Mecunio mentioned it – but I was beginning to realise my father knew more than he let on.

"Not sure I like the idea of you mixing with Crawlers," he said. "But it's a way out of your service in the mines. A way out of The Stain. What do you think?"

I had the arrogance of youth, the belief that I was destined for better things. "I like it," I said. "I could do it."

"You're sure you want to do this?"

I nodded. I wish now I could remember his face, but all I can see are his clothes, frayed at the edges and covered in oily streaks.

I didn't see Mecunio again for a few years. But a fingerspeak interpreter came to see me once a week, an old woman with knotted grey hair and a white armband on her right arm, and she began my training. Most families had to pay for private lessons like this, but I later learned that Mecunio had arranged it all – he took an interest in finding new interpreters.

The woman gave me three copper bands and we started by learning the different positions and signals – the taps, the squeezes, the finger trills. She didn't say a lot – she wasn't the mothering type, and we didn't have much else to talk about – but she was a good teacher. We would sit on the rocks, facing each other, holding each other's left arm. She loved the sun, and when we took breaks she would unravel her shawl and munch on dates, while I retreated to the shade. Once I had learned the positions and signals, she began teaching me the touches, and it started to get difficult. When I disappointed her or was too slow, she would show her displeasure with a tsk or a rap with a birch cane that she carried.

When I turned eleven, I left the black sands and The Stain for good. They moved me to a compound in the centre of Val Kedić to become an apprentice in the guild of interpreters. There were nearly thirty of us there, ages ranging from eleven to eighteen, and they expected more than half of us to fail.

On my first day, I realised how massive the city was. I saw Keda strolling up the broad avenues, and the alchemical plumes of silver smoke that hung high in the air. I met Borzu and all the other savvy apprentices, and for the first time I was ashamed of The Stain. I can draw a clear line between my life before that day and my life after.

My father left the city a year later. The Stain never really forgave him, I think, for keeping his son from the mines, for avoiding what they had all endured. The guilt became too much, and they say he sailed across the Southern Sea. I never saw him again.

I walk back from the High Chamber with Ira, along Victory Avenue, lined with palm trees. Until we reach the Bridge of Peace, we are on proper Keda territory – Val Firuz is an island-citadel at the heart of Val Kedić, and the only place in the city where they outnumber us. Some elders and high-ranking citizens are permitted to live here, but I'm not sure why you would want to. Ordinary, blue-robed Keda are all around us, though it's noticeable that they veer away from us as we cross paths, as though a bubble surrounds us.

"They seemed jumpy today," says Ira in a low voice.

"Who?"

"Council, of course. These visitors that are coming. They're nervous."

"How could you tell? Double was just ordering food for a feast. Yours?"

"Same, but xe was quite stressed by it. Got me to repeat back to xer what xe had said. And they were going in and out all morning, all these hurried conversations – Crawlers everywhere."

I glance at her in surprise. Most elders, interpreters and influential citizens don't use that word, not if they want to get ahead. But she's young, no children – she doesn't have the fear yet.

"Well," I say, "if it makes them jumpy, can't be a bad thing."

"Perhaps. It depends. An unhappy Crawler can be a dangerous one."

We pass the statue of Kedira, an enormous stone monstrosity that celebrates the victories of their ancestors. Keda are milling around in groups here, and we walk in silence. Nearby is the alchemical institute, and we both keep our eyes on the silver smoke billowing into the sky. Round the corner, and we come to the Bridge of Peace. A pair of iron gates frame either end of the bridge, with a Justice barring entry. Even if some foolhardy citizens managed to rush the first gates, the second pair would be long closed and bolted by the time they had crossed the bridge. Underneath, you can see the Little Firu, a horseshoe-shaped moat that winds its way around the island of Val Firuz, until either end meets the Firu River. This bisects the city in the east and rushes down to the Southern Sea. Between them, they lock the Keda in. Or us, out.

We approach the gates and come to a halt in front of the green-robed Keda. If the councillors are the Keda's brains, the Justices are the fists. Their job is to enforce discipline, exact punishments, and generally inspire fear in the populace. Like the councillors, I can't distinguish many Justices by sight – they all look the same to me. I know Scorpion, of course. Xe is one of the Justices who manage my quarter. Supposedly, xer name comes from how xe administers punishment – whipping with a studded belt, leaving the victim covered in xer "stings". But honestly, I wonder if they come up with these names themselves, and make sure they spread to build up their reputation. Any of the Keda who are particularly brutish or sadistic get put in line to be a Justice, that's for sure. The exemplar of this is Beast, a legendary Justice, known throughout Val Kedić for xer viciousness and rhino-like build.

The one here, however, looks like a run-of-the-mill Justice – xe takes xer time, checking our pass, despite the fact xe must remember us from earlier in the day when we entered Val Firuz. Eventually, xe lowers xer poleaxe, and allows us to pass through to the bridge.

The Little Firu is twenty paces wide here. We stop and watch the surface of the water, looking for the eels that swim there. I exhale noisily, and Ira smiles.

"How long you been doing this?" she says.

"Twenty-two years now."

"It get any easier?"

"Nope," I reply. A pause. I look at her curiously. "They say you quit, after you finished your apprenticeship. And travelled, before you came back here."

"They're right. I thought there had to be a better world than this out there. I went out to find it."

"And?"

"Turned out I was wrong."

I snort. "Didn't have you down as a cynic."

"Ah, I'm no cynic. Just a good old-fashioned disillusioned optimist."

"Right. What's the difference?"

"Don't know. Put it into fingerspeak, that'll get rid of the nuance for you."

"Was that a… *joke* about fingerspeak?"

"Don't sound so disgusted." She smiles. "I remember you, you know. When I was fifteen, you gave us classes for a year. We had you every few days."

"Really? I haven't had to teach for a while now. How was I? Was I terrible?"

"Not bad. Better than some, who were deathly boring. Mind you, you never looked like you enjoyed it much."

"No, I don't think I did. Imagine what it's like telling a group of hormonal teenagers how to touch and squeeze each other in the right way, *and* keep them all focussed."

She laughs, and we fall silent for a moment. I feel a wave of relief that working with Ira is going to be all right. She may play it prim and proper with the Council, but outside, she's a real human being.

I could stand here watching the Little Firu until dusk – the thought of having to see the elders bores me beyond words. But Ira jabs me in the ribs, nods at the Justice on the other gate, who is glaring at us for daring to dilly-dally on xer bridge.

"Come on," Ira says. "We'd better go before xe comes over for a frank exchange of views. Even your fingerspeaking skills won't get us out of that one."

2.

We make our way through the second gate into Five Bells, the meeting point with the elders. You can't help but notice the change as soon as you leave Val Firuz – the streets are shabbier, the buildings run-down. On the corner as we pass, there's a pile of masonry and two overripe melons split open and lolling in the heat as flies hover above them. A typical sight here, but it would look out of place the other side of the bridge. On the other hand, you don't have to endure the snuffling of the Keda, or their faintly sour smell. The elders may have their faults, but at least they don't physically repel me.

We find the meeting point, a square close to the bridge, full of juniper trees. The elders want their own official building, but the Keda won't let them. More status jockeying. So all the meetings and discussions have to take place in taverns, upper rooms and open spaces like this. There are a few benches in a rough pentagon around a shrivelled juniper; four delegates are here to receive the instructions of the Keda, and a handful of elders in their black sashes, including Mecunio – an old man now. He has a thin, well-manicured beard and better clothes, but still the same bland smile. He climbed and politicked his way to the top, and is now the de facto leader of the elders, the primary citizen of Val Kedić.

The elders are the citizens' representatives, an elite of sixteen old men and women who cling to their limited power. They are a pompous bunch and lord it over other citizens, but as interpreters we get the pleasure of seeing them bow and scrape to the Keda Council. The elected delegates are the next rung down the ladder, two for each of the twenty-five quarters of Val Kedić, and they take the jobs the elders won't touch – collecting taxes and trying to solve tedious local disputes. Grievances trickle down this ladder, and it's a common complaint in the interpreters' compound: the Keda harangue the elders, the elders harangue the delegates, and *everyone* harangues us.

We take a seat, and eventually they break off their discussions and ask for news. Each interpreter is assigned one of the quarters of the city, to be a conduit between the Keda and the citizens – mine is Wesson, and Ira's is Blackstone, adjacent to Wesson and on the coast. Katya is the long-serving Wesson delegate, we've worked together for over a decade; Urama, thin-lipped, ambitious, is the quarter's second delegate – transparently using this as a stepping stone to try and join the elders.

Ira relays the Council's messages to her delegates, and I pass them on to mine. As all interpreters learn early on in their apprenticeships, you don't editorialise, you don't offer an opinion, you just pass on the message and keep your mouth shut.

Katya is the first to react. "We're already at breaking point with our fish quotas. Where do they think this extra fish is going to come from?"

"Always, they squeeze and squeeze," says one of the elders. "It's the same with every quarter, Katya."

"We're not holding anything back. You want us to starve?"

Mecunio sighs. "There's no need for rhetoric. You're not trying to win over voters here, Katya."

"It's not rhetoric, it's the truth."

"There are times to negotiate and times to submit," he says, looking bored. "The visitors are ambassadors of the Dagmari. They are a strong people, who have conquered many cities. Understandably, the Keda are keen to impress them. So, we do our bit, and then it pays off long-term."

"And the girls?" Katya says, crimson springing to her cheeks. "You're happy for us to send them more of our girls? You remember what happened last time?"

Mecunio waves a hand. "We all make sacrifices," he says. "Yours is the responsibility you carry. You don't want it, there are others who can bear it."

It's an old argument, one that has been waged for over a decade, but not one that will be resolved today. Katya rises angrily, and leaves with a muttered goodbye to myself and Ira. Urama, silent throughout, gets to her feet as the elders do, and approaches one. She takes his arm to get his attention, and whispers in his ear. Soon the square is empty again.

Ira stays on the bench, looking thoughtful.

"What's up?" I say.

"The Dagmari. I came across them in my travels. Learned to speak Dagmansh – their language."

"Yeah?"

"Not a very pleasant bunch. Let's hope the Crawlers can come to some sort of accommodation with their ambassadors tomorrow."

"If not?"

"If not... Whatever you might think of the Keda, things could get a whole lot worse. Dark times ahead, my friend. Dark times."

Ira and I go our separate ways, through the patchwork sprawl of Val Kedić. The geography of the city is radial, with twenty-five quarters surrounding the central island of Val Firuz. The richer quarters like Sevanić and Roć are closest to the centre, while the slums lie on the fringes by the city walls: Wesson, Goathorns and Blackstone to the west, Queenstown, Saalim and Lekaan to the east. My route home goes through the Five Bells quarter, down the People's Market, a long road lined by wooden stalls. The market is not busy, and everywhere is the stale smell of desperation – wretched vegetables arranged in an attempt to look inviting; the listless expressions of the traders. It's profoundly depressing to see after the opulence of Val Firuz, and I look away.

At the end of the market is West Town, as some unimaginative Keda dullard named it when they took power. Most quarters retained their names, but sometimes, for administrative reasons, they grouped a load of streets together and declared it a quarter. Nobody calls it West Town, of course; it evolved into Wesson, and the name has stuck. And despite the arbitrary way the streets were shoved together, after a century or so, Wessonians have developed a sense of identity to rival that of the older quarters.

Wesson officially starts when the People's Market reaches Six Ways, a cramped square with five other roads leading off it. Even if I remove my white armband, people start recognising me a few hundred paces out – it's one of the hazards of being the quarter's interpreter. Like the delegates, you're something of a local celebrity. Some traders nod to me, and one group of men just watch me, squatting on the side of the road, smoking on their baat pipes.

As I approach Six Ways, one trader spits on the ground and scowls at me. It's my fault, of course. I'm the one that relays the Keda's unreasonable demands. As they squeeze and squeeze the city, it's the interpreters whose shoddy translation skills are to blame for all our problems.

When I was younger, I sometimes argued with citizens when their resentment spilled over into a comment or gesture. Now, I've given up. What is there to say? Nothing would convince them that I'm not a servant of the parasites, that I'm not one of the quislings that keep the system going. Which I am, really. But if we couldn't communicate with them at all, if we gave up on fingerspeak, where would we be then?

I cross Six Ways, take the path that heads south – a narrow alley that climbs up to my home, the interpreter's residence. A woman, brushing dust from her doorway, sees me and stops her work. I don't know her name, but she's spoken to me three times since her eldest daughter went to the mines a couple of seasons ago.

"What news?" she says. "Are they happy?"

"They're not *un*happy," I say cautiously. "No talk of retribution at the moment."

"It's my daughter," she says. "She's... delicate. She was a sickly child – the Shadows have always had their touch on her. I don't know how she's going to cope."

I don't have the heart to tell her it's the fourth time she's told me this, that I must know all the parents in Wesson by now.

"Have faith," I say. "She will come through this."

"How can you be so sure?"

"I have a son there too, remember," I say. "Six years now. I have to believe."

"I know. I just thought..."

"No special treatment," I say.

It's the opposite, if anything. Regular citizens, with a bit of luck or money, can get away with hiding their children. I've heard of kids living in cellars, or being abandoned to the Street Rats, then reclaimed when they come of age. But if you're an elder, delegate, interpreter, or anyone of influence in fact, you don't have a chance of keeping your children from the Justices and the mines. They can ignore a blacksmith or a trader, but they hold the elites of Val Kedić close with a remorseless grip.

Who knows when the Keda came up with their system of inspiring loyalty, but there's a brutal logic to it. If you look back in the history of our city, there have always been dissidents, rebellions. The ruling class have always punished them, but if you believe in a cause enough, the punishment becomes a badge of honour. Revolutions do love a martyr. And sometimes, eventually, the rebels are successful, and they wear their scars as proudly as any soldier.

The Keda, however, refused to punish the rebels directly, and saved it for their children. And everyone in Val Kedić – everyone – was treated as a potential rebel. So, at the age of eleven, every child, excluding the Street Rats, was transported to the mines of Riona, where they would spend the next seven years.

And so were created the Justices. Any transgression from an individual – theft, fraud, violence – would result in the local Justice punishing your child on one of their regular visits to the mines. Something more serious, such as any seditious activity, or failing to pay the taxes demanded by the Keda, would mean punishment for *all* the children of the quarter.

It was a dangerous balancing act for the Keda. In one stroke, they chose to be loathed as oppressors, instead of tolerated as benign dictators. But at the same time, they bound the citizenry to them, utterly and unquestioningly. Everyone became an informer, and the first hint of treason was snuffed out by honest people, desperate to save their child from beatings or starvation.

Despite being a masterclass in how to keep a city pliant, the system had two major flaws (neither of which, to be fair, would bother the Keda, since the system still worked). Firstly, corruption was rife. Having chosen the most vicious, sociopathic Keda to become Justices, it should come as no surprise that they were open to a little bribery here and there. A successful Wessonian merchant could slip Scorpion some coin to give their child extra rations that week, or to ensure his son missed out on the collective punishment. Mind you, it's anyone's guess whether the Justices would ever honour the bribes; it's not like you could quiz a survivor when they returned seven years later.

Either way, the Justices lined their pockets and became rich. Provided the population stayed docile, the Council knew about it but didn't care. Some ambitious would-be-politicians deliberately chose not to have children – but they soon found their nominations were blocked by the Keda until they procreated. I remember Borzu gossiping to me about Mecunio; how his parents had arranged a union by the age of eighteen, and the young man had diligently performed his duty every night for a year, until the girl had done the decent thing and got pregnant. Rumours that he had never touched her since then were unconfirmed, but it didn't seem far-fetched for someone as single-minded as Mecunio.

Anyway, you talk to travellers, they'll tell you every system is corrupt, one way or another. The second flaw, however, unique to Val Kedić, was the absence of youth. A city without teenagers is not dead exactly, but it is decrepit. Of course, there were children – you still heard shrieks of play and babies' cries – but the hole at the heart of the city, the flowering of our freshest, most vital citizens, hung like a pallor over the city walls.

When the teenagers return, aged eighteen or older – occasionally years are added as a punishment – they've changed, beyond repair. You can see it in their eyes – they've had their youth stolen from them. You see a mother, clinging to a hollow-eyed young man, stiff, awkward. It's written all over their faces.

Once, I saw a man on his knees, by the fountain in the centre of Six Ways, in front of Scorpion. He had stripped his tunic, and was baring his back to the Justice.

"Me," he was pleading. "Give it to me, not her."

Scorpion could not understand – xe just stared, and lazily pushed the man over with xer foot. But what really killed me, was the look the father gave me when our eyes met, across the fountain. Naked rage, not at the Justice, but at me. Because Keda are just being Keda; but in his eyes, I'm taking their side.

* * *

Always, after a long session interpreting, I go straight to the Western Glory, a tavern on the corner of my street. When Wesson was created, most of its neighbourhoods had their own taverns already. The Glory was set up as a central, unifying point for Wessonians – an artificial tavern for an artificial quarter. It was shunned by many locals but was perfect for travellers and citizens like me who wanted a drink without being bothered. Most patrons know who I am but choose to ignore me.

I head straight for the bar with a nod to the barkeep, Igor – a youngster who is stepping into his father's shoes, and still getting the feel of them. He passes me a frothy mug of chuka, the only drink served here – a bittersweet speciality of Val Kedić, brewed from barley. I thank him and he grunts. He's trying out being taciturn and competent, not yet confident enough to be the avuncular crony his father was.

I'm just settling into my chair, the tension of the morning easing away with the anticipation of the first sip, when a meaty palm slaps onto my shoulder.

"Razvan, aren't you supposed to be doing something very, very important?"

"Matters of life and death, Jakub. Why I still slum it with you remains a mystery."

Jakub: my best – only – friend. No children, so no awkwardness there. And a former Street Rat, so no experience of the mines or snobbery about The Stain. Not a member of the Keda Fan Club, nor does he treat delegates and interpreters as despicable collaborators.

"Dealing with Crawlers this morning, were you?" he says.

"Why else do you think I came here? The sparkling company?"

He laughs, the only person I know who does proper belly laughs – *Ha-Ha-Ha!*

"Go on then, pal, interpret this." He grabs my arm, gives a nonsensical impression of tapping, then makes a drinking motion.

I sigh. "It's a little more complex than that, Jakub." I gesture at the barkeep. "Another chuka, Igor."

Jakub pulls up a chair, it looks like a toy under his massive frame. "So," he says, with a rub of his bristling black beard, his pride and joy. "What's up? You're marginally more grumpy than usual."

"Ach. You know. It's the elders, not the Keda. Politicians always manage to suck the joy out of any situation."

"Mecunio still a bald, old prick?"

"He'll always be a bald, old prick. What depresses me is the younger ones, who'll crawl through shit for the Keda, and drag the rest of us with them."

Igor brings Jakub his chuka, and he takes a deep draught. A man I don't recognise passes our table, and Jakub clasps hands with him, greets him with a smile. Jakub is the kind of person who doesn't come to the Glory to be alone, but can count on bumping into someone he can have a drink and a laugh with. I don't know why he stays friends with me, but it works somehow.

"Aren't you on duty later today?" I ask.

Jakub is a sergeant in the militia, one of eight hundred or so citizens allowed to bear arms and keep order in the city, so the Justices don't have to get involved with every pisshead and dispute about goats.

"Nope – just a skeleton team tonight. The rest of us got the night off. All hands on deck for tomorrow though – some foreign bigwigs coming?"

"Right," I say, thinking back to Ira's comments about the Dagmari.

"So, if you're planning any larceny or arson – tonight's the night."

"I'd be a terrible robber," I say.

"Of course you would, you clumsy bastard. So, who are these bigwigs, then?"

"Ambassadors from the Dagmari. Don't know a lot about them, but they've got the Keda nervous. They're in a right fuss."

He takes my arm and does a frenzied series of taps. "Like that?"

"Well, firstly, you've got the wrong arm."

"Ah."

"And secondly, if you ever listened to my fascinating lectures about Spidertouch–"

Jakub mimes a noose, choking.

"–you'd know that *(Anxiety),*" I tap on his arm, "like *(Anger)* or *(Boredom)* isn't conveyed by how you fingerspeak, but by a secondary modifier at the start of–"

"Yeah, yeah, save it for your interpreter mates."

"I don't have any interpreter mates," I say, thinking of Borzu. "Even *they're* not interested in Spidertouch chat. They're a pretty boring bunch, if you ask me."

"I could have told you that, pal. That's why I decided not to bother with interpreter school."

"The only reason, eh?"

"Plus the fact girls love a man in uniform."

I glance at Jakub in his grey tunic. Sergeant in the militia is not a high-profile job, but from day to day he must barely give the Keda a second thought. For a moment, I feel a stab of envy, though it might just as easily be indigestion from the chuka.

Looking back at my time as an apprentice, I never would have made it through if it wasn't for Borzu. I was a decent enough linguist, but there's more to it than just that, and I would never have been savvy enough to survive seven years in the compound in Val Firuz alone.

My first night, I was allotted a bunk next to his in the dormitory. He was small for his age, with fashionable, braided hair and an air of confidence that set him apart from smelly fisherman's spawn like me. He chucked aside what he was reading and jumped down from his bunk.

"Oi, oi," he said. "What have we got here?"

He was only a year older, but it felt like an eternity.

"My name's Razvan," I said, in a husky croak.

"Oh, yeah? Me, Borzu. Going to learn Spidertouch, are you?"

Why he adopted me, I'll never know. Maybe he found the others a dull lot, less impressed by his charm. There are followers and there are leaders, and perhaps he could sense I would follow him. Either way, adopt me he did. The next morning, I clung to him like a limpet, and he kept up a low murmur as we worked in the kitchens, dispensing advice and picking apart the social hierarchies of the compound.

"That's old Stumpy," he said pointing to a hunchbacked teacher, "but don't call him that to his face, it's Omer to us. He hates the apprentices, doesn't see why he has to waste so much time with us. But it's just cos he's not that good at fingerspeak. They try and keep him away from the important Keda.

"Anyway, keep your head down in lessons and don't argue back, you'll be fine. After a year, we'll move up to compound duties, and after that the older ones help the interpreters to prepare for sessions with the Keda. Watch out for that group of fourth-year girls, they think we should bow down and kiss their arses, but they're nothing special."

I didn't take much in, just nodded and grinned at his asides. In my first class, he came over to my assigned partner and brusquely informed her they would be swapping. He was curious, I think, to see if I was any good, a bumpkin from The Stain who knew nothing of politics or the Keda. I quickly realised he had a gift for languages, but was let down by sheer laziness. He was never willing to sit down and learn a list of words, but the teacher would give him a phrase, and he had the knack of feeling his way through it and understanding as well as anyone. And as for his accent, he was, irritatingly, a natural. Over those seven years, I had plenty of apprentices and teachers squeezing and prodding my left arm; but there were few who could mimic the rhythms and cadences of the Keda as well as him.

If I had a plan, it was to keep a low profile, study hard, and survive my apprenticeship with a minimum of fuss. I was driven by the fear of having to return to The Stain and take up my father's trade. I'd be forever known as the lad who skipped the mines, who thought he was too good for the fish market, who came back with his tail between his legs all the same.

But Borzu put paid to ideas of keeping my head down. He was from Sevanić, one of the more wealthy quarters near the centre and bordering the Little Firu. Failure never really bothered him – the apprenticeship was just one big game. He enjoyed tweaking the nose of authority, and he must have seen me as a loyal disciple.

Of course, at that point, we were still yet to come face-to-face with the Keda. So when we got in trouble we only had to answer to the mild rebukes of our teachers and older apprentices. It would be some time before we saw how cruel and petty the Keda could be.

3.

The next day, I go up to the city walls in Blackstone to watch the Dagmari ambassadors arrive. The militia are out in force, as Jakub had told me, swarming around the backstreets in pairs. I find a section of the wall that overlooks the harbour and the Southern Sea. I make myself comfortable and people-watch. It is a fine, cloudless day, and the air is thick with the smell of grease and sweat.

From my vantage point, I can see around fifty militia scattered throughout the harbour. Some are shooing away the stray goats and dogs that plague the poorer quarters, others amble around aimlessly. A handful of Justices are directing operations to prepare the harbour, their dark green cloaks flapping behind them as they march around and point and gesture. Citizens are clearing detritus, broken wicker baskets and coils of rope, and mopping the cobbles with linen strips. It's a frenzy of activity to make the harbour look like something other than what it is: a shit-stained, ramshackle marketplace. On the fringes, I spot a few elders, standing in huddles, observing.

It is not until fourth gong has sounded that the Dagmari galleon appears on the horizon – the scuttling below me visibly speeds up, and the militia chivvies away the citizens. As the galleon approaches, councillors emerge from the Southern Gate, resplendent in their crimson robes. Even close up, I struggle to tell them apart, but I think I can make out Giant, and I recognise Double's gait. The gates close behind them, the militia line up at the edges of the harbour, and seven or eight Justices take up position in front of them, as well as assorted Keda in blue. I spot a couple of interpreters lurking in their white armbands – our most skilled, Silas and Talia.

The Council forms a semicircle. Below me, I can hear a couple of militia remonstrating with a drunkard, but apart from that, there is complete silence; though I can see several councillors are clasping the arms of their neighbours in animated discussion. Other citizens are watching too, from the walls like me, or with their heads craning from balconies and windows.

The Dagmari galleon enters the bay, its sails the colour of spoilt milk. The oars dip in time to a distant drumbeat and I can make out a figurehead on its prow, which looks like a clenched fist. The galleon doesn't seem in any hurry and takes an eternity to circle round into position, throw out ropes and dock. Still, we wait, and watch. The councillors have stopped their conversations now. Finally, the drumbeat stills, and a gangway descends from the galleon onto the cobbles of the harbour.

The man that steps down doesn't look like an ambassador, but a warrior. No weapons, but black lamellar armour and greaves down his legs. He folds his arms and faces the Council while eleven more men disembark, dressed in similar fashion, though not quite as ornate. Their movements are casual, unhurried, and you can see their heads moving as they eye up the walls and gate. A man and woman follow them, surely slaves, for they are thinner and wearing simple brown tunics. I can make out slim silver bands around their necks and smaller bands round their left arms. With a start, I realise I recognise one of them – I've forgotten his name, but he was an apprentice interpreter, a few years younger than me. Never finished, but left Val Kedić to see the world, just like Ira.

And indeed, while the twelve Dagmari inspect our city and stretch their legs, the two slaves approach the Council, and the one I recognise – Jordi, Jared, something like that – hesitates, and raises his right arm. Eleven steps forward and presents xer left. For some time, Jordi-Jared fingerspeaks. I've done enough of these things myself to know it will be full of "Your Excellency…" and "Allow me to…" and "It is with great respect…", and all that dross.

There's something absurd about the situation though – the militia and Council in their rows, hundreds of citizens watching in silence, the sun beating down on the cobbles; all while the poor sod in the middle splays and flexes his fingers, desperately trying to get across a garbled greeting to Eleven, probably in a horrendous accent. Some of the Dagmari must think so too, and I see a few of them sniggering, nudging each other.

Eventually, Eleven puts him out of his misery, nods, and summons Talia. Xer message is shorter, it could well be along the lines of "Tell the foreign dogs what I said earlier," followed by some tapping just to pad it out.

Talia steps forward, bows to the Dagmari ambassadors, and delivers the Keda greeting. The words don't carry this far, all I can hear is the rising and falling cadence of her voice. The leader looks to Jordi-Jared enquiringly, and he interprets for them. He nods, waves a hand, and issues a curt command in Dagmansh. The slave looks baffled, and the ambassador repeats it. Even though I can't understand, I can hear the note of irritation in his voice. Jordi – I'm sure it was Jordi – just stands there, frozen, and I wince in sympathy. I know this feeling when a Keda casually taps some obscure vocabulary on my arm and I have no idea what it could be.

The Dagmari ambassador breaks the impasse. He lurches forward, so quickly my arm muscle twitches reflexively, and he grabs the slave by his metal collar. Jordi gasps, and chokes as the Dagmari kneels and drags him to the ground. He straddles the poor bastard and takes a firm grip of the collar.

His eyes don't leave the Council; he gives a yank, and there's an audible snap as he pulls the collar loose. He stands up, one boot grinding Jordi's head into the cobbles.

None of the Keda fingerspeak, though there's a fair bit of snuffling. The other Dagmari laugh and one bellows back towards the galleon. Several more slaves disembark and stand behind their masters, but no one touches the interpreter.

The Dagmari leader turns his attention to the other interpreter, repeats the message, and this one doesn't pause; she hurries straight to Eleven to pass on the message. The whole nonsense is repeated, as Eleven's response is relayed back to the Dagmari with appalling slowness; a shocked silence rings on the city walls as we all watch the man lying in the harbour, bleeding and coughing.

A voice shouts a command, the city gates open, and our militia line up along the entrance. I have a sense that the assault on the interpreter was some sort of test, one that we failed. There's an unpleasant swagger among the Dagmari ambassadors, as they march up without invitation to the Southern Gate – our militia outnumber them five to one, and they are unarmed, but they move towards the city with a proprietorial air, brushing past the Keda with barely a glance down at them. The councillors are caught flat-footed – they are sticklers for ceremony and there was no doubt some convention as to how they should all process into the city. But the twelve Dagmari ambassadors have thrown that into chaos, and there's an undignified scramble as the councillors rush for the gates without getting too close to the Dagmari or looking like they're rushing. Behind them follow the other Keda, the elders and the interpreters, and I spot Mecunio putting his hand on the small of Talia's back, muttering in her ear. I don't envy her right now, interpreting at the meeting that is to come.

I share a glance with a citizen who is watching further down the wall, and she grimaces. Somehow, there's no pleasure in seeing the Keda humbled like this. Perhaps because, ultimately, I know we'll be the ones to pay for it.

Talia was the girl we had all looked up to – in my second year as an apprentice, she was eighteen and about to be formally accepted into the guild as an interpreter. Two of her friends, industrious but pisspoor at fingerspeak, had grimly hung on for seven years, and would go on to fail their final exams, never to enter the guild. It was probably a relief for them in the end. But Talia was the real deal, the great hope of our teachers during what was a pretty barren period. Even Borzu, who had a healthy disregard for most of his classmates and teachers, respected her. She was a short girl, smaller than me, with wiry black hair, but she carried herself with the poise of an older woman. Her friends ignored us, but she would always address me by my name, and I never forgot that. In my mind, she was the big sister I had never had.

The older apprentices spent their time in intensive practice – long fingerspeak conversations followed by tests to see how much they had understood. In the compound, they would work copying lexicons onto parchment – the giant records the guild kept with transcriptions of all the known touches and modifiers in Spidertouch. Borzu and I, meanwhile, were out of the kitchens. The afternoons were for lessons, and in the mornings our time was filled with mundane jobs that were designed to introduce us to the world of the interpreters: preparing their clothes for formal duties; accompanying them to meetings with the elders and taking notes; running messages when interpreters were urgently needed. We were kept away from the Keda as much as possible – "until you're toilet-trained", as one teacher put it – but, little by little, I was building up a picture of an interpreter's role.

Every sixth day we had to ourselves. Some apprentices would traipse around the compound or play games in the dusty terrace outside. But Borzu had something more exotic in mind. He was immune by now to the charms of Val Firuz or Sevanić and persuaded me that it was far more interesting to explore the slums and alleys of Val Kedić. Part of the reason he befriended me, I'm sure, was that, consciously or not, he liked the idea of his own personal urchin who could show him round the back streets.

By the time I was fourteen, I was regularly guiding him round The Stain and other slum quarters, either on our rest days or through the occasional skiving of lessons. Borzu had a knack for knowing exactly when it was safe to skive – which teachers, which days. He was always able to charm others into believing his stories as to why the two of us could not possibly attend that day. We kept to the quiet areas, since there was always the risk of someone confronting you, curious to see two teenagers – old enough to be in the mines, but not in the rags of Street Rats.

That was how we came to explore the sewers. One afternoon, we had gone past the harbour to the western shore, the other side of the wall from Blackstone. Nobody went there; it was a rocky coastline where the bay funnelled gusts of wind in to crash against the city. Borzu moved like a crab, bouncing between the rocks in bursts. I took the safer path, fewer jumps and awkward steps. In the distance, I could make out a huddle of fishing boats, and it struck me that it could be me and my father there, were it not for my old teacher, for Mecunio, and the decisions I made. Instead, my father had disappeared across the Southern Sea, and here I was, a tourist and a stranger to where I had grown up.

Borzu was forty paces ahead and had climbed up towards the sea wall. He beckoned me over, and I made my way there – a series of jumps, trying to avoid the thick brown algae and the crusty residue that gathered round rock pools. I was out of breath by the time I arrived. He pointed to a tunnel, just big enough to walk through if we crouched.

"What's this?" he asked.

I peered into the gloom. "The sewers," I said.

There was a rusting grille, hanging loose at the corners, and Borzu bent it to one side without any trouble.

"Under the city?" he said. "Holy Kedira! How have you never told me about these? We have to check it out."

I sighed. "Really? I don't know if this is a good idea…"

"Are you crazy? How much more interesting is this than learning modifiers?"

He entered the tunnel, held back the grille for me, and I squeezed round. A few paces on and the stench hit like a physical wall. I'm not precious, I grew up in The Stain, but even I gagged. "Can you not smell that?"

"It's just a smell," he said. "Smells can't hurt you, Raz. Let's go."

"I'll have no idea where we're going," I said. "Funnily enough, I never played in here as a kid."

"We can't go far wrong," he said. "Come on, it'll be a laugh."

I chose that moment to step forward and slip on a paving stone, landing face-first into something slick and wet. Borzu hyena-laughed and leaned against the tunnel walls while I tried to stand up and wipe it off.

"That's it, I'm going back."

"Come on, Raz," he said, still laughing. "That was brilliant. Let's just get to the end of the tunnel. Please, I need you with me."

I scowled and grumbled but went along with him, as he knew I would. Bent over, we advanced up the tunnel, hands on the walls as we steadied ourselves. It was dark, but still possible to see through the gloom, even as the tunnel curved round to the east. We didn't hear any rats, just the irregular drip and plop of water. The smell didn't get any worse, just that solid, eye-watering stench. We held our tunics to our noses when we could.

Eventually, we reached an opening that looked onto a far

larger tunnel, with sewage and liquid floating at its base. There was a narrow path running alongside; Borzu gingerly pulled himself through the hole and down to the path. He offered his hands to help me down.

"Do we really have to?" I whispered.

"Why are you whispering?" he said.

"Dunno. Just feels like we should."

"Look," he said, "we're past the walls now. This tunnel is headed north, to the heart of the city. It's an underground network, begging to be explored."

"Whenever you're excited like this, I *know* it's a bad idea."

He strode along the pathway, and I followed. After a hundred paces, we came across another opening, another small tunnel branching off. But by this point, it was getting too dark to see, and Borzu had nearly toppled into the river of sewage twice. He came to a sudden halt. Tendrils of smoke were twisting down to us from a grille in the roof of the sewers, silver fingers creeping and exploring.

Rumours had always been rife about the Keda's alchemical smoke. All we knew for sure though was that Keda alchemists wore black robes and you hardly ever saw them outside their institute in Val Firuz. There weren't many of them, and it was thought that the Keda held them in as high a regard as the Justices. We knew the smoke had been instrumental in Kedira's victory over a century ago, and that if you inhaled it, it had terrible effects. Not for the Keda, of course, who seemed to be immune thanks to their flat noses. Some said it sent you mad with hallucinations, that you would try to rip out the smoke that drifted through your body. Others said that it led to a protracted death, paralyzing your limbs but keeping you alive. It was just rumour-mongering and speculation: the Keda had not used their alchemy as a weapon for a century. But one thing was for certain – they carried on experimenting and producing smoke in the institute.

The wisps of smoke told us we were closer to Val Firuz than we realised. Borzu pointed at them and stepped back.

"Maybe that's enough for today," he said.

"For today?"

"Next time, we bring a lamp," he said.

"Borzu…" I said as I grabbed his arm and squeezed some of the new modifiers we had been learning.

(Disgust) / (Negative) /.

"Lovely technique," he said, "but we're doing this. Now – start counting steps, we're going to get the maps out when we get back."

Only Borzu could have found glamour and intrigue in the sewers. That was the moment to argue; he never would have come here by himself. But of course I didn't. I turned around and prepared for the long slog back to the beach.

I go home after the arrival of the Dagmari because there's nothing else for me to do. My working schedule has been thrown out; all I can do is wait to be summoned. So all afternoon, I wait. I'm too on edge to relax; the Dagmari unnerved me more than I care to admit. The sound of the snap, as the ambassador ripped off Jordi's collar, keeps coming back to me. I can't get the picture out my head. In my imagination, his face becomes Talia's, her bloodied neck on the marbled floor of the High Chamber, a Dagmari crouching above her while the Keda watch and snuffle.

For as long as I can remember, I've had a horror of my head being squashed, teeth shattering, skull fracturing, as a boot stamps down. I'm no coward – I've faced beatings before, held my nerve in front of an armed thief – but the skull, membrane like an egg-shell, that's always made me squeamish.

That's all I can picture now – that boot, that skull – snap, thud, grind. Once you get stuck in a loop like that, you might as well write off the afternoon. I stare out the window, watching as citizens stop to talk; wondering whether the topic of conversation is the arrival of the Dagmari ambassadors, or whether they're oblivious to it, stuck in the same cycle of gossip and small talk that fills each day.

Dusk comes. In distant Val Firuz, I hear the gong crash eight times. Eventually, a knock on the door. I hurry down and there's an apprentice outside, a fifth year I vaguely recognise.

"Yes?" I say.

"The elders want you," the girl says. "At the High Chamber. Talia and Silas need a break."

"The Keda are still negotiating with the ambassadors?"

"No – they've just left. Back to their ship. The feast is off."

"That doesn't sound good."

"Well, the elders didn't look too happy."

I slip the girl a copper, grab my bronze bands, and hurry through the streets, past Six Ways, along the People's Market, and over the Bridge of Peace into Val Firuz. When I arrive, everyone is seated at trestle tables, where the feast had been due to take place. The Keda are on a raised dais, fingerspeaking with each other and picking at food. Most of the elders and delegates are gathered round lower tables, deep in mumbled conversation. Ira has been summoned too and is standing to one side. I catch Talia's eye, and she wanders over. She looks exhausted.

"The Dagmari are gone?" I ask.

"Yeah." She nods grimly. "Negotiations didn't go too well."

"The Keda not giving them what they wanted?"

She lowers her voice. "Not sure they had much choice. They were practically begging the Dagmari at one point. The demands were crazy."

"What did they want?"

"A tribute. In return for them not invading us, from what I could gather."

"What happens now?"

"Ask the elders. Good luck." She pats me on the shoulder and makes an exit, hurrying after Silas.

I find a space next to Katya, who is with a few other delegates.

"So the talks collapsed?"

She nods. "The tribute they were demanding was ridiculous. I'm not sure even *they* believed we could pay it. Maybe they were just here to get a measure of us." She sighs. "As the ambassador left, he uttered something in Dagmansh, at all of us. Nobody translated, but I recognise a threat when I hear one."

"What are the Keda going to do?"

"That's what you're here for. They're going to tell us what happens next."

She takes a handful of dates, chews, and spits out the stones. We look around – everyone is watching the Keda, whispering and muttering. The silence of fingerspeak always makes you quieter and more self-conscious.

The Keda begin breaking up their discussions, and get to their feet. A few councillors process out the room, and a Blue Keda gestures towards us. From our tables, some of the elders rise and beckon Ira.

A group of councillors gather around Eleven, and a servant clears the food from the table around xer. Mecunio nods at me from down the table. "With me, Razvan."

Along with a few other elders, we climb the dais and bow to Eleven. I go round the table, and present my arm to xer. I spot Double in the group and our eyes meet for a moment. I've only fingerspoken with Eleven once before; it was no different to the others to be honest, but you feel a bit more nervous in the presence of power. *True* power, that is, in the way that some of the Keda know how to wear it.

Eleven wastes no time. *Talk / Foreigner / Disappointing /.*

"The negotiations with the Dagmari were disappointing," I say to Mecunio.

(Future) / Attack / Val Kedić / Many / Death /.

"They will attack the city. Many people... will die."

Foreigner / Strong / Many / Soldier /.

"The Dagmari are strong and have a big army."

(Imperative) / Prepare / CityWar /, xe says, eliding xer touches together to make a compound touch.

"We need to get ready for a siege."

Justice / Lead / (Future) / Day / Instruction /.

"The Justices will be in charge. They will give their commands tomorrow."

(Imperative) / Acquire / Mura / MoneySoldier /.

"We should send for the Muranese mercenaries."

"The archers?" Mecunio asks sharply.

(Question) / BowMan /, I ask.

(Positive) /, xe responds.

I nod, and Mecunio mutters something to one of the elders. "Is there no other way?" he says. "Maybe this is just all just part of the Dagmari's negotiation tactics?"

I pass on a rough version of the message.

Eleven raises xer eyes and shakes xer head at me. There's a flash of remorse in xer eyes as xe taps and squeezes xer answer.

(Future) / (Positive) / Attack / Foreigner / Animal / (Conditional) / Enter / Val Kedić / (Future) / Kill / Man / Rape / Woman /.

"The Dagmari will attack," I say. "They are animals. If they get into the city, they will kill the men and rape the women."

Eleven squeezes something complex and unintelligible. I look at xer helplessly. Xe sighs and tries again with a euphemism.

(Question) / City / West / Mountain / North / Sea /.

I gesture recognition. "You know of the city of Sensasha?" I say.

"We heard," Mecunio says. "It's ashes now. Last year... they defied the Dagmari."

I pass on the reply, and Eleven nods.

(Imperative) / Prepare / CityWar /, xe repeats. Then rises to xer feet, a clear dismissal.

4.

I leave the High Chamber with Ira, several paces behind the elders. The evening is dense, an oppressive mugginess in the air. I feel lethargy crawling up my spine, a pang of regret that I ever left The Stain. Ira wears a grey cloak over her tunic despite the heat. She glances at me. "Not looking good, is it?" she says.

"We can't fight the Dagmari," I reply. "The Keda just want to batten down the hatches and ride it out."

"My lot were talking about food supplies," she says. "They want to requisition all the grain, to bring all the animals inside the city walls. They're talking about abandoning the farms and villages. We're looking at thousands of extra homeless, swarming through the city."

"Better than being butchered by the Dagmari," I say.

"What, better to starve on the streets?"

I don't answer, and we walk in silence for a while. It's always quiet in Val Firuz, without the hum of conversation you hear in other quarters. Blue Keda watch us from street corners, but in an eerie silence that you never quite get used to. Cicadas buzz, but other than that our footsteps are the only sound. We pass a Keda on xer own, and xe puts a hand to xer *cantu*, the slim silver whistle that all of them wear on their necks. It emits a low-pitched tone, inaudible to us, but is their best way to signal danger to each other or to draw attention. Ira looks at me and smirks.

Once we're outside Val Firuz, she speaks again.

"Interesting, though, isn't it, getting to play a big part in all this? Making a difference to all these lives?"

"We don't take part, Ira. We facilitate, act as a conduit. Don't ever forget that."

She rolls her eyes. I can hear how pompous I sound; I'm trying to be the wise mentor figure, but it just doesn't fit me.

"We are a cog in the machine, though," she says. "When we speak to the elders, we make a choice how to translate. We give a message to the Crawlers, we decide which taps to do, which squeezes. And... nobody can say whether we're right or wrong."

I feel uneasy at what she's insinuating. "What are you trying to say?"

She shrugs. "We shouldn't forget it, that's all. We're more powerful than we think."

"Right now, I want the same thing the Keda do. Survival. Knowing the city will still be standing by the time winter gets here."

There's a pause, then she says, "You do hate them, don't you? The Crawlers?"

I look at her, surprised. "Why do you ask?"

"Humour me."

"I mean... I hate the rain. I hate the Grey Fever. And yes, I hate the... Crawlers. But they just are. There's no point dwelling on it. We've got to work with them. Fighting them is like shaking your fist at the storm."

"This business with the Dagmari, though. Interesting times ahead."

"Not sure interesting is the word I'd use."

"Can't you feel it?" she says. "Change. This might be the best chance we ever get."

"To do what? You want to walk into the arms of the Dagmari?

The Keda might be parasites, but at least they're not going to kill off their host."

"Think of your son, in the mines–"

"Don't tell me about my son," I say, cutting her off sharply.

The silence is strained now, no longer peaceful. We walk along the deserted People's Market. Nearby, the road splits and heads towards Goathorns, and its night market – a busy jumble of beggars and thieves, chuka and gambling. There's a famous dogpit too, that attracts punters from all over Val Kedić. But here, the awnings are down on the stalls and we are the only people in sight. We walk behind the backs of the stalls, where broken crates are piled.

"Haven't you come too far?" I ask Ira. "You're that way, aren't you?"

I point south, in the direction of Blackstone. She mutters something, and I'm about to ask her again, when we pass the entrance to an alley. A figure jumps out at my shoulder – small, lithe – and brings out a stiletto knife, which she puts to my throat. Her other hand grabs me round the neck – I snarl something inchoate, twist away, but she grips me tight.

"Don't move," she hisses. "I'll hurt you if I have to."

"Ira!" I shout.

In the corner of my eye, I can see that Ira is not in fact moving to help me, but calmly taking what looks like a hood from somewhere within her cloak.

"Ira?"

"Take it easy, Razvan. There's someone who wants to talk to you. In private."

"You what?"

I feel the edge of the knife against the base of my throat, cold, and the bitter tang of metal. I stop struggling with the girl.

"We can't have you seeing where we're going, Razvan," Ira says.

"If this someone's got something to say, they can say it here," I say, panting. "Tell your lackey to drop the knife."

Ira proffers the hood to me. "Forgive the theatrics. We've learned the necessity for secrecy. The hood is needed. And without the knife, you might not be… convinced to come along with us."

"Just do as we ask," the girl says.

"Doesn't feel like you're asking," I spit at her, moving my head away from the hood. "Who the fuck are you?"

Ira raises her eyebrows, waits for me to get it.

"Bloody hell," I say. "You're Camonites, aren't you?"

The girl loosens her grip a little. "Yeah," she says. "Blessed be the name, and all that goatshit. Now are you coming, or not?"

I give Ira a hurt look, but I shouldn't really be surprised. She's prime age and background for the Camonite order – the closest thing we have to opposition to the Keda.

It started nineteen years ago, with the Riona Revolt. It was led by Camun, an eighteen year-old, who was about to leave the mines and has been deified ever since. It was doomed from the start, but they certainly gave it a go; they tried to overwhelm the Justices and local guards with sheer weight of numbers, armed with chains and pickaxes. Of course, the revolt failed, as all slave revolts have to – Camun died, no doubt far less heroically than the tales say, as did countless other slaves, already weak from hunger and punishment. There have been ballads and epic poems written about him, his battle cries as he led this rabble of teenagers, whirling his chains above his shaven head. Even a quasi-religion was set up in his memory, all mythologised and exaggerated I'm sure; I never paid it much heed.

Although the revolt failed, in a sense it also succeeded. Twenty escaped, the only successful mass breakout from the Riona mines in history. They returned to Val Kedić, and spread their message, and the resistance began. They took part in minor acts of civil disobedience, assaults on Blue Keda, and the public shaming of particularly egregious examples of collaboration. Their heartland was the slums, quarters like Goathorns, Queenstown and The Stain, and it was believed they were mainly ex-miners, disaffected and in their twenties. They were a shadowy group, and no one would admit to being a supporter, let alone an actual Camonite. But they were there, and made sure the Keda didn't forget it.

For their part, the Keda made a show of not noticing them, irritants who barely deserved their attention. But on the rare occasions they fingerspoke of them to the elders, I could tell it galled them. It was clear that even after nineteen years, they hadn't been able to extinguish the Camonite spark. Every so often, one would get caught – and the Justices made sure their executions were very public, very messy, and very painful.

There is a noise in the distance, further down the street, and the girl stiffens. "Come on," she says, "we don't have time to argue the toss. Is he coming or not?"

Ira holds the hood to my head. "Hear us out, Razvan," she says. "We only want the best for this city, like you do. We need people like you."

"Like me?"

"I told you, we can change things. We'll never have a better chance, with the Dagmari at the gates."

"Can we save the moral debate for later?" the girl says. "I'm getting edgy here."

I push the knife away from my throat. "Fine. Hurry up, then. But no more threats."

Ira lowers the hood over my head. It's rough hessian, and it itches at my neck. The girl spins me around, and with a firm hand on my arm, guides me forward. With the two of them at my side, we walk several hundred paces twisting left and right every now and then. I stumble twice on the uneven paving stones, but the girl's grip is strong and she keeps me upright.

Eventually, they come to a halt. There's a squeak of a door opening, and we go inside. Finally, they let me go and I rip off the hood. We're in some sort of warehouse, hemp sacks piled high by the walls. A few crates are positioned in the centre, and a single oil lamp is flickering on one of them. I take a proper look at the girl, but she's pulled up a scarf. All I can see are her narrow brown eyes, and cropped hair.

"So, what do I call you?" I ask her.

"Let's leave names out of it for now, Mr Interpreter," she says. "Until I know whether you're with us or not."

"With you lot?" I snort. "Religious cranks? Trashing people's livelihoods and beating up Blues?"

The girl sneers at me, and Ira puts a hand on my shoulder. "Razvan, I'm sorry. Maybe this wasn't the best way to do this. But we have to have secrecy – you know what happens to us if we're caught. I've told him you're a good man. At least hear him out."

"Who?"

"Me," says the Camonite, striding in from the other side of the warehouse. He's slightly younger than me, wiry frame, not hiding his face like the girl. Gaunt cheeks, and a fuzzy beard that does a bad job at covering them. He gives the sign of Camun: a double tap of two fingers on his belly, supposedly where Camun was pierced by the spear that killed him. The two girls return it.

"And who are you?" I say.

"You can call me priest. I'm one of the Twenty, who escaped from Riona."

"So you knew Camun?"

"Yeah, and I saw him die too, choking on his own blood. I'm no cultist, Razvan. I leave that to the true believers, the ones who need it. We're far from perfect, I know that. But we're doing the right thing. The only thing."

"And what do you want with me, 'priest'? What's with all the cloak-and-dagger crap? Why didn't my colleague here," – I glare at Ira – "just ask me what you wanted to know?"

"It's the way we work," he says, pulling up a crate to sit on, and gesturing for me to do the same. Ira and the girl sit too, but I stay standing.

"This is dangerous, what we do," he continues. "Enough of our followers have died at the end of a Justice's spike."

"And what, you're recruiting teenagers now?" I say, glancing at the girl.

"I'm fresh out the mines, so what?" the girl says. "At least *I* did my service, interpreter."

I laugh. "And sorry, you want me... to *join* you?"

"You believe in change, Razvan," Ira says. "I know it. Right now, with the Crawlers under pressure, it's an opportunity. To have two interpreters working for the Camonites–"

"And give the city to the Dagmari? Are you out of your mind?"

"Nobody's saying that," the priest puts in. "But it's a time of pressure, of flux – we could actually get some leverage on the Crawlers."

"Leverage? For the last twenty years you've been an irritation to the Keda, I'll grant you. But you can't seriously believe you will ever actually change anything?"

"Someone has to stand," the priest says. "They told Camun he was mad–"

"And remind me how he ended up?"

"He started the only meaningful resistance to the Keda in over a hundred years," the priest says.

"Look," I say. "Believe it or not, I'm not unsympathetic to your cause – even if I disagree with your methods. But you cannot beat them. Not while they hold the mines."

"You're right," the priest shrugs. "So that is what we have to do. Take the mines. But to do that, we need you."

"Me?"

"You see the Council every day, Razvan. You know what goes on in the High Chamber. You could be the key to this."

I scowl at them all, angry to be put in this position, hating that feeling of being steered again, towards a path that I would never have chosen.

"I'm sorry," I say. "I'm not the man you think I am. I wish I could help, but–"

"I knew your son in Riona," the girl says. "Rico."

I turn on her. "Don't you dare do that," I say. "Don't you use my son as a lever on me."

"And why not? It's what the Keda do."

"Is that supposed to make me feel better about *you*?" I ball my fists and look away from her, heat rising in my chest.

"How was he?" I ask a bit more softly.

"I'm not going to sugarcoat it," she says. "Not great. It's not the Keda that's the problem, it's the guards. He's got balls, your son, he stands up to them. He's with a group of lads from the Wesson barrow, and the guards have it in for them. I've seen them beat the shit out of him, piling in with pickaxe handles."

I stare at her. "Why are you telling me this?" I say, spitting the words. "Would it have killed you to tell me he's coping fine?"

"I tell you because you need to know! People like you, you have no idea how bad it is. And you can help stop it!"

"You're not being fair," I say.

Ira puts a hand on my arm. "I wish we didn't have to do this, Razvan. But you need to wake up. These are good people. There's been idiots in the Camonites before, nobody's denying that. You can trust us, though, we're doing this for the right reasons."

"How long has he got left?" the priest asks. "Your lad?"

"Year and a bit," I say tonelessly.

"You know the most dangerous times down the mines?" he says. "First year, and last year. The guards settle a lot of scores at the end."

"You want Rico safe, out of the mines?" the girl says. "Help us. We can get him out. Before it's too late."

It's emotional blackmail, but it's effective. "Of course I want him safe," I say. "I'd do anything to get him out of there, you know I would. But... do you even have a plan?"

The priest looks down at his hands, and in the lamplight I notice for the first time his scars and the raw stump where his left little finger should be. "The plan," he says, "is to blow that whole fucking place apart. The mines. An end to them. Perhaps the Crawlers are here to stay. But the mines are... an abomination."

"How?" I say.

"With Ira," the priest says, "we finally found someone in the inner circle of Val Kedić. Most of our followers are from the slums, or Street Rats. We've been trying for years to place one of us among the delegates, even the elders. But it's hard work. Most of the delegates are political climbers – good family, ambitious – and they cling on until they die. An interpreter, though, is perfect – within the inner sanctum, yet also without. But Ira's junior. I want the two of you, working together at the heart of the city. The priesthood *is* formulating a plan. You won't hear it unless I know you're with us."

There is silence for a few beats. "I need to think about this," I say. "And I want to talk to you," jutting my chin at Ira. She assents. "And I want your name," I say to the girl. "Whatever happens, I'm no snitch. I want a name."

She hesitates, then her eyes soften, and she pulls her scarf down. I see her face properly for the first time, a thin, stubborn mouth and a pointy chin.

"Naima," she says.

"Naima. Well, Naima, I'm going to have some more questions for you about my boy. But first, Ira and I are going for a chat."

Naima looks at the priest, and he nods imperceptibly. "We need an answer soon," he says. "Time is not on our side."

"The hood–" Naima starts, but I glare at her.

"Don't push it. I've told you, I'm no snitch."

We leave the warehouse – I soon recognise where we are, one of the tributaries of the People's Market. We join back onto the main road, and walk along it at a brisk pace.

"You had no right," I say to Ira.

"Ah, give it a rest," she says sharply. "It was the only way. I've said I'm sorry. You think you would have listened if I had just casually mentioned I was a Camonite? And did you fancy joining me for a quick spot of revolution?"

"I don't–"

"You had to meet them, to see that we were serious. That we weren't just a load of holy fools. Where are we going, by the way?"

"The night market. I need a drink."

"I've taken a big risk, you do realise that? If you're not interested, I'm risking everything!"

"Am I supposed to care about that? You ambushed me. I hardly know you," I say.

"We haven't got time for get-to-know-you games. We've been preparing for war from the moment we heard the Dagmari were coming."

"It was a hell of a gamble."

"I trusted my instinct," she says simply.

The road splits and we head into the Goathorns night market. Plenty of citizens are out, squatting by stalls and barbecue pits, watching the world go by. We come to the dogpit, barrels shoved up against each other to form the walls, and a raucous crowd placing bets as the two dogs are brought out and displayed. One mongrel, mangy and scrawny, is straining to be released, and I stare at its foam-flecked muzzle, already smeared with blood by its trainer. The one closest to us is a stocky mastiff, standing there, impassive, staring down its opponent.

I can't see the attraction in seeing dogs rip each other apart, but I'm strangely fascinated by the crowd.

Ira looks away with disgust. "Please," she says.

I spot a stall selling chuka, and lead her over there, gesturing to the barkeep for two mugs. We find stools and sit facing away from the frenzied snarling and shouting in the dogpit.

"You haven't told me everything," I say.

"Well, obviously."

I ignore her snide remark and continue. "How did you wind up in bed with *them*?"

"I was an orphan when I started my apprenticeship," she says. "My parents got caught up in the middle of some stupid riot, something about grain shortages. Wrong place, wrong time. The Justices went wading in – I saw them kill my mother, then my father as he tried to save her. One of them was Beast. I haven't forgotten xer. I see the bastard sometimes when I'm in the High Chamber, you've no idea the self-control it takes…"

"I'm sorry," I say.

"Yeah. Anyway. My father had already proposed me for the guild, and this made it final. No reason for me to go to the mines now, and some delegate figured it was better to try me out in the guild than leave me as a Street Rat. So I did my apprenticeship, and when I was eighteen, I left the city. No way in hell was I serving the Crawler bastards. But when I was on my travels, I met a Camonite. Another of the Twenty, like the priest. He convinced me to go back to the city and to serve the order by becoming an interpreter. He had properly caught the religion bug, though: Camun was a martyr, we're in a holy war, etcetera, you've heard it all before. I was nearly convinced too, I'll be honest, but the priest and Naima put a stop to that. They're both pragmatists. You should get along with them fine."

"So you decided to put my name forward – and told them I had a son in the mines?"

"Everyone looks down on the interpreters, Razvan," she answers. "The Crawlers, the elders, the citizens. But think of the power we have. When we pass on messages to a Crawler, we can speak with the voice of the Camonites, not the elders. And vice versa – when we translate for the elders, we can give it whatever spin the order wants. The reason I suggested you is that you can actually *do* something. You're not just some clown who worships Camun and wants an excuse to kick things over."

"It's dangerous," I say.

"So it is. And that's exactly why I need you. One more thing – I told you, I learned a fair bit of Dagmansh when I was out there. I think I'm the only interpreter who speaks it, and I'm going to let Mecunio know. If you tell him you know a little too, the two of us will be entrusted with the negotiations when the Dagmari arrive–"

"Woah, woah," I say. "Slow down. I haven't even said if I want any part of this."

"It's a chance to get them back, Razvan. For my parents, for your son–"

"Stop bringing him into this!"

"But he *is* in this, Razvan. There's no escaping that. He is the hold the Keda have over you, the only hold."

We sip our drinks without further words. There's a roar from the dogpit, and I turn round. Through the throng, I can make out the mastiff, worrying at the throat of the other dog, fur matted with gore.

Despite myself, I know she speaks the truth. Her words are starting to hit home. I can't get the image out my head, Rico curled up while pickaxe handles rain down on him. If I can save him, I have to try.

"How many of you are there?" I say.

"We operate in cells of four. Every Camonite knows no other followers except for the three other members of their cell, and their priest. So far, just me and Naima."

"If I did do this," I say quietly, turning back around, "I'd want to choose the fourth member of the cell. Someone I know I can trust."

"Why – have you got someone in mind?"

"Maybe," I say. "Depends how open-minded he's feeling."

5.

"You're not serious," Jakub says.

"Jakub–"

"The Camonites?"

I scratch my head. Maybe I should have gone for Ira and Naima's knife-and-hood approach.

"I mean, we are talking about the same people, right? The ones with the scourges, the hymns about some shaven-headed little miner twat?"

"That's a bit over-simplified–"

"Terrorists, Razvan? *Terrorists?*"

I had found Jakub the following morning. My shift had not started yet, and I located him off duty by the militia barracks. It was deserted, with many soldiers summoned to briefings by the Justices.

"Look," I say, "clearly some of them get a bit carried away–"

"Carried away?"

"All the religious mania, the Camun-worship – I'm not condoning any of that."

"Well, that's a relief."

"But the principles, what they stand for, it's all... pretty sound."

"Kicking down stalls, setting fires and getting into fights is 'sound' logic?"

"No, that's not what I said. Not *all* the Camonites are nutters. The ones I've spoken to–"

"Who are they?" he says suspiciously. "Give me names."

"I can't. You know I can't," I say.

He scowls, and it looks unfamiliar on his broad, warm-hearted face.

"Jakub," I try again, "what they say is right. We should be trying to get rid of the Crawlers, not working *for* them. We should be trying to destroy the mines and setting our children free. Now, I admit, the Camonites haven't always used the most sensible tactics in the past, but…"

Two beggars are having an argument, a hundred paces away on the other side of the square. Jakub sighs, marches toward them, then puts up a hand to me as I move to follow. He breaks up the argument and moves one of the beggars on.

He returns, clearly deep in thought. "It's one of our main jobs," he says, "trying to root out the Camonites. We don't make a big deal about it publicly, but the Justices are always pushing us to find them."

"Not been a roaring success," I say. "Unless I've missed all the arrests and show trials."

He gives a wry smile. "Nah. They're tricky little buggers. Keep to themselves, don't mix with other citizens. And on the rare occasion we've picked one up, they can't – or won't – give us names."

"Are you going to arrest me, then? A nice little prize to show your commanding officer?"

He ignores the question. "You're serious, then? You're joining them?"

I sigh. "I thought a lot about it last night, and I'm tired, Jakub. Tired of the way they look at us. Tired of all the pain tens of thousands of us go through, all the misery we endure – for what? So that a thousand or so Crawlers can live in luxury. In power."

"I know. But now, Razvan? With a barbarian army on its way?"

"Now more than ever. We can actually put some pressure on them for once. Influence them, force a change."

He shakes his head. "I'm not strong enough for this, mate. I've managed to climb all the way from being a Street Rat to a sergeant of the militia. I don't want to throw that all away now."

"Don't give me that. I grew up in The Stain, now I'm in the High Chamber most days, interpreting between the elders and the Council. You think I want this? I'm a coward, not a religious nut!"

"Then why–"

"Because enough is enough. The Dagmari will arrive, and the Keda will see us all dead as long as the city walls hold. It pains me to say it, but the Camonites are the only answer I can see. And I need someone I can trust at my back."

He grumbles a bit longer, but he's softening. Eventually, he says, "I can't join the Camonites, Razvan. It'd be too much of a betrayal, to all my mates in the militia. We're supposed to hunt them down." A pause. "But... I do need to look out for you, you daft bugger."

"So?"

"So, I will help you. If you are set on joining them, I'll be there when you need me. Weapons, backup..."

"Information? On what the Justices are telling you to do?"

He nods stiffly. "If that's what you need. But I'm not joining any order. No ceremonies, no chanting, no new poxy Camonite name."

"I'm not sure they do that any more."

He waves it away. "Whatever. Nobody's going to say I'm a Camonite."

"Just a Camonite sympathiser?"

"It's an important difference."

"Okay."

I feel a sickness stir in my gut. Part of me wanted him to talk me out of it, to show me I was being a fool. But, I reason, I've already committed myself now.

Last night, I lit a candle to the Shadows for Rico, as I do every night. Usually, I sit in a numb despair, knowing I am helpless, that I can't do anything for him. The guilt is overwhelming. But even worse than that, is now knowing that I *could* do something. It's dangerous, it's not guaranteed, but it's still a chance. And no matter how hard I tried to shut it out, Ira and Naima made sure I could not forget it. I would never have chosen them, but it seems like they've chosen me.

Jakub shifts uncomfortably, adjusts his spear. "So?"

"What?"

"So what now, you prick?"

"Let me talk to the others, work out what our plans are. In the meantime, find out all you can about the siege preparations. And I'll grab you when I need you. The great thing about being friends already is that we can meet without it looking suspicious."

Jakub gives a long-suffering sigh. "This is a mistake, my friend. Definitely a mistake."

"That's the spirit," I say, patting him on the back. "Blessed be the name."

Borzu and Jakub had a lot of similarities, and I looked up to them both. But whereas Jakub listens to me, Borzu was never really interested in another opinion if it got in the way of his plans. He insisted on us going down to the sewers on a regular basis – we found a map of Val Kedić, and then, on thin yellow vellum, we drew the tunnels that we explored, tracing them on top of the map of the city. The tunnels were ancient and labyrinthine in places, but in surprisingly good condition. The whole system was split in two by the Firu – the section in the east of the city sloped down into the river, but we spent most of our time in the central and western section, which ended up disgorging sewage into the sea. The tunnels were at their deepest in Val Firuz, going underneath the Little Firu, the moat that the Keda had coerced citizens to dig after their triumph one hundred and thirty years ago. They were dank, lonely places, those sewers – but I think from the very start Borzu recognised the possibilities in them.

The second time we explored, we brought a lamp, and retraced our steps all the way from the shore. Deeper into the main sewer system, we came across rats and other unseen animals that scuttered and splashed around us. There was space to stand at full height now, though the sewage and standing water was deeper, and our tunics stank. Every so often we found grooves in the walls, heading up to exits; and pipes surrounded us, clambering over each other like roots, bringing the sewage from different buildings. At one point, we climbed up to one of the exits, and were peering through the hole in the masonry, trying to work out where we might be. Somewhere under Goathorns, we believed. But we were wary of climbing out into some sanitation building, or somewhere restricted where we might get caught. We were whispering to each other when a voice boomed up from below.

"Ho! What are you boys doing up there?"

I was startled, and nearly dived through the hole. But Borzu was calm, and effortlessly able to manage adults who he thought of as below him in the social scale. He started to climb down the grooves.

"We're from the sanitation guild, just checking on maintenance," he said. "There's been some blockages lately. What about you, old-timer?"

I saw that the man was indeed old, with a curved spine and grizzled beard, and he was carrying a wicker basket.

He ignored the question. "Rather young for that, aren't you?" he said.

"Old enough. They send us young'uns down to do all the dirty work. Don't worry, we won't get in your way."

We both climbed down and faced the old man. He seemed to relax, realised we weren't a threat to him, and showed us his basket. It was full of junk and dripping with water and shit.

"Amazing, some of the stuff you find down here," he said with an avuncular smile. It turned out he was a scavenger, spending his time searching the tunnels for anything that had found its way down there, then re-selling it to a scrap merchant in the city. He rattled off a list of some of his most impressive finds – jewellery, part of a mosaic, a crossbow bolt – and let us follow behind him as he continued his work. He must have soon realised Borzu had been talking nonsense, that we had little idea where we were going, but it didn't appear to bother him. He seemed content to have an audience who were not going to obstruct him or were disgusted by his finds.

The underground engineering of the sewers was impressive, far more so than what existed overground, and he took pleasure in pointing out to us the mechanisms that managed the water flow. He showed us one of the tunnels that connected the sewer to the stormwater tanks in Five Bells, which, when opened by the guild, would come flushing down in a torrent, and clean out the tunnels.

"But you'd know all that, wouldn't you," he said to us with a wink.

The tunnel was closed now, but he showed us the levers that opened and closed the sluice gates, and I could tell Borzu was itching to investigate them and see how they worked.

"Don't you ever get caught up when they release them?" I asked him, looking nervously at the barrier. In my imagination, I could already see the black water, crashing and foaming down towards us.

"Nah," he said to me. "Don't you worry about that, boy. I've been doing this for years, and they run regular as clockwork – every fifteen days, at dusk. And then only in the rainy season. Your guild's not very spontaneous."

He carried on up the main sewer, rarely straying into the side tunnels. Occasionally we asked him the location of various exits, but he always professed ignorance.

"No idea, lads," he would say. "I come and go the same way – could be Crawlers doing their business up there for all I know."

We found ourselves competing to help him, showing him scrap metal and broken trinkets for his judicious review. "No, no, that's no good to anyone," he'd say, or "very good, boy, shove it in the basket."

Eventually, deep in the bowels of the sewers, and facing a particularly rank-smelling passage, we realised we had to head back to the compound. He bade us farewell, and waded off whistling, ankle-deep in sewage, with all the insouciance of a man strolling through the park with his lover.

We saw the scavenger again a handful of times. He'd always greet us like old friends, and chat to us as though it was perfectly natural to be ambling through the sewers together – which I suppose to him, it was. But for Borzu and me, the fascination of the sewers became the network of exits and entrances. Whatever had first attracted him to the place, I started to get it now – the idea that you could remove a manhole cover, slip down into the tunnels, dash under the city and come out in some latrines thousands of paces away – it was quite a buzz. It felt like we'd found a secret world that nobody else knew anything about.

The Justices don't waste any time. We don't know how long we have before the Dagmari army arrives, but there is much to prepare. The one advantage we have is that, despite sending their ambassadors by sea, the Dagmari are not known to be a major naval power. It would be a nightmare having to manage a full defence of the coastline, at the city's rear. Although we have a fleet, it is poorly equipped and with no experience of war.

There are three gates to defend, excluding the Southern Gate, which opens onto the harbour. The principal entrance is in the north at the Gate of Triumph, an enormous, bombastic barbican, with gargoyles and grotesque facades, trimmed by a mosaic detailing Kedira's triumph. The barbican sticks out twenty paces both sides of the wall, so for an army to enter Val Kedić, they need to go through a tunnel fifty paces long, bookended by portcullises. Either side of the walls are slits for archers and spears, and above are murderholes for molten tar and scorpions. If an army did attack, it would be far easier to go over the city walls or through one of the smaller gates – the Queensgate or the Western Gate. There is also the river Firu, of course, which enters under the city wall in the north-east, but we have two manned jetties there, so a river-bound assault would be full of risks.

This afternoon there are fifteen Justices out in action, issuing commands all over the city, each with an interpreter and a squad of thirty soldiers from the militia. I am with Scorpion, translating for a captain called Ansić, who seems to know what he is doing, and sometimes gives tactful advice to Scorpion disguised as questions. Scorpion has marched us to the Queensgate, and we stand outside the walls, surveying the dusty scrubland beyond the city. To the north-east, the mountain road disappears into the horizon, ten paces wide in places, carrying a trickle of wagons and carts. Later, it will split into a dozen routes that connect to the Riona mines, the mountains, and the villages scattered across the plains.

Scorpion points to where ditches need to be dug – xe draws a line in the dirt with xer foot, and two men start to mark out lines. Xe takes my arm with xer crooked fingers, the brittle scratch of nails on my skin.

Man / Leave /, xe says, with a peremptory gesture at some of the homesteads and farms in the vicinity of the gate.

"We need to inform these citizens," I say to Ansić, "that they will need to leave their homes."

He murmurs instructions to his sergeant, who is writing on parchment. Then he motions to me, and says, "Ask the Justice about the woods. A league or so north of here. We should chop them down, so these Dagmari bastards can't use them for battering rams or siege towers."

I address Scorpion and place my hand on xer bands.

Wood /, I say and point north. *(Question) / Do /*.

Xe cocks xer head to one side. *(Question) /*.

(Danger) / Foreigner / Use / Wood / (Question) / Stop / Foreigner /.

If I was more fluent, I could feed xer the answers more subtly, be more disingenuous with xer. As it is, I have to speak to xer with the subtlety of a child trying to fool its parent.

(Positive) /, xe replies. *(Imperative) / Destroy / Wood / Use / Many / Man /*.

(Approval) / Excellent / Plan /, I say, wishing there was a modifier to indicate sycophancy.

"Yes," I tell Ansić. "Xe says you can get some citizens to help you chop down the woods."

He grunts and we follow Scorpion, who is wandering away from the city walls, looking at the land with suspicion. I watch xer back. This Keda, I remind myself, will have beaten my son. Xe will have punished Rico, no mercy given.

Xer robes have a stain on the back; it looks as though xe tried to use some alchemy to remove a burn or a mark, but it bleached the green dye. Xer cowl is frayed. Xe walks with a slight limp – xe returned with it after a visit to the mines last year, trying to hide it. Xe is not invincible, I have to keep telling myself. With the help of the Camonites, the Keda can be beaten.

Every so often, something catches xer attention, and xe issues a curt command, which I pass on to Ansić. Xe's not as comfortable fingerspeaking with interpreters as the councillors are; there's more misunderstandings in both directions. But xe is at least patient and does not seem bothered by having a conversation in what sometimes must be baby-talk for xer, free of grammar or fluency.

By the time we reach a hamlet, several thousand paces

from the city, Ansić's sergeant has scribbled down dozens of instructions to keep the squad busy. Some are crucial defensive fortifications, others are more whimsical tasks that I can't help feeling Scorpion invented more as a display of authority than anything else.

The hamlet looks to be little more than a collection of six farms in a circle with a well in the middle. We approach down a dirt track, twelve of us still with Scorpion. We pass an olive grove – recently picked clean, with some fruit discarded and a black pulpy mess on the scrub. Ahead of us, we can see five men and women who have gathered by the well to watch our approach. Scorpion comes to a halt twenty paces away from them, and gestures to Ansić. The farmers watch in sullen silence, one of them fiddling with a hoe. Ansić steps forward, a glance at the Keda to remind the farmers whose authority is speaking.

"An army is coming," Ansić tells the farmers. "They wish to destroy Val Kedić, and they will destroy you with it."

The farmers say nothing. They must have heard the news already on the winds.

"We will need your goats, your grain, to feed the city. Our supply routes will soon be cut off. As for you, you will have to leave your homes. Those who are able to bear arms, you have the choice of joining us, and defending the city against the foreign scum."

"And if we can't?" says the man with the hoe, eyes burning hate.

"Then you should prepare to leave, before the foreign scum get here. Go and stay with family. Visit sunnier climes."

"What did they do?" one of the women asks.

"Who?"

"Who do you think? The green one and xer friends. What did they do that means we're now at war? No army has dared attack us before."

"There have always been wars, woman," Ansić says. "We've

had peace here for a few generations, it's true. But we have got flabby and idle. Now the enemy are coming. And you chose to live outside the security of the city walls."

"I curse the Crawlers," the woman spits. "The Shadows take them."

Scorpion looks up sharply.

"Tell your woman to hold her tongue, friend," I say. "The Keda do not speak our language. But they can recognise gestures. And certain words."

(Question) / Problem /, Scorpion asks.

"No, there's no problem, is there?" I say to the people in front of me.

Two other farmers have wandered over to see what is happening. There's a tension in the air, and some of the soldiers are eyeing each other, preparing for trouble.

"You may not like it," Ansić says, smoothly taking control again. "You may well curse us and our green-robed friend here. But we will take your goats, and your grain, and those who wish to put their farming days behind them and give soldiering a try, are welcome to. You'll get comrades, a uniform of sorts, a sword, and the chance to die a glorious death defending the walls of our blessed city."

One man spits on the ground, and stalks off to his farm. There is still a fair amount of protesting, haggling, and cock-waving to get through, but it makes not one jot of difference. Eventually, the farmers bring out grain and goats, which are inspected by the soldiers. Three men volunteer to join the militia; the sergeant takes down their names and gives them instructions.

Scorpion turns away – xe has long lost interest in the hamlet. I want to be sick, but most of the people around me despise me enough already, and I hold it in.

6.

The city thrums. Everywhere is movement as Keda, soldiers, artisans, messengers and refugees fill the streets. The militia is recruiting all the time, with the intention of growing into an army of several thousand to defend the city. Our guild is busier than ever, and for the first time since I joined, there are not enough of us to go round the councillors and Justices who require interpreters.

For two days, I do little else but accompany Keda throughout the city, passing on instructions and plans. Once, I see Ira in the High Chamber, and our eyes meet, but we do not get the chance to talk. My head throbs from the concentration and effort involved in so much fingerspeak. I hear nothing from the Camonites, and I wonder if they've forgotten about me. All I can think of is the Keda – in the last two days, I've had to translate from fourteen different fingerspeakers, each with different accents. Most are new to me, with the exception of Scorpion and Chicken, who draws a bead of blood on my forearm from xer nails, and stares at me with no remorse and naked contempt.

On the third night after I met the Camonites, they summon me. I am about to turn in for the night when a boy comes to my house with a message. The parchment is folded, and as I open it, a scrap of hessian cloth falls out. Two words are scrawled on the parchment: SAME PLACE. For a moment, I consider ignoring it, crawling into my bed, and collapsing. But I know I cannot. I pull on my boots and find my way to the warehouse, along the moonlit streets.

When I get there, Ira is already waiting across the street, in the shadows of some steps. She raises a hand and the two of us enter. She looks exhausted, and slumps down onto a bench that has been pushed up against the walls. We don't say much, just stare at the opposite wall where there are several coils of rope, artfully wound, as if someone was trying to create pyramids. At last, I say, "Where's Naima? The priest?"

"Naima will have been watching the entrance. To check nobody's following."

"You think?"

"I know. She loves all that stuff. She says it's for security, but it's all part of the game for her. She's never happier than when she's doing a coded message or passing on a secret package."

"And the priest?"

"No idea," she shrugs. "We won't see so much of him. It's all about the cell." She sighs and gives me a weak smile. "I'm a wreck. The Dagmari aren't even here yet, and look at me. Doesn't bode well, eh?"

"Not enough interpreters," I say. "They're going to have to bring out the apprentices. Or maybe the Keda will just back off, let the militia handle the defence and the elders run the city."

"Some chance," she says. "The elders can't fart without the Crawlers giving their approval. They don't trust us, you know. They're not fools, they'll be expecting some kind of insurrection. Giving all these weapons to citizens, it's asking for trouble."

There is a movement to our left, and we turn to see Naima padding towards us.

"Where did you come from?" I say.

"There's a window at the back. In case anyone's watching the front. Don't think there is, but it never hurts to be safe."

I sense Ira giving me a look, and I ignore her. "So, what's up?" I say. "No knives? No hoods? No speeches?"

"The priest's not coming," she says. "We won't see him unless we have to. Do I take it from your presence here that you're joining us?"

"Can we dispense with the ceremony, the hymns, all that?" I ask. "It's not really me."

"Sure. I don't have much time for it myself. I'm more concerned with the present than the afterlife."

"Good," I say. "Then I'm in."

Naima doesn't show any particular emotion, just nods.

"What about the fourth member, Razvan?" Ira says. "You said you had someone in mind."

I explain about Jakub, and Naima frowns.

"Militia is good, the priest has been talking about infiltrating them. But we don't want an informer, we want a proper cell member. Cells should be four."

"Why?" I say, a sudden wave of irritation washing over me. "Is four a sacred number? Did blessed Camun decree something while he bled to death? No? Because a cell of three will work perfectly well. Jakub will support us when we need it. Lest we forget, this isn't a typical cell – we're more about linguistic subterfuge, rather than brute force."

Naima puts up her hands in mock apology. "All right," she says. "Calm down, Grandad." A pause. "In any case, we're out of time. We have to get moving."

"Doing what?" says Ira.

"I spoke to the priest this morning," Naima says. "There was a special convocation of all the priesthood – they've decided on a course of action. And our cell will be at the heart of it."

It's like I'm watching this happen to someone else. I've taken a step now, and I know I can't turn back, no more than I could walk away from the guild after first arriving in the apprentices' compound.

"The plan is in three stages," says Naima, eyes shining – she's in her element. "Stage one is procuration of weapons. In seven days' time, a shipment of weapons will arrive at the harbour. Swords, shields, pikes – all for equipping Val Kedić's growing army. Where they're from, I don't know. Some trade deal the Crawlers struck. We are going to steal a load of their weaponry to equip the order."

"We, as in..." says Ira.

"We, as in we three. Our cell is going to facilitate it."

"How, exactly?" I ask.

"We have sources who work on the docks. There's a system for managing the requisition of weapons. Some Blues control the depot where the weapons will be stored – and you need chits to take weapons away, stamped by the Justices. Now, if the militia was cooperating, we could easily make a few crates of weapons disappear, for us to use. But they won't be cooperating, so it's up to us to fool them. We'll have to engineer it carefully, but at some point, when we're speaking with the Justices–"

"And with this we," I say, "presumably you mean..."

"Okay – you two. When you're speaking with the Justices, you're going to give a creative interpretation of one of their instructions. As in, you're going to tell the militia captain that the Justice wants to transport some weapons to a particular location. At that location, our people will be waiting in militia garb.

"As for the Justice's actual instructions, obviously you'll give those separately to make sure they're carried out too. Meanwhile, you reverse the process to get the chit stamped. You tell the Justice that the captain needs more swords for his squad, can xe stamp this chit please? The Justice won't look at it twice. You take the chit to the captain, his men move the weapons from the depot. A few crates go missing, nobody's any the wiser."

"And what happens if some Blue in the depot does notice there's been some funny business and that the numbers don't add up?" I ask.

"You've seen what it's like out there," Ira chimes in. "It's chaos. And when the Dagmari get here… nobody's going to be demanding what's happened to a few swords." She nods. "Might just work."

"Let me worry about the chits, and how we manage it," Naima says. "That's my job."

"All right," I say. "Stage Two?"

"Stage Two. We kidnap a Justice."

"We kidnap a…" I laugh. "This gets better and better." It is a relief that Jakub choose not to join the cell – he would be having a fit right now. The Justices are thought to be fearsome fighters – skilled with the two short scimitars they carry at all times, and trained to be strong, vicious, relentless. I've never seen anyone foolhardy enough to fight a Justice, but stories abound of their cruelty. In the end, their reputation is enough.

"I know, I know," Naima says. "We're getting on to the more dangerous elements of the plan now. But really – raising a hand to a Crawler is death already, so what else could they do to us if we're caught?"

I think of my boy, in the mines, and say nothing.

"Now," she says, "no one's suggesting we actually fight a Justice – if nothing else, it gives xer a chance to blow xer *cantu*, and then we're really screwed, as well as dead. But we can trap xer. Again, our cell is crucial here. You two can communicate with xer, you can get xer into a position where we trap and disarm xer, then take xer *cantu*. The priests are still working on the plan mechanics."

"Torture?" I ask.

"Torture, if necessary. Again, we will need you two to translate."

"And what's the purpose of this?" Ira says. "Kidnapping a killing machine?"

"It's all building up to stage three." Naima pauses. "We're going to send a small Camonite army to liberate the Riona mines. Capturing a Justice will give us the information we need to storm the mines. Many of us were slaves in Riona, of course, but we know little about their resources, their manpower, the routes in and out. And the weapons we steal will properly arm us for the battle."

"And what of the war with the Dagmari?"

"The timing couldn't be better. That's why we have to do this now. All the Justices will be recalled to Val Kedić, so the mines should be undermanned. When a Camonite army breaks out of the city, and takes the mountain road to Riona, do you think the Dagmari will have any incentive to get in our way? Will the Crawlers pursue us? Of course they won't. We leave the Crawlers and Dagmari to their war, while we free the slaves. And we destroy those bloody mines in the process."

"I want to go," I say, "when we liberate the mines. I'm not a fighter, but I want to come. For my boy."

"And so you will," Naima says. "We'll need every available pair of hands with us. You may not be a swordsman, but you can point a crossbow. How about you, Ira? What do you think?"

"It's a bold plan. But it's a lot of pressure on me and Razvan. A lot of people depending on us to not cock things up."

"I know. But the priest trusts in you. And I'm behind you, all the way. What we're doing here, what the priests have dreamed up... we're finally going at it the right way round. All my life, the order has tried to change things from within Val Kedić. But we've only ever been nipping at their heels, an irritant for the Crawlers to brush away. This time, we're going to take the fight to Riona. The mines have always been the bind that controls the city. And we're going to cut the bind."

After that, there isn't much more to say. Naima tells us it's the last time we'll meet at the warehouse. The Camonites have a safehouse for us next time: two rooms above a butcher in Val Varin, the quarter just north of Wesson. That will be our meeting place in future, and a hideout should we need it. We make arrangements for the evening before the weapons arrive at the harbour. Then stage one of the Camonite uprising will roll into action.

The Dagmari outriders arrive two days later, five days before the weapons shipment is due to come in. I am with the elders and two other interpreters when the news filters through. It is raining, and we are in a room above a tavern in Sevanić. All sixteen elders are there, seated on benches while they discuss the preparations and construction that is still unfinished.

A messenger arrives and tells the gathering the news of the outriders – five hundred men on mounts, split into three groups, setting up position on the three roads that lead into Val Kedić. I watch from the back of the room as Mecunio fumes and paces in front of the benches.

"Those bastards, this is too quick! There's no way they had time for the ambassadors' ship to return, and then raise an army!"

"What were they doing here then?" someone asks.

"I said it all along, the whoresons had no intention of cutting a deal. They were just here to check us out, take a look at what was inside our walls. Their army was all ready to go. And now they hold all the roads in and out!"

A militia captain, here to liaise with the elders, stirs. "Should we talk to the Justices about mounting an attack on them? Before the main body of their army gets here?"

"No," Mecunio snaps. "Can't you see that's exactly what they're hoping for? They want to fight us on the plains, their riders against our ragtag army. We'll outnumber them seven to one, but it'll be a bloodbath. Farmers with shortswords against elite Dagmari cavalry. We might kill some of them, maybe even most of them. But they'll have cut our forces to shreds before the siege even begins."

There's a lot of opinions thrown about, by old men who fancy themselves as military commanders. Then it's agreed that we will go to see the outriders for ourselves.

We set off north for the city walls, through the rain, a group of twenty men and women. I walk at the back, with the other two interpreters: Silas and Darius. The latter is a shy young man who has the misfortune to typically interpret for Chicken. Silas jabbers the whole way, about what the Dagmari strategy will be – and although this is frightening, there's also an undeniable excitement in the air that this is happening. It has started, something outside all our experience, something that will shape the rest of our lives.

By the time we reach the city walls, a thousand paces or so west of the Triumph, the rain has eased and there's an earthy smell in the air. We climb the steps and spread out, looking out at the men who have come to destroy us. There must be three hundred of them there, horses and riders, setting up camp, stretching their legs. They're around four hundred paces due north, grouped around the Ilić Royal: the road for over half the travellers and traders who come to the city. They're too far for professional archers to reach, even if we had any, which we don't. The Muranese archers are on their way, due to arrive in the next few days. Even with just three hundred men, the outriders look like a horde, all in the same black armour, bristling with lances and steel.

"If that's the outriders, how big is the army?" Darius says under his breath. He must be reading my mind. Neither Silas nor I reply.

The messenger mentioned five hundred of them, so it's safe to assume that a hundred have gone west to the coastal road, and a hundred east, to cover the mountain road. But the bulk have come here, to face the Gate of Triumph, and confront the city head-on. The Ilić Royal is empty, all the way up to their camp, and I shiver, for it seems unnatural to see it free of travellers and carts so close to the city. The space is paralysing, a giant lacuna, like a beach waiting for the waves to crash over it. A long way behind the outriders, you can see a gathering, presumably travellers and merchants who were on their way to the city, now at a loss for what to do.

I look over the top of the walls and see there are still dozens of men and women working on fortifications. Ladders are scattered all the way to the Triumph, and the citizens keep looking nervously back at the outriders, as though ready to drop their tools at any moment and go scampering up the ladders. Some are driving lines of sharpened stakes into the ground, others are digging what look to be fire gullies, by the most vulnerable points of the wall – packed with barrels of oil, ready to explode into flames if needed. Normally the noise here is steady and raucous: a marketplace just inside the walls, and all the hubbub outside that comes with a transient population.

Today however, it is quiet – many other citizens are standing on the walls, pointing out the outriders to their neighbours. The elders are silent too, except Mecunio, who is still ranting about the treacherous Dagmari. He seems personally offended by their early arrival.

I ask aloud, "Does anyone know how long we've got before the rest of the army gets here?"

One elder, who is standing by me, and is known to have travelled a lot, sniffs and replies, "You'd think they'll be five, six days behind. Maybe longer, depends how much they're bringing with them."

"Siege towers," puts in one of them knowledgeably. "Trebuchets."

Two sentries march past, in the colours of the Val Kedić flag, yellow and cobalt blue. Their uniform is not properly matching, and their swords droop down on belts that are too big. I look out again at the outriders – even at this distance they reek of professionalism and murder. Even their horses – I know they're just animals, but I make out one armoured destrier galloping around without a rider , chanfron over its head, black metal barding down to its legs – and for a moment, I imagine it pounding towards me, a horse from the bowels of hell.

7.

As the group disperses, Mecunio takes me by the arm and steers me away.

"The Dagmari have outmanoeuvred us," he says, guiding me towards some steps. "We have to get ahead of them. The Keda can control the city, but they have no idea how to manage savages like these."

I say nothing, wait to hear what he wants from me. He finds a shingle wall to lean against, takes out his baat pipe, taps it twice and begins to puff.

"This will end in one of two ways, Razvan. One, they breach the walls. Nothing you, or I, can do about that. We leave that in the hands of the militia, the thousands we've drafted in for the defence. Or two – we negotiate a settlement with the Dagmari – give them what they want, and they leave us in peace."

He exhales, and the smoke drifts under my nose, thick and cherry-sour.

"Your colleague," he says. "Ira. She speaks Dagmansh. And I understand she's been teaching you a little as well?"

I incline my head in assent, wondering exactly what Ira said to him.

"So," he says, "we need to open negotiations. To start the conversation. The Council won't wish to treat with Dagmari outriders – it's not appropriate. But I hope to convince them to send me. And if they do, I want you and Ira with me, my own interpreters."

"It'd be an honour," I say.

"Spare me. Let's be frank, Razvan. I'm not sure how much Dagmansh you know, how much you can help. But it seems you do know Ira."

"I do," I say carefully.

"I could do with a pair of eyes on her. A pair of ears, in fact. As you no doubt know, she's flaky. Left the city after her apprenticeship to travel. Idealistic, a little naïve, perhaps. Of course, when she came back, we gladly took her on as an interpreter. Can't afford to turn anyone down these days, not if they're any good. Anyway. I don't fully trust her, not like I trust you. You're a Val Kedić man through and through, aren't you, Razvan?"

"To my bones," I say.

"This could be a time of great change," he says. "When it's all over, we will remember, Razvan. Those who were loyal and those who were not. You've handled Wesson a long time, haven't you?"

"Fourteen years," I say.

"After this," he says, "it might be time to move you to a new quarter. Somewhere more suitable for someone of your experience. Somewhere with more... opportunities. How would that sound?"

"Super," I say, and he pats me on the shoulder.

"I'll let you know about the negotiations," he says. "I'll talk to the Council, and you'll hear from me this afternoon."

This is how Mecunio got to the top of the tree, promises and handshakes, private agreements and knowing smiles. I want to sneer, to turn my back on him, but I see how easy it is to nod, to smile and go along with his oily hints. Hundreds of citizens in his thrall, basking in his approval and enjoying his petty favours. This wily old man, I realise, will be just as dangerous as the Keda to the Camonite plot.

* * *

I never thought much about what it would be like, to finish my apprenticeship and become an interpreter. It was simply the track I was on, and I followed it in Borzu's shadow. He was a year older, and so at eighteen I saw him accepted by the guild and take his place as one of the city's interpreters. He left the compound, to share a residence with another young interpreter, slumming it in Lekaan.

I, meanwhile, had a whole year to get through on my own. I had hitched myself to him so thoroughly, that I realised I had few friends left among the other apprentices. I still saw him, of course, since all interpreters used the compound as a base, a library and a rendezvous to gossip and break bread. But, as you might imagine, membership of the guild gave him a swagger, and he would only stop by to brandish his white armband, and tell me anecdotes of his adult life, dealing with the elites who ran our city.

I put my head down and focussed on my fingerspeak, determined to be accepted at the end of the year. Understanding the language was the easy part. If you ever talk to someone about fingerspeak, they scoff and shake their head, often ascribing some mystical, innate talent to you, if you can master the Keda's tongue (insofar as 'tongue' is a suitable word for fingerspeak). But really, learning a language is nothing more than repetition and habit. If I ever had the mind to have a linguistics discussion with a Keda, xe might marvel at the way our babies acquire speech – after just a few dozen times of hearing a double air vibration, formed on the lips and with a nasal exhalation, the baby can recognise the word and point at their "Mama". Is it really so hard for us to see the reverse? I must have felt a triple tap on my lower band hundreds of times over my seven-year apprenticeship, so I didn't have to consciously remind myself it meant /Man/, the sensation just conjured up the image of a man. Three

taps on the middle band meant /*Woman*/. Two taps on the
lower band, /*Boy*/, two taps on the middle band, /*Girl*/. As
a language, it lacked elegance, but it had a certain unfussy
logic.

So, after seven years, I was competent at understanding
my teachers' careful messages. (Understanding the Keda
themselves would be another story. Nobody forgets their first
time with a Keda. Their hand crawling over your arm – their
accent, slang, the slurring together of touches.) The challenge
as a senior apprentice was learning to string together your
own messages. You could quiz me on vocabulary, and I could
tell you the touches for /*Ship*/, /*Afternoon*/, /*Four*/, /*Crate*/ and
/*Onion*/, but there's a certain verbal dexterity needed to recraft
them on the spot into a delegate's message: "The ship arrived
this afternoon, but it's missing four crates of onions."

Much like the understanding, habit is key. If you don't have
the head for it, you don't have the head for it, and in the years
between Talia and Borzu's acceptance to the guild, I saw many
who failed to make the grade.

At the end of that year were my exams. Borzu had been
blasé about it, but told me what to expect. The vocabulary test
was straightforward: thirty words or word combinations to
translate into fingerspeak, and then thirty touches to transcribe.
Then they sent me to an administrative building near the High
Chamber, where I had my first experience of fingerspeaking
with a Keda. Xe wasn't a councillor, just a Blue – to xer, it was
just a chore to get through; but although I towered over xer,
my palms sweated and I noticed nothing of where I was or
what the Keda looked like. All I could think about were the
two strips of flesh between my bronze bands.

Xe gave me three messages, a pause between each one.
Nothing to write on, for retention of the messages was part
of the skill. Then xe dismissed me with a wave of xer claw-
like hand. Outside, waiting for me, was Nuray – at the time,
the most experienced interpreter of the guild, some seventy

years old. Like the Council, we had no formal leader, but the others deferred to her age, and she spoke for the guild. She's been with the Shadows more than ten years now, but she was a good woman who the entire guild trusted. I told her my translations of the three messages, and she went to confer with the Keda. I heard nothing more, but the next day they invited me back and the process was reversed. Nuray took me into the antechamber and gave me three eccentric sentences, packed with modifiers and compound touches. I still remember one of them: "Val Kedić is not a small city – it's a pity all the dogs eat rats in Blackstone." I remember too that in full hearing of the Keda, she put a little stress on the word "rats" and elongated it to two syllables – a reminder to me that it was a tricky compound touch, and I needed to use /Mouse/ and /Evil/.

Surprisingly, I found this part of the exam easier than the previous day. Perhaps I got lucky with the sentences, or perhaps my nerves had calmed after the rush from my first proper experience of fingerspeaking with a Keda. Either way, Nuray had a short conversation with the Blue while I waited outside. Then she came out beaming and told me I was accepted into the guild.

There was a celebration that night, which all the interpreters attended, as was tradition. Nuray made a short speech and there was a ceremony as I received my white armband. Borzu slapped me on the back and teased me non-stop. Once the older generation left, it got raucous, and some of the men made me a noxious chuka spiked with spirits, then roared with laughter as I snorted it out my nose. It got very bawdy, and it may all sound a bit tribal and immature, but I was happy to feel like I belonged, part of a gang at last. Borzu was at the heart of things, though later he was dismissive of our colleagues and told me he found them tiresome. Tongues loosened, and some of the interpreters gave their honest assessment of the Keda, and the elders – and the men and women who had been my teachers and superiors suddenly became more human. By the end of the night, I was drunk for the first time in my life. Borzu had agreed to let me sleep on his floor until my quarter was settled – it was my first night outside the compound in seven years – and he helped me back home on his shoulder, laughing most the way. I vomited once into the river, as we crossed the Bridge of Sorrow, and once in the street gutters. It seemed to take us the best part of the night to find our way back to Lekaan.

The next day, my life as an interpreter began. I returned to the compound with a stinking hangover, to learn they had assigned me to be junior interpreter for the quarter of North Ash. In those days there were forty-two of us in the guild, more than enough to cover responsibility for the twenty-five quarters of the city; so a few worked full-time as teachers or administrators, and ten of the quarters received both a senior and junior interpreter. In the last decade, our numbers have dwindled to twenty-eight, with old-timers dying or incapable of carrying on with the demands of being an interpreter, while not enough apprentices have come up.

Back then, however, there were enough of us that a new interpreter, green and terrified, could have a year or two shadowing a more senior colleague and avoid the crimson-robed councillors. I had nearly two years sharing North Ash, an inoffensive sinecure near the Gate of Triumph. And then, there was an opening in Goathorns, which bordered Wesson, right by Six Ways. It was during my time there that I was to gain a woman and a son, but lose my dearest friend.

As promised, a messenger from Mecunio comes to me at the end of the day, summoning me to the Gate of Triumph. As I hurry through the streets, dusk is falling, and the sun is blood-red, something which superstitious citizens will delight in analysing.

When I arrive, there must be over a hundred soldiers milling around the portcullis and the various slits and traps around the gate. There's a panic in the air, soldiers toying with their new blades – but even I can tell there's no way three hundred cavalry are going to launch an attack on a fortified gate. Mecunio, carrying an oak staff, pushes through the crowd, men and women making way when they see his black sash. Five militia are with him, and at least they look like they mean business, a cut above the conscripted citizens and refugees who are playing at soldiers.

"Razvan," he says. "The Council approved me trying to open a dialogue with the Dagmari. Who knows whether it'll do any good. But at the very least, it's an information-gathering exercise." He looks around. "Where's Ira? We should go before dark."

We wait for a while, and one of the soldiers takes the opportunity to rip the white linen he has brought and tie it to a stick for our flag of parlay. Eventually, Ira arrives. Mecunio runs through with her what he's planning to say, the militia adjust their weapons, and suddenly I find myself walking under the barbican, about to leave the security of the city walls. There's a hush as the crowd sees what's happening. A few stand to attention, and some clap the accompanying soldiers on their backs.

"Go on Mecunio!" someone yells. "Good on yer!"

Others cheer and applaud; it's more in line with a champion going into battle than an emissary going to plead for peace. The thought flickers that I might die out there, but it's not helpful and I shove it to the back of my mind. Four men run to the gatehouse and turn the wheels that open the gates, grunting and straining. Out we go, Mecunio in the lead, flanked by the five soldiers, one holding the white flag high in the air, Ira and I together behind them.

"You all right?" I mutter.

"Shitting myself," she says, eyes dead ahead.

Four hundred paces ahead, the Dagmari outriders have stopped what they're doing. There are a few sentries, but most seem to be eating, chatting or tending to their horses. When it's clear there are only eight of us, many of them go back to their tasks. From behind, I watch Mecunio, walking straight up the Ilić Royal with his oak staff, no falter in his step. For a moment, I can't help but admire him: an old man striding out to the enemy camp, unarmed, clearly the one in charge – if the Dagmari do decide to ignore the parlay flag, he will be the one they slaughter first, while the rest of us sprint for the walls.

He stops halfway to their camp, and the soldier waves the flag. I can make out faces now, hear some of their shouts. For a horrible few moments, it looks like the Dagmari will ignore us, and we'll be left like lemons in no-man's land. But then a single rider confers with his comrades, waves away one of the others, and rides out to meet us, alone. I glance backwards and see that citizens are lining up along the city walls, watching.

The rider approaches us at a steady pace. He carries an enormous stabbing spear, loose in his right hand while his left holds the reins. The horse is unarmoured – a grey stallion, magnificent. He snorts as the rider pulls him up, and comes to a halt a few paces away. Mecunio starts to speak, but the Dagmari gives a short bark in Dagmansh, and Ira and I slip between the soldiers to stand by Mecunio.

Ira calls out to him in Dagmansh, and he replies.

"First he asked if anyone spoke his language," she says, "now he's asking what we want."

Mecunio smiles pleasantly. "Perhaps he could dismount from his horse, and we could discuss face-to-face."

"He says he will not dismount. We should… say what we have to say."

Mecunio looks coldly at the Dagmari warrior. "Your riders are blocking our roads," he says. "What are you trying to achieve?"

"He asks if you know the name… Shakan, I think it is?"

"I do not."

The rider jabs a finger at us, starts to talk fast, points at the city and laughs.

"Shakan is the Dagmari warlord," Ira says. "Lots of honorifics – Master of the something something, Breaker of the something else, you get the picture. Then he says… Shakan is bringing his army here. They will crush our puny walls. They will enslave us, we will bend our knees and lick their feet. Ha-ha-ha."

Mecunio gestures at the walls. "Our walls are high and strong. We have grain and water to last a long time. Shakan may find us a tougher egg to crack than the other cities he has conquered."

This takes a bit of time to translate, but the rider sneers, and utters another couple of clipped barks. It really is an ugly language.

"Fine words."

"There is no need for many men to die," Mecunio says. "Better to come to some arrangement."

"The war has not begun, and already the southern dogs shrink from battle. Men will die – such is war. We are, ah, I'm not translating that, but the gist is we are cowards."

Other men might have lost their temper, but Mecunio has had a lifetime of negotiating with unreasonable demands.

"Come the winter," he says, "you may see things differently. Can you tell Shakan that we should like to talk with him?"

"Talk, talk, talk," Ira says. "That's all you southerners do. I can tell you now the mighty Shakan's answer. Open the gates, and we will be merciful."

Mecunio raises himself to his full height, stamps his staff on the dusty ground, and says, "I will remember you, rider. I will know your face when I talk to Shakan. For the last time, will you deliver the message to your leader?"

The rider gives a mirthless grin, and eyeballs Mecunio. After a pause, he delivers one last bark, then wheels his horse around, and gallops back to the camp.

"I will," Ira says softly.

"Well," Mecunio says. "At least we're making progress."

8.

Three days pass, and the outriders do not move. The Muranese mercenaries finally arrive and take up position on the wooden hoarding lining the city walls. The Keda have instigated a curfew, with no citizens allowed out on the streets after dark, apart from soldiers on duty. I am mostly interpreting for the militia now, and see little of the elders. I am billeted with Ansić and his unit on the western wall. It is tiring work, as I have long periods with nothing to do, watching the soldiers training, then suddenly there is a flurry of communication with a Justice, or a Blue, about sorting out equipment or similar. Unlike elders or the Council, none of them have much experience of the tortuous back-and-forth involved in using an interpreter, and tempers are starting to fray.

All the city is on edge, knowing Shakan's hordes are inching closer every day. When I'm in the south, I find myself looking out to sea, scanning the horizon. The weapons shipment is due to arrive tomorrow, to kickstart our uprising – and, just as importantly, I look for the Dagmari galleons that could disrupt our supply channels. The sea is the city's only source of food now, and rationing has started; already citizens grumble at the meagre amount of grain they are allowed to buy.

The cell meeting is scheduled for tonight in the Val Varin safe house, when the gong crashes ten times. The curfew starts on the ninth gong, which is a pain. Ira has a friend in the quarter, so she is going to stay there until it's time. To try and cut the chance of being caught, I go to an abandoned building I know nearby, and wait it out. When the tenth gong sounds, I sneak through the back alleys until I get to the butcher. I see one pair of soldiers striding towards the walls, but otherwise the streets are empty. I slip through the unlocked door of the butcher; to get to the stairs, you have to pass through the abattoir, which has goat carcasses piled high in one corner. Traces of blood line the stone gutters by the walls. I gently touch one of the cleavers – this takes me back to the days of my father's fish stall. Sometimes, he would let me wield these to chop enormous sunfish into pieces – it was my favourite job.

I hear murmurs upstairs and climb up. It's a sparse room, no furnishings or decoration. There is no light, to avoid the risk of nosy neighbours. I blink, my eyes accustoming to the gloom. Naima and Ira are there; they both greet me with the sign of Camun.

"You look tired, Grandad," Naima says.

"Well, the guild keeps us busy. Remind me what it is you do all day? When you're not revolting and advancing the cause?"

"Don't you worry, I have plenty to keep me occupied. Were you okay getting here? Bloody curfew is all we need."

"Fine. I know Val Varin."

"Not much military presence here," says Ira. "My friend says people are sneaking out every night."

"Even so," says Naima, "can we hold our next meeting in the day?"

"Too busy," I reply. "They're working us non-stop. We can't just sneak off."

"It would raise alarm bells," Ira agrees. "How about we meet on the ninth gong? At least then we'll only have to break curfew to get home."

Naima nods. "Fair enough. Now, to business. Everything is in place. The shipment is due to arrive tomorrow, Camun willing. Looks like the Dagmari army will be here soon though – could have done with a few more days, but we work with what we're given."

She takes two squares of cream fabric, marked with annotations, and hands them to us. "There's your chits. Now, a forger's been working on these the last few days. They look genuine, nothing that will make the Crawlers suspicious."

"And we get these stamped by a Justice?" Ira says.

"That's right. I'm telling you, xe'll stamp it without even looking at it. And once it's stamped, no Blue or militia captain is going to quibble with it."

"So where do we take these weapons?" I say.

Naima gives us an address in Blackstone – chosen for its location close to the harbour, so the job can be done as quickly as possible. She makes us both memorize it and repeat it back to her several times.

"Now," she says, "we don't want to pull this job tomorrow. The ship arrives in the afternoon – by the time everything is unloaded and sorted out, it'll be the end of the day. We can't have you rushing in, trying to move a load of crates at dusk, it would be too visible. Time it for the day after, when dozens of teams will be picking up weapons. Give the instructions to the militia first thing in the morning, then get the Justice to stamp the chit as soon as you can."

We run through the plan a few more times. Two Camonite cells and possibly a priest will be waiting at the Blackstone warehouse. Naima warns us to avoid entering the building and seeing them – for our protection and theirs. Naima tells us she'll be at the harbour herself on the day, in case anything goes wrong. "But believe me, nothing'll go wrong."

I want to ask how, exactly, one nineteen year-old girl, Camonite or otherwise, will be able to help if the Keda realise we're trying to steal weapons to arm an uprising. But since she's already taken risks for the order, and been in the mines, she has the moral high ground, so I say nothing.

"What about stage two?" says Ira. "Any news?"

"The plan is pretty much ready. Another cell will deal with the trap and neutralizing the Justice. All we have to do is give xer the location and lure xer there. Let's get stage one out the way first, though. And think about which of those bastards we want to take down."

We agree to meet here after the job is done, on the ninth gong, to debrief and prepare for stage two.

"I want Jakub there," I say. "We could do with some inside information from the militia, and more importantly, he can bring us some gear. This is starting to get dangerous for us. I'm going to ask him for crossbows and leather armour."

"Not sure we want to share details of the weapons cache with him," says Naima. "Might not be happy that we've ripped off the militia."

"Fine – we can discuss that when he's gone. But let's have him here at the start."

The others agree. We're about to leave, when I ask Naima about Rico again. "Tell me about him," I say. "What was he like?"

She chews her lip, looks uncomfortable. No one ever likes talking about the mines.

"Look, I can't pretend I knew him that well. He was, what, sixteen when I left? And I was in Val Varin barrow, he was in Wesson. But he was sometimes on my shift, and I do remember him. Hard-working, tough, hated the Crawlers. One thing I can remember, he wasn't a weeper. He was hardy, that kid – he hated being there, but he was one of those that was damned if the mines were going to break him."

"And what did he... look like?" I say. For some reason it feels embarrassing having to ask.

"He was, you know... tall, quite thin. Had a bit of a crooked nose, which some of the girls liked. Quite serious-looking, but always a smile in his eyes. Bit like you, I suppose?"

I know she just added that to please me, but I like it anyway. Hearing about my boy, from someone who knew him, it gives me a sort of peace.

Naima leaves out the back of the abattoir, as is her way. By mutual consent, Ira and I leave together – the curfew means the streets should be empty. We're walking south – down a dirty passage, with steaming dung in the gutters. We're talking quietly, when we're interrupted by a shout from behind. On the major road that connects Val Varin to the city centre, a patrol is crossing our side street. It's cursed luck – even more so when I realise two Keda are with them. There's a moment when we could run. But the soldiers are probably fitter than me, and in any case interpreters are too valuable to punish for minor indiscretions, whereas running really would be suspicious. So we wait as the patrol marches down toward us, six soldiers, a Justice and a councillor.

"What are you doing?" a soldier calls out. "Don't you know there's a curfew?"

He's about to say more, when the councillor puts out a hand to stop him and takes over, approaching us with feline grace. I look in xer eyes and realise it's Chicken, who has recognised me. Xe raises xer right hand, and reluctantly, I hold out my left arm. The soldiers watch as I apologetically point to my bare skin, unadorned by bronze bands. But xe waves it away and xer hand encloses my lower arm.

(Question) / Outside / TranslateMan /, xe says. *(Question) / (Negative) / Home / (Question) / Break / NightLaw / (Question) / CityWar /.*

It's a lot of questions. And I'm in no mood for fingerspeak, but I know how much trouble I could be in, so I summon up my most unctuous accent.

(Regret) / Excellency / (Shame) / Outside / (Negative) / Home / (Shame) / Break / NightLaw /.

I gesture to Ira and take a gamble.

Woman / Love / However /... I sigh theatrically. *Other / Man / Possess / Woman /.*

I bow to Chicken, my forehead at xer chest. *(Imperative) / See / Woman / (Shame) / Excellency / (Intensify) / (Shame) /.*

By this point, the Justice is growing impatient. Xe reaches out and takes Chicken's arm from me. They fingerspeak, but Chicken's gaze never leaves me. The Justice snuffles, looks at me and xer shoulders rock up and down – I think it's the Keda equivalent of "Nice one, mate, get in there."

The soldiers look perplexed, and the Justice turns to go. Chicken isn't finished, however, and xe leans back to me. With xer left hand, xe points to the city around us.

Val Kedić / In / CityWar /, xe says. *(Negative) / Brothel /.*

The touch for */Brothel/* involves an extended squeeze, and xe pinches my skin, leaving a red welt.

War /, xe continues, *(Negative) / Love / (Conditional) / Break / NightLaw / (Consequence) / Punishment /.* Xer tone is riling me now, and I hold xer gaze, just long enough to let xer know I'm not quite as spineless as I appear.

(Positive) / Excellency /, I reply.

Xe turns xer back on me and follows the soldiers in the direction of Val Firuz.

"What the hell was that?" Ira asks me when they're gone.

"We're having an illicit love affair," I tell her. "It was all I could come up with. Sorry."

She stares at me.

"No need to look quite so horrified. And by the way, you now have a union with another man. In case a Keda mentions it. Might be best to have him killed off in the first wave of Dagmari attacks."

"Right," she says. "I suppose it's just about plausible."

We continue south, keeping to the shadows, headed for the boundary with Wesson. On a couple of occasions I see people looking out at us, but I've faced down a councillor tonight and don't really care what these citizens might say.

"I'm not sure I'm cut out for this, Razvan," Ira says.

"What do you mean?"

"I froze up. Just then. When they were coming towards us, my mind was blank. I panicked. If xe had spoken to me, it would have been a disaster."

"Come on, Ira—"

"And going out to negotiate with the outriders today? Inside, I was a mess. My heart was beating so fast I thought it was going to explode. All along, I thought I would be cool in a crisis. But I'm really not, Razvan. What the hell am I doing in the middle of a bloody revolution?"

"Ira," I say, gripping her by the arm. "Only fools are never afraid. But you didn't show it. And with the Dagmari, you nailed it."

"Eh. I was doing some pretty liberal translation. Just as well he had no interest in negotiating."

"I'm serious, Ira. Look, I'll let you into a secret. Twice I've seen men die in front of me. Both times, I was sick straightaway. All those soldiers I work with, they'd laugh at me if they knew. This pansy interpreter who can't hold a sword or cope with a bit of blood. I could never have imagined myself joining the Camonites, but here I am."

"What about next time, though? What if I freeze up and put everything at risk?"

"Dammit, Ira – you're the one that got me into this! Don't get flaky on me now. Look, we're all weak – but what we're trying to achieve here is massive. And the end result is all that matters. Who cares if we panic or puke our guts out while we're doing it?"

"All right, boss," she says, and takes a deep breath. "Good pep talk. Now, what about that Crawler – did xe buy your story? Is xe going to cause trouble?"

I think back to Chicken's gaze; I think back to when I knew xer as a Blue, eighteen years ago. If anyone was going to cause trouble, it was Chicken.

* * *

My first few years in Goathorns were possibly the happiest of my life. For the first time, I had my own place to live – the interpreter's residence in the centre of the quarter. Borzu had his own quarter now too, Ganzić in the south, not far from me. My quarter's delegates were experienced but not jaded, and I worked well with them. And then, of course, there was Margrethe.

With love, as with all things, I followed in Borzu's footsteps. He had scorned the Sevanić girls his family had intended for him, and was instead courting one of his delegate's daughters, a sweet girl called Nikoleta. The delegate was a climber, and to outsiders it may have looked like a political match for Borzu – but he had fallen hard for the girl. Like all cynics, he was a romantic really, when you scraped away the carapace. Aged eighteen, he used to make world-weary comments about the pitfalls of monogamy, but as soon as he met Nikoleta, he was as lovesick and foolish as anyone. Our duo became a trio, and any thought of popping down the sewers was a million leagues away. Other girls might have tried to push me away, but Nikoleta adopted me – I think she knew how besotted Borzu was, and that I was no threat. And whenever we shared a chuka down the Goathorns taverns, a regular topic of conversation was finding a girl for me.

It was on my twenty-third birthday that I first met Margrethe. It was the year of the Riona Revolt, the birth of the Camonites – not that any of us paid much attention. Borzu insisted on celebratory drinks at the Seven Goats, the oldest tavern in the city. In stone cellars, you could drink at giant trestle tables, and the barkeep turned a blind eye to the high-stakes dice games that took place in the dark corners.

A few other interpreters came along, and a couple of local friends – this was before I met Jakub – and Nikoleta brought her cousin Margrethe. The setup was transparent – they arrived late, giving me a chance to have a few mugs of chuka, then Nikoleta introduced me and chatted for a short while, before dragging Borzu away with a wink at me. I was embarrassed. The two of us had a whole trestle table to ourselves, but Margrethe was unfazed.

"Nik thinks we'd be a good match," she said breezily. "You're nothing like Borzu, are you? He's nice enough, but a bit loud and showy."

"We're completely different," I said. "Two Borzus in a conversation would be intolerable."

"Good. Now tell me about this Spidertouch business. It looks damned creepy to me. I don't know how you stomach it."

It was the first time anyone had asked me about my skill. When I was with Borzu and the other interpreters, we never discussed it. We might bitch about particular Keda, delegates or senior interpreters – but nobody would think of talking about fingerspeak. I found I loved telling her about it. She listened seriously and asked intelligent questions. I took her arm and explained how modifiers worked. I saw Borzu look at me with raised eyebrows. "Really?" he mouthed at me.

I didn't care. I liked talking to her. She told me about her life as a folk singer, performing at various city functions and celebrations, with a friend who played the mandolin. It was traditional music, from centuries before the Keda arrived and renamed the city. So her music was not favoured by the Keda, and she spent her time performing for the wealthier citizens of the city, in quarters like Sevanić and Roć. It was an alien world to me, just as mine was to her. We talked most of the night, until the last gong rang, and the barkeep kicked us out.

We stayed in contact via Borzu and Nikoleta, who formalized their union shortly after, with Nikoleta moving to his interpreter's residence. Our relationship, however, was slower and cooler – I would see Borzu and Nikoleta together, flirting and with their hands all over each other, and envy it a little. But it was the way we were, we weren't going to fake it. We courted the best part of a year, in the gardens of Ganzić, or on long walks along the city walls, or I'd go to watch her perform. We were serious together, pragmatic. There didn't seem to be the fireworks that others talked about, but we didn't mind. It was more of a slow-burner, and I felt comfortable with her in a way that I never was with anyone else.

In the winter, we formalized our union, a couple of seasons behind Borzu and Nikoleta. She didn't move to my residence in Goathorns – I was embarrassed by my shabby quarter, and she was happy to carry on sharing a house in Ganzić with her friend who played the mandolin. We spent our free time together, and I would often stay at hers. In the back of my mind was the fact I was expected to have children as soon as I could. It wasn't like the elders or delegates, where the Keda would block progression unless they had children. Interpreters were needed, and they wouldn't discard me because I failed to procreate. Even so, it was simply an expectation, and at that stage I didn't challenge it. I just knew I ought to breed soon, so that the Keda could have a threat to dangle over me. If it sounds absurd, it shows how thoroughly the thinking had permeated our society.

It was the following season we encountered Chicken for the first time – still a Blue at that point. I say the first time – perhaps we had fingerspoken before, but as I've said, they all look the same. Unless they had a particular habit or did something memorable, it was hard to distinguish them. But I heard about xer when Borzu told me about an incident he had witnessed. It had been in one of the clerical buildings, so he told me – he was there to translate some Blue instructions to delegates. The two of us were in his residence, preparing dinner as Nikoleta was not yet back.

"So this Blue – nasty type, very full of xerself. Do you know xer?" He trilled Chicken's name on my arm, and I shook my head. "Rather like the touch for /Chicken/, isn't it? I don't usually have a problem with Blues, but xe was correcting my

Spidertouch, and I swear xe was speaking fast to put me off. Supercilious bastard. Anyway, the delegates leave, and xe tells me to wait for another pair xe needs to speak to, so I'm standing in the corner. Then a councillor comes in. One of the old ones. You know xer, horrible wrinkly skin, moves so slowly it's painful – the one who's always getting angry with the elders. Straightaway, I can tell something's up. The councillor goes to this 'Chicken', grabs xer arm and starts speaking. Jabbing with xer other hand. Chicken's standing up, stiff as a rod, taking it. I can see xer eyes dart to me once or twice, but the councillor hasn't spotted me. This goes on for a bit, and I'm trying not to watch, but I can see xe's arguing back. Suddenly – the councillor hits xer! Holy Kedira – I couldn't believe it!"

"Xe never! That old Keda?"

"I swear. You wouldn't believe how fast xe moved. Sideswiped xer. Chicken staggers back, crashes into a desk. Then the councillor brings up xer staff – and starts beating xer. Three times xe hits xer!"

"I would pay to see that…"

"Chicken can't do anything. Xe's bigger, but xe can't fight a councillor. The old Keda's wheezing away, looks knackered, then xe walks out. I'm left on my own with Chicken."

"What did you do?"

"What could I do? Both of us are still for a bit. Xe's snuffling on the floor. Eventually, I figure I've got to leave. But as I slink out, I glance over at xer. Our eyes meet. And I can't help it, I give this little half-smirk. It's so awkward."

"Ah, Borzu, you didn't… did xe do anything?"

He waved it away. "I mean, xe looked pretty pissed off. But you know, xe's just a Blue. What's xe going to do?"

I didn't share his relaxed attitude. Even a Blue Keda was capable of cruelty. And the humiliation xe must have felt, for a citizen like Borzu to witness xer being beaten by a councillor… I was uneasy. Borzu called me an old woman and told me not to worry. He told the story again to Nikoleta over dinner that evening, but she didn't laugh either, and told him not to turn it into an anecdote.

A few days later, Borzu and I were in attendance in the High Chamber. It was a quiet session, lots of Council discussion while the elders sat like lemons, taking no part. A Blue came in and Borzu nudged me. "That's xer," he whispered. "Chicken."

The wizened councillor raised xer arm, and Chicken went over. Borzu gave me a mischievous grin, but in the corner of my eye I could see Chicken, looking at Borzu with pure fury, for xe had seen his grin, and xe must have known in that moment that Borzu had been spreading the story. Afterwards, as we left, Chicken even accosted us – xe marched straight up to Borzu and gave him a talking to.

"What did xe want?" I said afterwards.

"Ah, you know, whingeing away, telling me if I breathe one word of what I saw, blah, blah… honestly, I don't care for xer. Very pompous attitude."

I was worried now, even more so because Chicken had seen me with Borzu, and knew that I knew. What I thought xe might do, I wasn't sure. I just knew that it was best not to antagonize the Keda, any of them. For a time, however, nothing happened. Perhaps ten days passed, and each day I worried a little less, until it was just a vague anxiety at the back of my mind.

And then, Chicken struck.

I was with Borzu after a morning in the High Chamber – we had crossed the Bridge of Sorrow, and were walking back through Roć, towards his quarter. Borzu nudged me and pointed – for Margrethe was running up the street towards us.

"It's Nikoleta," she shouted. "Come, you've got to come!"

Borzu broke into a run, and I chased after him. The three of us hared south as Margrethe explained. A Justice had arrived at Borzu's residence, and arrested Nikoleta. Two militia had accompanied xer, but said they did not know the charge. She didn't resist, and they dragged her to the market square, the central point of the quarter. They were holding her there – Margrethe had run north to find Borzu.

We ran through the Ganzić gardens, jumping over flowerbeds, brushing past groups of citizens. I figured it was political – something to do with her father being a Ganzić delegate. I reached the market square five paces behind Borzu, Margrethe at my shoulder. About thirty citizens were stood watching, silent. The Justice was standing by a fountain, holding a thick club, xer foot on Nikoleta's neck. She was on the cobbles, wearing just a torn cotton shift. Her tunic was floating in the fountain, and you could see a livid bruise on her arm. She glanced up, gave us a despairing look.

And then I saw Chicken. Xe was standing to one side with the militia. Xe nodded to the Justice, eyes on Borzu.

Once, the club hurtled down, and Borzu yelled out in horror. Twice, and he made to run towards her, but I grabbed him round the chest.

"Don't do it!" I said, as he struggled with me. "Can't you see what xe is trying to do?"

"She's pregnant, you fool!" he hissed at me.

A third time it came down, and Borzu tore free, running at the Justice.

I'm not sure what he planned to do – arms outstretched, maybe he just thought he could knock xer over. But as he came running in, the Justice was prepared and swung a fist, cased in a black leather gauntlet. Borzu grunted as he hit the ground.

He got to his feet almost immediately. Maybe the Justice would have let him live, but Borzu raised a hand, aiming to strike xer. In one fluid movement, the Justice stepped away from Nikoleta and sliced at Borzu with xer scimitar that was sheathed by xer green robes. Nikoleta screamed, and Borzu collapsed.

I made a half-movement towards them, but Margrethe stopped me with her arm. "Don't be a martyr!" she said fiercely. "What good are you to me as a corpse?"

I let her hold me back as the Justice took xer second scimitar, and delivered the killing blow, running it through Borzu's gut. As for me, I promptly vomited in the brown scrub at the side of the market square.

Nikoleta lost the child. Whatever charge was against her – whatever Chicken had bribed the Justice for – it went away. Xe had got what xe wanted. Sometime later that year, Nikoleta committed suicide. She drowned herself in the Southern Sea. Her body washed up on the beach, another victim of the Keda.

So, yeah, I always thought Chicken was a vicious little shitbag. And I knew xe might cause us trouble.

INTERLUDE (1)

The wind is bitter in Riona, especially at night. It snakes through the crags and buffets you from all sides. Whitehair squints as a gust of sand stings the scar on his cheek; he hurries past the towers that loom over the colony's scattered buildings until he arrives at the dovecote. A youngster is waiting for him, a boy really – pink-cheeked and fresh from the hills to the north.

"So?" Whitehair says.

"A pigeon from the south," the boy says. "They say the city is under attack from the Dagmari. They're summoning all the Keda back."

Whitehair frowns, takes the tiny scrap of paper from the boy. Not that he has any notion how to interpret the scratches. He sucks his cheeks in and his mind whirrs.

"Ill news," he says. A candle is guttering, and he holds the scrap over the flame. It shrivels in a black and orange spasm. "Best if you don't say anything about this," Whitehair tells the boy. "No need to worry the Keda about it right now."

The boy blinks. "But... can we do that?"

Whitehair takes a seat and rubs a hand over his scalp. He is bald now, no sign of the startling blond locks that gave him his birthname. "You think seven Keda are going to turn the tide, defending their city? Course they won't. But they make a difference here." He nods in the direction of the barrows, the long, one-storey dormitories where the southerners' children sleep. "You think they fear us?"

"Ye-es?" the boy says. "No?"

"They hate us, and can't say I blame 'em. But they *fear* the Keda. It's the Keda that stops 'em from turning on us. How many are we, lad? Seventy-five? You think two thousand southern brats couldn't take us on if they put their mind to it?"

Whitehair turns his head ninety degrees, and the boy swallows. Whitehair taps the scar that runs from his chin to his right temple – livid and bloated like a slug.

"Know where I got that?"

"I heard it was… from the revolt?"

He nods. Nineteen years, now. Only three of them still here who remembered Camun's day in the sun.

"That's right. Wasn't Camun himself who gave it to me, but one of his mates. Took me out with a swing of a chisel. Out stone cold I was, missed most of the action. Never got it treated properly, that's why I'm such an ugly bastard. But there you go. Those little waifs – they might look broken and dead behind the eyes, but I promise you, if they get half a chance…"

"All right," the boy says, "but the southerners will expect an answer. Won't they keep sending messages?"

"Maybe they will," Whitehair replies. "But you keep on burning 'em, and the longer the Keda stay, well, that's another day we get through."

"Yessir." The boy does a clumsy salute.

Where does he think we are? Whitehair thinks, as he gets to his feet and leaves. *The bloody army?*

As a boy, he had dreamed of being a soldier – his fantasies revolved around glory on the battlefield and dying acts of heroism. There was little honour, however, in a lifetime spent guarding malnourished children – though everyone tried to spin it to themselves some way or other when they started. For most, it was a stopgap of five or six years to earn a bit of silver before returning to the hills to marry. The Keda paid well, that was for sure. So once you had your fill, you left the mines behind you and tried to forget the whole shameful episode. But not Whitehair.

Twenty years on, and he was still here. Only Bearhide had been here longer. *One more year.* That had been the refrain for over a decade. *Just one more year, then I'll call it a day.*

He stalks past the barrows. They are ugly, lumpen buildings, designed purely for solidity. Aesthetics didn't get a look-in. Between seventy and ninety kids in most, though a few of the slum barrows topped a hundred, like the kids from Lekaan and Goathorns. Why they are called barrows, nobody knows – long before his time. Roć barrow is the one he watches out for – as is his custom, he unbolts the door, and peers round to check up on them. A few tiny faces look up at him from their bunks.

"Everything okay?" he asks in the southern tongue, and one of the older ones nods.

He retreats and locks up. Beyond the barrows, a stony valley drops and twists through the mountains. Rocks jut out at jagged angles, blissfully unaware of the inconvenience they cause the colony. He hawks up some phlegm and clambers up an escarpment. Everything is a trial here. Just walking from the dovecote to the barracks is a mission.

Below him, in the valley, are the entrances to the mines, adits that are driven into the mountainside and slope slightly upwards to help drainage. Even in the dark, you can make out the logs that hold up the openings, in angled table-shapes. They look precarious, but have held for dozens of years.

Although he's a senior guard, Whitehair spends nearly half his time on the road – accompanying eleven year-olds from the city to Riona, and then their future-selves, grown men and women, back to Val Kedić. Not to mention security for the caravan of wagons that transport coal and marble to the city, where it will be traded and sold across the Southern Sea. Some of his countrymen see it as a chore, but not him. If it wasn't for the Roć agreement, he would spend even more time travelling back and forth, across the plains. On the road, he's free, driving the horses forward, pace after pace, until they reach their target. Here, aside from the unforgiving landscape and wind, he has to contend with the looks in the kids' eyes, has to see them begging for mercy and their tears of frustration as the Keda dish out their arbitrary, twisted punishments. Or some of his over-zealous compatriots, let's not forget them. And yes, he's been here twenty years, he's as guilty as anyone. He could walk away tomorrow. But always, that rotten refrain: *One more year. Just one more year.*

If he didn't do it, someone else would. Someone crueller, someone with fewer scruples. He scowls. *Stop trying to justify yourself,* he thinks.

The Roć business, at least, was making him a wealthy man. Why go back to being a shepherd, or join the roving band of mercenaries, or whichever hell passes for life in the hills these days?

It was a decade ago he had encountered a Roć delegate in a Queenstown tavern during an overnight stay. Over the years, he had learned enough of the southern tongue to get by, and the two of them were able to scratch out a proposal over several mugs of chuka. In return for a stipend paid by the Roć parents, he agreed to look out for their kids. Extra rations, one of the cushy mines to work in, and no fear of beatings from the guards. They even arranged the delivery of letters to and from Riona.

Whitehair had to square it later with the other senior guards, of course, and they would get their cut. There was plenty to go round, though. The next time Whitehair visited the city, he brought a half-empty barrel of apples on the wagon, nestled among the barrels of water and dried meat. He left it overnight by the Queensgate, and the next morning, the bottom of the barrel was filled with silver ingots, and covered with apples. They would melt the ingots down later in the colony, and share out the wealth.

It was risky, cutting a deal without the knowledge of the

Keda. But it had paid off. The quarter seemed to pay their taxes, and the Roć Justices were uncommon visitors compared to in other barrows. So the Roć kids got through their time in the mines relatively unscathed. And during his marches along the mountain road, it just about kept his guilt at bay.

My conscience is not clean exactly, he would tell himself, *but not dirty, either. Mud-spattered, perhaps.*

A nightjar calls out – an implausibly long trill, punctuated by chirrups. The wind burns. Night is the only time he can stand this bloody place. No cries, no unpleasantness, no tortuous attempts to communicate with the Keda. He sighs and moves on.

He carries on past the Keda's quarters. A single Keda is leaning against the clay wall, looking up at the stars. Xe is just a dark shadow, even at ten paces. He can make out xer curved fingers, tapping on the wall. They don't acknowledge each other. They hardly ever do, even on the eight-day trips between Riona and the city. Sign-language and gestures are usually enough. Like all the guards, he's learned a few basic touches – /Number/, /Boy/, /Girl/, and so on. The one who usually communicates with them is Half Moon, who's managed to pick up more of the touch language than the rest of them.

Whitehair pauses as he approaches the barracks. The atmosphere sounds lively, he can hear shouts and songs. He is aware he dampens the mood sometimes – slightly too old, slightly too serious. The others respect me, he thinks, but they won't fully relax around me.

So instead, he continues walking. The ground rises sharply, an incline that leads up to The Noose – a massive rock formation in an oval shape, hollowed out over centuries to take on the appearance of a noose. Nobody comes here – there are no mines, and escape would be impossible, for the land falls away in a dizzying drop beyond. He climbs methodically, looking for each foothold in the moonlight. He used to bounce his way up here, barely pausing for breath – twenty years have taken their toll.

At the top, he sits at the base of The Noose, underneath a thin arch. The view over the valley is vertiginous, but he is immune to it. The conversation earlier is making him think of Camun again. The Keda had not paid the boy any attention – his parents must have been no trouble. But the guards had his number. They clocked him as a troublemaker, and some of the senior ones had taught him a lesson or two. He was a sinewy, gangly thing – all limbs and muscle. A small head, with a constant sneer that flickered at his lips. Whitehair never spoke to him, but the boy made him uneasy. He had the sense that Camun knew him, knew the lies he told and the compromises he made. Of course, everything was different then. *He* was different, a twenty-three year-old who had never gone further south than Riona, not yet made the journey to Val Kedić.

Simpler times, he thinks. All the southerners he had ever met were rich, arrogant, lazy sots. The Keda were his employer. The kids were the opposition, the southerners' whelps who they had to control. The Miners, some guards called them, as if to try and forget they were children.

Despite their youth, the mines made the children grow up fast. Under Camun's direction, they took the guards by surprise. They might have even taken over the colony, if Camun had been able to rope in all of the barrows, or if there had been a few less Keda present. Whitehair can't remember which barrow Camun had belonged to – Saalim? Ganzić? – regardless, he had set up a simple decoy in the night. A few guards had gone to investigate cries coming from a barrow – a girl, feigning violent sickness. As they went to calm the child, the barrow overwhelmed them, and they streamed into the colony, with weapons they had secreted.

Thirty of the biggest, with Camun in the lead, had skulked over the rocks to the armoury, while the rest released as many of the other barrows as they could, and caused chaos. Not all of the barrows were on board with his plan, but still, hundreds of teenagers with sticks and axes were on the rampage. He had been one of the guards who ran into the chaos, where demented eighteen year-olds were lashing out with seven years of pent-up fury.

Then had come the chisel. He only regained consciousness the next morning. Fifty-seven miners killed, twenty escaped. Eleven guards dead, and one Keda. Camun had taken the armoury, but he hadn't quite had the will and momentum for the revolt to succeed.

Retribution from the other Keda afterwards had been merciless. Whitehair couldn't watch – he holed himself up in the barracks and waited it out.

Less than a year later, he had to make his first trip to Val Kedić. By the Queensgate, he had watched as the southerners let their children go. They weren't like the southerners he had met before. Shabby, poor and stricken with grief. He had felt a prickle of shame.

Just one more year, he had told himself, for the first time.

9.

I hunt down Jakub the next morning. He's outside his barracks, at the side of the road, sharpening his sword on a whetstone. It is early, not yet first gong, and I feel rough after a poor night's sleep worrying about Chicken, remembering Borzu and Nikoleta, thinking about Margrethe. Rico.

"Jakub," I say.

"Razvan," he says, looking guarded.

"How you doing?"

"How d'you think? When I joined the militia, it was to break up tavern brawls and catch cutpurses. Not to fight in a war."

"What are the new recruits like?"

He snorts. "Some of them are a complete liability. More likely to cut their own throat than a Dagmari's. But who cares? They're just bodies for the bastards to kill. Distract them from getting over the wall."

"Well, I guess we'll know pretty soon," I say.

He draws the sword savagely, and it gives a shriek against the whetstone. "This is the last bit of calm we're getting, I reckon. Once it starts, they'll have us taking shifts up on the walls non-stop."

"Listen," I say. "You know what we talked about?"

"Ah," he says. "And there was me thinking you'd just stopped by for a natter with your old pal."

"I'm going to need your help, Jakub. This is getting serious."

"I honestly don't know how you can think of–" he lowers his voice to a stage whisper to say "terrorist activity", before raising it back. "Not at a time like this. You do know there's a war on?"

"If we can get rid of the Keda," I say, speaking softly, for there are other people in the street, "then we can give the Dagmari what they want. And the war goes away. The Keda just don't want to give up their life of luxury."

"Perhaps. But don't forget; there are plenty of elite citizens out there who don't mind things the way they are. And in the militia, come to think of it."

"I liked you better when you were happy-go-lucky, not this miserable sod."

He gives me an obscene gesture, half-heartedly. "So. What is it you want from me? That will doubtless end in a grisly death for both of us."

"First – can you put your hands on some gear? I need three crossbows, and bolts. And some leather armour."

He raises an eyebrow. "What the hell are you planning?"

"Can you get them for me?"

"Sure. I can get hold of them."

"And I want you to come to our next meeting. It's tomorrow, at ninth gong."

"Do I have to?"

"I want you to meet the others, Jakub. You'll understand why we're doing this."

"Well, I'm not on a night shift. Though if the Dagmari army have arrived by then, who knows. Where is it?"

I give him the butcher's address in Val Varin.

"And what will we talk about?" he asks. "With these terrorist scumbags you want to introduce me to?"

"We'll want some information from you. About the militia, what the latest strategy is. And we'll tell you our plan – you might be able to help with it, suggest some operational changes."

He holds his sword up to the sun, and it catches the glare. "Just don't ever say I don't look out for you," he says.

I grin then leave him to get his armour on, and take a walk around Wesson to clear my mind. The weapons shipment arrives today. The city gates are closed for the first time in my life, and an army is drawing in on us. The Keda want to throw citizens' bodies at them. And the Camonites want to tear it all up and start again. It's a lot to process.

I circle round the quarter, trying to unpick the problem, to find a way out. I go past the Western Glory, eyes down, not wanting to see anyone I know. The streets are still busy, though enemy riders are just a short walk away. Until the gates are breached, life must carry on.

I reach the walls. Tufts of brown grass are sticking out the brick joins in bunches, like nostril hair. They look solid, these walls, unbreakable. They have the agelessness of a giant cypress tree. But the Dagmari don't have to knock them down. They just need to get over them. Or starve us out.

I stand and stare at the walls. I wish I could get out of here, out of this bloody city. I used to come this way with Margrethe – up to Val Varin, out the Western Gate, to explore the black sands and the olive groves on the other side of the walls. For all the good it does to think of her. I had Margrethe just seven years before I lost her to the Grey Fever. Long enough for her to bear me Rico, long enough to move to Wesson with me. It was just as grubby as Goathorns, but still somewhere we could call home.. At least she never had to see them take our boy, see him leave on the dusty road to Riona. A small blessing.

First gong sounds and breaks my thoughts. I'm facing the wall, slack-jawed, and I realise two boys are staring at me curiously. I wheel away and head home – I need to get to the interpreters' compound and find my business for today.

* * *

In the afternoon I am with a Justice, who is inspecting troops in the barracks, when a Blue enters with a message for xer. They fingerspeak, the Justice snaps xer fingers at me, and heads in the direction of Val Firuz. Xe is in a hurry, and I walk a few paces behind. Men and women make way as xe pushes through the People's Market. Off the main streets, the earth is dank and crumbly after a heavy rainfall last night. The rainy season has arrived which will, at least, make life miserable for the Dagmari in their tents.

Over the Bridge of Peace, into the High Chamber xe goes. It is busy in there, and I lose xer as xe goes through several doors and round a corner.

Silas passes me and catches me by the arm. "Have you heard?" he says. "A pigeon came from one of the towns on the Ilić Royal. They're a day's march away."

"Did the message say how many men?"

"It just said 'Big army', apparently." He laughs.

"Well, we knew it was coming." I look round at everyone milling about. "What's going on here?"

He gives a sour smile. "You know how it is. Like flies to a turd. No one wants to miss out. The Keda, the elders – everyone wants to be involved." He nods at a black-robed alchemist who is fingerspeaking with a councillor. "Even one of *them* turned up."

"They're going to help defend the city?"

"Just a last line of defence for Val Firuz, so Eleven says," Silas murmurs. "They're too valuable to risk on the walls, and the Keda see the value of not gassing our own soldiers."

I ask him what I should be doing, but he has no idea. Our schedule is in tatters, and it looks like it's going to stay that way for a while, interpreters running harum-scarum round the city to whoever shouts the loudest. Even with the apprentices, there's not enough of us to go round.

For the last three years, Silas has been the most senior interpreter and the voice of the guild. He's a prim, fussy man, not given to banter with the younger interpreters. He's a first-class interpreter, but a reluctant leader, and has never quite won the respect of the whole guild. In peacetime, it wouldn't matter, business still runs smoothly. But in a crisis, he's not the right man for the job. I don't think it's vain to say our guild is the gossamer-thin thread that holds the city together, and enables dialogue between the Keda and the citizenry. But this siege could break us, and, if the guild falls, what hope is there for Val Kedić?

I would mention this to Silas, but I know he has no appetite to fight our corner. If the Keda demand some interpreters, all he will ask is "How many?"

He takes his leave of me and I walk purposefully through the halls, as if I've got instructions to go somewhere. I'll have to hope the Justice forgets about me in all the chaos that is brewing. I'm looking for Ira, but she is nowhere to be seen. Up on the dais, I see Chicken. Xe is with Eleven, and many of the more influential councillors. I'm uncomfortably aware that this crisis has been good for Chicken: xe has risen as one of the strongest voices of the Council, always issuing instructions and at the heart of discussions. Darius, Chicken's usual interpreter, is with xer – as I pass, there's a horrible moment when xe spots me. Xe is fingerspeaking, and Darius looks over at me, as though Chicken has pointed me out. What the hell is xe saying about me?

I up my pace and get out of there. I have to remind myself that we are under siege, and a councillor surely has bigger fish to fry than me.

I head out to the Seven Goats, which is a popular haunt of interpreters. My plan is to avoid the Council as much as I can, and interpret for Ansić and whichever Keda are with his squad. Everywhere I look, there is a strange calm which is in stark contrast to the buzzing of the High Chamber. Citizens must be aware that we're surrounded, that the city will soon be under attack, but also that life must go on. Children are playing, and old men squat on their haunches, smoking and spitting. Black markets had sprung up in the days after rationing began, and with the militia occupied they don't even attempt to hide their activity. There is one right outside the tavern, doing a brisk business in flour, eggs, and grain under a makeshift awning.

There are only a couple of interpreters around in the tavern, no one I know that well. The weapons must be at the harbour now, and I'm tempted to ignore Naima and do the job straight away, before the Dagmari arrive. But I have to hold my nerve. Rico is depending on me to do this right.

I spot one of the administrators, drinking by herself at the bar. I ask her, and she confirms that the interpreters' rota no longer bears any resemblance to reality – they're just sending us out whenever a messenger comes to request one. I have visions of infuriated Justices, helplessly trying to communicate instructions to soldiers, as the enemy horde advances on the walls, and projectiles go flying overhead. Or even worse, the pressure of a Keda giving me complicated battle commands while fighting rages around us.

Jakub was right – getting involved in a rebellion right now is a shockingly ill-conceived idea.

When I wake the next morning, I know from the noise the Dagmari are here already. I dress in a hurry, and head straight for the walls. Militia are crawling everywhere – shouting at citizens, sending them home. I cross from Wesson into Val Varin – Ansić's squad hold a section of the wall just south of the Western Gate. As I get closer, I can make out a low rumble beyond the walls. I reach the steps, where most of the squad are found, busy with their weapons and armour. Ansić gives me a curt nod, but there's no sign of any Keda yet. The sergeant, a lugubrious man, who I now know goes by the name 'Bones', sees me and takes pity on me.

"Here we go, then," he says. "They arrived in the night, the sly sods."

"Any Keda here?"

"Nope. Don't worry, they'll be along soon enough." He looks in the direction of the walls. "Want to take a look? They're not doing anything yet."

I agree and he takes me up the steps. There is an archer every ten paces, locals mixed in with mercenaries. Quivers of arrows are at their feet. Some militia are marching along the crenellations, barking commands. I look out and see the source of the rumbling.

The three hundred outriders that we had previously stepped out to negotiate with were just a cluster compared to this. The Dagmari form a giant semicircle that surrounds the city. To the south, they stretch nearly as far as the sea. To the north, they curve round towards the Ilić Royal. It is a solid wall of men. Mixed among the swarm are wagons, and I can make out soldiers unloading them. The rumble I heard is an amorphous noise of chatter, creaking, chopping, hammering, yelling, goats bleating. In places, cavalry are bunched together, not heavily armoured like the outriders, but smaller, sleeker colts. In front of them, slaves are digging ditches and setting up palisades; beyond them I can see huge, wooden constructions. I count three trebuchets – I've seen drawings, but never in the flesh – a couple of bridges on wheels, and other contraptions I don't recognise. And all the time, new arrivals are pouring through. To a man, they take a good look at the city, then find a space and start setting up.

"Holy Kedira," I hear a man whisper behind me. I glance round and see two soldiers who have mounted the steps. I can tell from the accent they're farmers, yokels from far beyond Val Kedić.

"Yeah, something like that," says Bones, with a pitying glance.

"Are we ready?" I ask him.

"If they attack now? Well, the archers are primed. We're ready to man the walls if they come at us with ladders." He shrugs. "As ready as we'll ever be. None of us have lived through a siege before. What worries me are the things we don't know we're not ready for. If that makes sense."

"What about those?" I say, pointing at a trebuchet. "Don't look as terrifying as I'd thought."

"Wait till you've got boulders and blocks of limestone flying at you," he says. "Then tell me how you're feeling. And we'll find out how well our ancestors built these walls." He claps me on the shoulder. "I wouldn't worry though. They won't attack today. Give us a bit of time to stew."

A drumbeat starts up in the distance, a relentless *tum-tum-tumpity-tum*. I shiver. "This city's lasted hundreds of years. Survived plague, floods, the Keda. Scary to think this bunch of animals could pull it all down in a few days," I say.

"Aye. A lot easier to destroy than it is to build," Bones says.

Ansić appears at the stairwell and beckons me.

"Interpreter," he says. "Justices are circulating. You're needed."

We go down together. "If we're under attack," Ansić says, "I'm going to need you to relay messages efficiently. I don't care about you getting it word-perfect, I just want the gist of it. Just tell me, concisely, any information I need to know. Got that?"

"Of course."

"They sent me some kid yesterday. He was fussing around, trying to explain different possible meanings of something a Blue was telling us. I couldn't make head nor tail of it – ignored him, in the end. The bare bones, that's all I need. If you jeopardise the lives of my men cos you're taking too long dicking around with words and meaning–"

"Hey," I say, tired of his speechifying, the high self-regard of this militia grunt. "I'll do my job, you do yours. I'll translate, you keep the bad men out, okay? You do realise, by the way,

I'm the only one up here without a weapon? What exactly am I supposed to do if any Dagmari scale the walls?"

"Do?" He smirks at me, he's the kind of man who doesn't mind backchat if it shows you have a bit of spunk. "You run like fuck, interpreter – that's what you do."

10.

The Justice is another one I don't recognise. Xe's standing away from the soldiers, inspecting a sword, weighing the heft of it. Xe notices my white armband – so I hurry to xer side, and xe begins to fingerspeak.

(Negative) / WestGate / Defend / Good /, xe says. *(Imperative) / Soldier / Go / WestGate /*.

(Question) / Number /, I say, an easy phrase, one of the first questions you learn as an apprentice.

Ten /, comes back the reply.

I nod and withdraw my arm. My skin is suddenly prickling all over. I know this is it, I'm about to deceive a Justice and a militia captain; the Camonite uprising and the road to Rico's liberation starts here.

I walk over to Ansić, who is conferring with Bones, arms folded.

"So?"

"The Justice says ten men are to accompany me to the harbour. A shipment of weapons arrived yesterday – we need to distribute them to another squad."

Ansić frowns. "Weapon distribution? We're not delivery boys, interpreter."

"Xe was very clear–"

"A barbarian army is on our doorstep, my men need to

116

protect the walls. Ask xer why these soldiers can't go and collect the weapons themselves."

I swallow. "Captain, I–"

He puts his hand on my back, and guides me towards the Justice. "Go. Talk to xer."

My cheeks burning, I place my fingers between xer bands. Xer flesh is coarse, and xer eyes are regarding me, impassive.

(Question) / Justice / Choose / Ten / Soldier /, I say, aware the syntax is appalling, I've definitely messed that up. *Or / ChiefSoldier / Choose /.*

Xe waves at Ansić impatiently, before replying *ChiefSoldier / Choose /.*

I keep our arms in the fingerspeak position as long as I can, dragging it out so the conversation looks longer than it is.

(Positive) / Justice /, I say. *(Future) / ChiefSoldier / Choose /.*

I turn to Ansić. "The Justice's message is not to be questioned," I tell him. "The other soldiers are occupied elsewhere. Those weapons must be delivered. The Dagmari will not attack yet, the ten men can be spared."

He fixes me with a hard stare. The militia aren't used to the Keda interfering much with them, and I can see Ansić weighing up his options. Unwilling to back down in front of his men, but unable to argue with a Justice.

"Very well," he snaps. "But you're taking some of our new recruits. Bones, round them up."

Bones moves among the squad, tapping the chosen ones on their shoulders. As he's finishing, there's a roar from the north – a guttural noise, more taunt than war cry. The Justice reacts first, and bounds up the steps, limber as a cat. How fast they move! Ansić and a few soldiers are behind xer, and I follow them up. As I get to the top, a clashing of shields starts, a rhythm that seems to drive the shouting.

When we look out, however, the horde has not moved. They're still unloading, wagons and soldiers streaming through their ranks. Further up the wall, we can see our own men, craning necks, looking to the north. Clearly, something has happened at the front of the city, but there's no way for us to see.

"What happened, archer?" Ansić says to one of the men.

"Nothing here, captain," the man replies. "There was shouting up north, but I'm just keeping an eye on my section."

Everyone's looking north now, there's a palpable mixture of relief but also frustration, a sense of being left out. Ansić goes back down the steps, shouting at someone as he goes. I take the chance to get the Justice to stamp my chit. Xe looks at me distractedly, as I take it from my pocket and hold it out to xer with my left hand.

Councillor / Command / Man / Collect / Weapon /, I say. *(Negative) / Enough / Weapon / Soldier /.*

Xe peers north again, for there are still ragged shouts and that clashing noise. On xer belt is a ring with various keys and a stamp. Xe takes the stamp and presses it down on the chit, not troubling to look at it. I turn around, exhale, and hurry down the steps before xe can talk to me again.

Ansić tells Bones to accompany the ten recruits to the harbour. I don't think he likes the idea of his men going off with me nominally in charge. The soldiers he's given me are a sorry-looking lot, underfed and appearing uncomfortable with their weapons. Bones leads them out with me at his side. They've been well-drilled at least, and march in step as we go south, back through Wesson, towards the Southern Gate. We're cutting through Goathorns when I spot a patrol, and suddenly remember the Justice's instructions. There's seven of them, and they don't look like regular militia.

I nudge Bones. "I've just remembered – the Justice also wanted some men at the gate. We didn't have enough to spare but this lot will do."

"Hey," I yell at the recruits. "I've got a command from a Justice. I need all of you to go to the Western Gate immediately. We need more men there."

"But we're meant to be manning the wall at Blackstone," one of them objects.

"Forget that. This is a direct instruction from a Justice."

A couple of them look at each other, but they don't move.

"Men!" Bones shouts. "You're in the army now! There's a chain of command, get yourself to the bloody gate! You," he points at a soldier at the rear, "I know you, you worked in the smithy by the market. I'll be checking later that you went to the gate."

They salute, and set off in a new direction, with a sour look at me.

"Thanks," I say.

"Don't thank me. Got to have discipline or this siege won't last three days."

We continue south. I'm relieved to have what passes for an ally among these soldiers.

"How do you rate our chances?" I ask. "Of surviving more than three days?"

"Well, if we tried to meet them in the field, it'd be a massacre," he says. "But behind these walls... doesn't matter if our soldiers ain't the best. If the sea stays open, and we keep our discipline... give me 2-1 odds that we outlast them, and I'd take it."

"Still," I say dubiously. "Those aren't amazing odds, for not dying."

"They're not, I'll allow you that. But you just concentrate on keeping yourself alive. I ain't got much time for the crawling buggers – but we need them right now, and you're our only way of talking to them. So you, we can't afford to lose."

"Will do, sergeant."

We march down the hill to the Southern Gate. There's no sign of Dagmari galleons yet, but there's still a high military presence here. We pass the fish market, and I see a few stalls open. Above us, gulls swoop and shriek. When I was a kid, I used to hate those gulls, glaring down at me. They always seemed to be biding their time, scavengers eyeing me up, hunters of infinite patience. If supplies run short, soon we'll be shooting the little bastards down for meat.

I point in the direction of the depot, and the soldiers follow. When we get there, it's not as busy as I thought it might be, but immediately I know we're in the right place. Crates are piled high, and one has split open so that a dozen pikes have cascaded out in a fan formation. I approach a Blue sitting at a desk and present the chit to xer. Xe inspects it, and we have a brief conversation, before xe shows me the four crates I can take. Naima's forger has passed the test before I even have a chance to get nervous.

The crates need three men each, so I pitch in and get under the corner of one. I tell Bones the address of the Blackstone warehouse, and his trio lead the way. The two soldiers with me are friends and ignore me while they banter together. The crate's awkward rather than heavy, and the corner juts into my armpit. I wince with discomfort.

As we cross a street, I tell the other two we need to stop and reposition. They look at me with mild contempt while I rub my arms and try to get a better grip. We carry on through Blackstone, a little behind the other trios, my arms aching. Finally, after several hundred paces, when I'm sure I'm on the verge of dropping my end, we reach the warehouse. There's some militia there, who must be disguised Camonites, taking the crates. I keep my eyes down. We put the crate on the ground and I turn away, letting the soldiers sort it out. It's done. I've dropped a pebble in the ocean, and the ripples are spreading out. Six years ago, I watched my son leave this city – I felt the powerlessness bubble up under my skin like a rash. At the time I wished there was something I could do, anything. Now, there is.

My grief for Margrethe lasted years, but in time I forgot the details of her last few days – sweating and delirious, before she succumbed to the Grey Fever. The day Rico left Val Kedić, however, was a particular type of trauma, and is stamped on my memory forever. We had to present ourselves at the Queensgate at first gong. So Rico had a tearful farewell with Baba Shika, the old woman who had been nanny, cook and tutor to him for the past eight years. Then we walked all the way to the east of the city. Over the river Firu, into Queenstown, past the Palace of Shadows. We didn't speak much. What was there to say, that wasn't trite or a lie?

Traders were calling out from their stalls, and I remember two men laughing together hysterically at some joke, holding each other in mock support. I wanted to smash their faces, to push over their stalls and send their wares flying. It was just another day for them.

I had already given Rico a huge breakfast, but before we arrived at the gate I spotted a Street Rat selling figs, which were a favourite of his. We stopped, bought a bunch, and sat at the side of the road. Rico munched them contentedly – he was apprehensive about the mines, but not overly anxious. He lived day by day, as I suppose most kids do. I just had the one fig, but it was overripe, and I spat some of it out. When he had finished, we walked the last few hundred paces to the Queensgate.

A dozen eleven year-olds were there already, and a Justice. Accompanying xer was one of the older interpreters, who gave me a sympathetic grimace; also a Blue, and five guards from the hill tribes – paler skin than ours, and all sporting thick moustaches and beards, as was the fashion for the hillsmen. Everyone was in groups of two or three, the child and their parents. There was no talking between the groups. By the time first gong sounded, the gathering had swelled to thirty or forty children. The guards checked their lists, and called out some names. There were six who had not turned up – "there's always some runners," as another parent had confided in me a few nights ago. One came sprinting up just after the names had been called, the father right behind her, eyes red. For the rest, the Blue recorded the names, and left us, along with the interpreter. Then, too soon, it was time for the children to leave.

There were some wailers, mainly mothers, who gripped their children and gave great gulps of bitter, impotent rage. Some pressed their children close, and gave them urgent pieces of advice. Others cursed and shouted at the sky. Me, I just held Rico in my arms, hugged him tight, and let him go.

The children drifted through the crowd to where the Justice and guards were waiting by a wagon and horse, with supplies. Parents were left in ones and twos, more alone than they had ever been in their lives. A few of the children looked back, but I'm glad Rico did not, for I could not have borne it. The guards shouted some instructions. The Justice surveyed us all, slowly, deliberately. A reminder of who xe was, the power xe held. Then a guard slapped the horse on its haunches, and they were off, through the Queensgate.

A few of us ran up to the wall, to watch them down the mountain road. Most other citizens nearby gave the procession a respectful silence, for many of them had been here before. I watched Rico's back, retreating towards the mountains. In my mouth, the fig's sweet taste had curdled, and I badly wanted water. I wept silent tears and as I watched, I heard a mandolin player strike up a tune that was very popular at that time. "This Burning Fire", it was called, a mournful love song with an inexplicably jaunty chorus. The minstrel's voice drifted up from the street, clear and bright as the first rain of summer. I've never been able to listen to that bastard song since.

That evening, Jakub and I walk to the Val Varin safehouse together. He comes to mine first, and drops off my crossbow, bolts and leather armour. I admire it all, and try on the armour – it's good quality. He has brought gear for Naima and Ira too, and we take half each before setting off. It turns out Jakub was one of the hundreds of militia stationed by the Gate of Triumph this morning, and I ask him about the shouting and disturbance.

"Ha!" he says. "That was just a bit of silliness – poking each other in the chest before the fighting starts. Three Dagmari envoys came riding up the Ilić, all decked out in their finery. All the citizens had gone, it was just soldiers around. The wall was packed, everyone wanted to see what was going to happen. Anyway, the central rider could speak our tongue, and he yelled out, 'You have until dawn to open the gates! If you do, Shakan will be merciful!' Well, nobody replied. There were a few Justices around, even a councillor – and interpreters with them. But nobody knew what to do – waiting for a Crawler to take the lead, I guess. Who knows, maybe the interpreter was about to give a message for someone to shout back. But as it was, we just looked like bloody idiots – threatened in our own city, and all standing there in silence.

"The Dagmari must have thought so, because they started laughing with each other. Then the central envoy turned his horse to leave. But then one of his escorts – must have planned it in advance – brought out our flag, unrolled it, and it floated to the ground. He kicked his horse, and it lets drop a steaming dump, right on the flag. I mean, fantastic trick. First class. Full respect to the guy. But of course, everyone on the wall was furious. I was screaming and shouting along with everyone else. Thousands of Dagmari cheering. That might have been that, but some gimp of an archer lost his cool. One of the conscripts, I bet. An arrow went whizzing past the horseman, several paces wide. Then everything went crazy. Two units of their horse archers came charging towards the walls. Captains were shouting commands, most of us went diving for cover. Our archers let loose, theirs let loose. I saw a lad on top of the barbican, he took one in the arm. Apparently we hit a few horses. They were all banging their shields, making a horrible racket. Then the horse archers retreated." He laughs. "Oh, boy.

What a clusterfuck. Great start to the siege. Omen of things to come, I fear."

"So, it'll be tomorrow, then."

"Tomorrow, then. I could really do with a drink, to be honest. I know a place that's doing a lock-in. Sure I can't persuade you to drop all this?"

"You could, Jakub. But I'm trying very, very hard to do the right thing. So please don't."

We arrive at the safehouse just before ninth gong sounds. I had timed it as close as possible – I wanted to be last, as waiting there with just Naima felt awkward. We pass through the abattoir, and Jakub mutters something which sounds sarcastic. Upstairs, Naima and Ira are already there. The introductions aren't as difficult as I feared: Jakub can be jovial with anyone, no matter what he thinks of them. Naima seems guarded at first, but warms up considerably when he passes her a crossbow.

We talk generally at first, of the Dagmari and the strength of their army; then Jakub tells us what the militia leadership is arranging for the city's defence, and what he has heard from the Justices. Then the conversation circles around to our cell and what we're planning.

"Before we go any further," Jakub says, "I want to know what you're up to. If you're not out to hurt us, if you're just after the Crawlers, then we can work together."

"That sounds fair," Ira says.

"And if it's secret society goatshit and weird ceremonies, you can count me out. I'm taking enough of a risk – this has to be serious."

"Don't worry, we're serious," Naima says. "What we're planning is nothing less than to liberate Riona, and everyone in it. You weren't in the mines, were you, Jakub?"

He shakes his head.

"But you must see, this is a just cause. Break their power over us, and we can correct some of the wrongs done to this city."

"You're ambitious. That's good. Do you have enough weapons?"

"We do," Naima says. "Now, before we attack, we need to get information from a Justice. The plan is to kidnap one, with Razvan's help."

"Kidnap a Justice? With him? No offence."

"None taken," I say. I turn to Naima. "Hadn't realised it would definitely be me."

"You're more experienced than Ira," Naima says. "The Justices know you, less chance of them being suspicious."

"In that case," says Ira, "can I nominate which Justice we take? I want Beast. Xe killed my parents."

Jakub whistles. "You couldn't choose anyone tougher," he says.

"I'll put your suggestion to the priest," says Naima. "Xe's recognisable, I suppose, so should be easy to track xer movements."

"And how exactly will this work?" I ask.

"You'll go to xer at a set time," says Naima. "Beforehand, our people will have circulated a rumour that there is a Dagmari traitor inside the city, sending information to the enemy and trying to find a way to help them in. You will tell xer some soldiers have trapped the traitor – xe will come running. We've secured a location by the Little Firu, in Five Bells. That is where you'll take xer. Once inside, another cell have prepared a trap to disable the Justice, take xer *cantu* and scimitars. We'll hold xer there, right under the Crawlers' noses."

"The Justices move fast," says Jakub. "Damn fast. You'd better be sure your trap works, and that you've got enough people to take xer down."

"We will," says Naima. "We're not taking any chances."

"And you know they wear chain mail under their robes? Beautiful craftsmanship, from across the Southern Sea."

"Good to know. But we're not trying to kill xer, just overwhelm xer."

"All the same," says Jakub, "don't underestimate them."

It's at this point there's a sickening creak from the stairs. Our eyes all turn to the door. Ira has the presence of mind to keep on talking.

"And what will the next steps be?" she asks.

Jakub moves with a grace that belies his size. Silently, he edges to the door. Naima has taken up her crossbow.

"Well," Naima says, "that all depends."

Jakub flings open the door. Staring at us, eyes bulbous in the darkness, is Darius. Chicken's interpreter. For a crazy moment, I wonder if he's come here to ask if he can join the Camonites. Then he springs back and scampers down the stairs. Naima's crossbow bolt buries itself into the wall, where his head had been a moment earlier. And I know this is going to end very badly for one of us.

11.

Jakub pushes through the doorway in pursuit, with me right on his tail. I hear Naima behind me, cursing, shouting at Ira to clear the place out. Down the stairs we go, through the abattoir. Instinctively I grab one of the cleavers – Jakub has his sword, Naima has a crossbow, and without a weapon I feel pretty useless. I'm not sure I could hurt Darius – he's not a friend, but he's a colleague, and he's all right really. I know he has a daughter in the mines, so if Chicken told him to spy on me, he'd have no choice, the poor bastard. But all the same, if I had to choose between him and me, I'd choose me, every time.

Jakub barrels out into the street, and looks left, right – I see Darius, running east, and I think I know where he's headed. The three of us chase him up the street, but Darius is light on his feet and moves like a hunted animal. Naima and I overtake Jakub, and Naima is fiddling with her crossbow, fitting another bolt. It's curfew now, and if we bump into a patrol we really are screwed. Darius looks over his shoulder, sees the crossbow, and darts into a side street.

"He's an interpreter," I say to Naima, between breaths. "A Keda put him on our tail. Xe saw me and Ira leaving the safehouse last time."

"You are shitting me!" Naima spits. "How much did he hear just now?"

"We were, ah, talking about the plan to kidnap a Justice. And then to march an army on Riona."

She curses under her breath, and we zig-zag, following him as he cuts a chicane. "It's my fault," she says. "I thought the safehouse would be secure."

I look behind, wave at Jakub, who is still following at a steady pace.

We are on a straight now, and Naima winds the crossbow. Darius must hear it, for he gives a little yelp, and cuts towards an alley. Naima aims, fires, and it clatters into the limestone wall. We follow up the alley, which winds up a hill. At the top, there is no sign of him, and we look around desperately.

"Where's he bloody gone?" Naima says.

"He's headed for Val Firuz," I say. "He must be. Only place he can get sanctuary. He's trying to get to Chicken. This way."

I call to Jakub, and we dart down another alley, downhill, the streetlamps blacked out. I stumble on the cobbles and Naima slows, pulls me to my feet. We are in Five Bells now, between Val Varin and Val Firuz. My mind is flashing ahead, already planning for worst case scenarios. Suicide? Sneak out on a boat? Go back to The Stain and pretend to be a fisherman?

We get to the bottom of the hill and jump a drystone wall. On our left are the city's stormwater tanks, on our right are gardens. Naima points. "There he is," she whispers. He's fifty, sixty paces ahead, and my legs are burning but we keep running, quietly so he can't hear us. I spot two soldiers on a street corner, but their backs are to us. On we go, through a small orchard, the leaves brushing against our faces. We follow him, over the canals that weave their way through Five Bells, and I watch him, jogging into the juniper tree square where Ira and I met with the elders, what seems a lifetime ago. We put on a last burst of speed, follow him into the square –

Darius is calmly walking towards the Bridge of Peace, where a Justice stands guard. He gives one last backwards glance, and

I grab Naima, before anyone sees her. We watch, as he takes something from his tunic, and presents it to the Justice. There are only two bridges into the citadel, and both are guarded by two Justices at all times. We've lost him.

"He's got a night pass," Naima says. She crouches down. "I don't believe it. We're finished."

Jakub arrives, panting. "Where's he gone?" he says.

"A councillor. Chicken. Xe sent him to spy on me," I say.

Jakub swears. "That's it," he says. "He saw my face. He's not going to forget me."

"We need to wind everything up," Naima says. "I need to find the priest."

"Maybe not," I say. "We might still have a chance."

I've forgotten plans of suicide. I know what the Justices do to a child whose parents don't pay their taxes. What will they do if your father helps plan a revolution?

"What?" says Naima. "How?"

"I know a route into Val Firuz. Through the sewers."

She chews her lip. "Seriously?"

"And I know where Chicken's mansion is. I attended a function there once – some ceremony, they needed interpreters."

"It'll be too late," Jakub says. "We can't possibly beat him there by the sewers, even if he's walking."

"No," I say carefully, "we can't. But we can get there before Chicken tells anyone else."

"And... kill a councillor?" says Naima. "In the middle of Crawler Central?"

"Has anyone got any better ideas?"

"Let's do it," says Jakub. "It's all or nothing now. If we fail, I'm going to have to go on the run."

Naima is about to say something, but I interrupt. "You need to wait behind, Naima. To deal with the interpreter when he comes back." I can't bring myself to name him. "And if we don't make it back, you need to be here to tell the priest, sort things out. I know the sewers, where Chicken lives. And Jakub is expendable."

"Thanks," he says.

Naima shakes her head. "I should–"

"No time to argue," Jakub says. "He's right. You don't have to try and be a hero. Let's go, Razvan."

"Wait – the interpreter lives in Ganzić. Don't wait for him here, he's sure to leave via the Bridge of Sorrow."

Naima watches us forlornly, standing with her crossbow. I lead Jakub over the road. A hundred paces away are some latrines – we used them as an entrance maybe three or four times, during our days in the sewers. I find the panel at the back, it's not as loose as it was more than twenty years ago. Jakub shoulder-charges it and grunts as it breaks.

I climb though, and down into the sewers we go, with me pointing out to Jakub the grooves in the brickwork where he should put his feet.

"I hate to be proved right," he says in a sing-song voice, "but I did say this was a terrible idea."

"Let's save it for later, eh?" I reply, looking up at him as he nearly steps on my fingers.

We splash down into the tunnel. Despite the years, the network and the routes come rushing back to me, without any conscious thought. I point left.

"This way."

Along the main tunnels are dim oil lamps, but the side tunnels are just shadows and night. I can see the rats all over the pipes, running for cover as they see us coming.

"We'll have a bit of time," I say. "But not long. He'll think he's safe, he'll walk through Val Firuz. And then it'll take a while for him to convoy all that information to Chicken in fingerspeak."

"And how do we get into this mansion?" Jakub asks.

"Xe has a garden. That's where xe held the ceremony. If we can climb the wall, we can get in at the back."

We plough on, through the slime. The only sound is Jakub, dry heaving behind me. I can tell when we're past the Little Firu and into Val Firuz – the tunnel is better maintained, everything is cleaner. Borzu and I didn't dare come here often – too much risk of being caught – but I remember a route that took us up to some administrative facility.

I point right, and we crawl through a side tunnel. It's so dark here my right hand is flailing in front of me, in case of a turn or an obstruction. My legs are wet and coated in slurry, and I can feel bile rising in my throat. We keep going. I'm sure we've gone too far, but then I see a chink of light above us. Groping for the wall, I find a ladder. I call out to Jakub and, exhausted, climb up to the opening.

I push open a trapdoor and climb out into a sparsely furnished room. The building seems empty. Jakub and I find a back door that is bolted on the inside.

"So," he says. "That was disgusting. Where do we go now?"

I don't know the Keda's residential area so well – my regular haunts in Val Firuz are the interpreters' compound and the administrative buildings around the High Chamber. But we have to find Chicken.

"Just follow me," I say. "I think I can find it."

"Keep to the shadows," he says, "and don't make a sound."

We unbolt the door, and step into the heart of the city. The streets are straight and wide. There's no sign of anyone. Militia are supposed to patrol the riverbank and the walls beyond the moat, but there should be no one around here. The Keda are in their homes, many with lights extinguished. To the west, the alchemical institute looms up, and I can see one room still lit. Through the window, I can make out the black cowl of an alchemist, still at work – though no silver smoke drifting out from the window.

We go in the opposite direction, east towards the residential area. I make a couple of wrong turns and have to double back, but I know I'm on the right track as the houses start to increase in size and develop walls and gates. Footsteps ring out, and Jakub pulls me behind a balustrade. We watch as the figure of Darius appears, walking down the road opposite at a brisk pace. I glance at Jakub, and he shakes his head.

"Trust Naima to sort it out," he says. "We've got to move fast."

We follow the direction he came from, and sure enough there is Chicken's mansion. Lamps are lit in several windows. I beckon to Jakub, and we circle round the back to the wall. Jakub gives me a leg-up, and I pull him up. If a Keda is looking in this direction, we're done for, but we're too far down this road now, and we jump into the garden.

Chicken, or whoever xe paid to decorate, has taste, I'll give xer that. Since the ceremony I attended, xe's done plenty of work on it. There is a spiral design of paving in the centre, covered with what looks like an elaborate mosaic; and Judas trees are arrayed around it, with their heart-shaped leaves. In the corners, bronze statues of animals stand – oversized and fearsome. One is a boar, another an eagle, and I can't make out the other two. At the back is the least tasteful part, which looks like a shrine to Kedira. It's ostentatious, framed by two enormous junipers, and steps leading up to it. A few dim candles dot the trees and light our way to the mansion.

Jakub takes the lead now, unsheathing his sword and edging round the garden, his back to the wall. We reach a courtyard, just twenty paces wide, with doorways into the house and various outbuildings.

"What's the plan?" I whisper. I'm holding my butcher's cleaver tight.

"Let me deal with xer. Be on my shoulder – your job is to make sure xe doesn't get to xer *cantu*."

Inside, we find ourselves in a room with a circular pool, surrounded by pots of oleander. I dimly remember being here, and discussing the pool with another interpreter later – it might even have been Darius. Do they take their robes off when we're not here, we wondered, and splash around in it?

There is no sign of life. Normally, you'd expect to find some servants in a residence like this, but the citizens would have returned to their quarter at the end of the day. We pad through the room, into a hallway. But, try as we might, we can't help making slight noises, the creaks and swishes of motion. We hear movement in an adjacent room, and Jakub signals to me. We back away into the pool room, and the steps come closer. Jakub gets behind the doorway, and I'm right behind him.

A figure moves through the doorway, and I nearly call out, for the robe is blue, not crimson. But Jakub has already moved, lunging forward and thrusting his blade between the Keda's ribs. The Blue looks at us, a startled expression on xer eyes. Xe crumples and falls to the floor. I lean down, grab the *cantu* and pull it off xer neck. Jakub has closed his eyes. He opens them, gives me a look. Raises his eyebrows.

It's nearly fifteen years since a citizen murdered a Keda, and that was a father, mad with grief after his daughter died in Riona. This Blue was innocent, as far as any Keda could be called innocent. Technically, Chicken is innocent too. But I have no qualms being party to killing xer.

Blood is bubbling out from under the Keda's cowl. I think about fingerspeaking something to xer, but it's too late. Xer eyes flutter, and shadows pass behind them. Jakub gently moves the body out of the doorway. He shrugs at me, points onwards. We go back into the hallway, and this time we hear a shuffling of parchment, then a clink as a glass or a plate is placed on a table. Jakub creeps towards the chamber where the noise came from. The hallway is well lit, and I feel horribly exposed. Blood is dripping off Jakub's sword, leaving red explosions on the lilac carpet. I can see Chicken's crimson robes over Jakub's shoulder. He puts three fingers up.

Three... two... one...

He darts into the room. As I enter, a pace behind, I see our reflection in a silver goblet by xer hand; Chicken has spotted the movement too, for xe has jumped to xer feet. Jakub snarls, jabs with his sword, and Chicken skips to the left. Jakub uses his bulk and bounds forward, blocking off all exits. This time he cuts down with a savage hack. But there's a metallic *ching*, and Chicken staggers back into the wall. Xe gives us a triumphant, hateful glare, as xer chain mail appears over the lip of xer cowl. I'm not close enough to do anything – too wary of Jakub's lunges – and then Chicken goes on the attack. Xe hurls xerself at Jakub, so close he can't use his sword against xer. Xe drags Jakub down to the floor and rolls over with him; xe uses his size against him and propels him away so he crashes against the desk. Xe grabs xer silver *cantu*, and I see a flash of xer mouth: tight and lipless, with rotting teeth. On the floor, xe blows the *cantu*, though I can't hear it.

As Jakub gets to his feet, I fall on Chicken. I'm not even thinking, as I take my cleaver and bring it whistling down –

And I chop off xer right hand.

We look at each other for a horrified moment, as the blood starts spraying all over me. Then xe starts what must be a Keda scream, a wheezing, high-pitched keening sound, straight from my nightmares. But I take the cleaver again, and chop off xer left hand. Xe is convulsing on the floor now, flapping xer arm stumps in spastic rhythms. Xe is a fingermute.

Jakub touches me on the arm. "We've got to go," he says.

I jump to my feet, impulsively putting one of Chicken's hands into my pocket, and we run into the hall. As we leave the mansion, into the courtyard, we hear a battering at the front door. We're running through the garden, and I can hear the battering getting louder, more insistent. There's no need for a leg-up this time; there's a bench by the wall, and I lift myself up onto it. Then I jump straight back down, for I can see several Keda, running towards the house, it's a mercy they didn't spot me.

"The back," I hiss at Jakub, and we run past the shrine, to the back wall. It is lower and easy to climb. I have no idea where we are now, and we blunder through the darkness – shrubs, walls, the occasional gate. My heart is pumping. I look west, finding the towers above the High Chamber, from where the city's gong sounds. As long as we head that way, and avoid Keda, we may get out of this alive.

Eventually, after a mindless rush through gardens and outbuildings, we get back onto a street I recognise. Another Keda is fifty paces away, running in the direction of Chicken's house – I wonder if the first responders have broken in now, and blown their *cantus*. By their very nature, we don't know how frequently the Keda use them, but we believe it's only supposed to be for emergencies, not just when someone falls over and needs a hand getting up.

Everything aches. My lungs are in agony. I try to stop, but Jakub grabs me by the elbow and keeps me moving. Fifty paces to the sewer entrance, and I see another Keda further down the road. I think xe sees us, but it's just a Blue, by xerself, and xe doesn't challenge us. Out of sight, we go round the back of the administrative building, get inside, and bolt the door. We look at each other. We haven't spoken since leaving Chicken's garden. I smell of sewage; my face and arms are speckled with a fine mist of blood; and my tunic ripped somewhere during our escape. I gingerly touch a gash along my gut – some spiked tree I brushed past.

"You look," Jakub says, "like shit."

We go back the way we came, through the tunnels. Not stopping at Five Bells, but all the way back to Wesson. We are breaking curfew, after all, and the last thing we need is to be stopped by a patrol. It's a long, weary slog. I'm running on automatic now, but that image keeps flashing through my mind – Chicken's eyes, when I cut xer hand off. The horror, the strangled scream.

Finally, we reach the exit by the Six Ways latrines. We stop, and sit down on the tunnel's stone path, by the grooves that lead up to the city.

"Bloody hell, Jakub. We killed a Keda," I say.

"Two Keda," Jakub says. "Chicken won't survive that. And xe can't tell them anything. Good thinking with xer hands." A pause. "I'm sorry – I didn't know councillors wore mail under their robes. Maybe it's recent, since the Dagmari arrived."

I wave away the apology. "It's just as well there's a siege on," I say. "Can you imagine the fallout if this happened in peacetime?"

He gives a short laugh. "Yeah. How about if we both die when the Dagmari attack tomorrow? That would be an irony, wouldn't it?"

"Whatever happens, we kept it going. We made sure the Camonites can still free Riona. That's something."

"I guess so."

"Join us, Jakub. When we march on the mines, you could come with us. Don't you want to get out of here?"

"Maybe. But the city, first. We've got a siege to fight."

I nod, and we sit in silence for a while. I need to speak to Naima, I need to get some sleep, but I can't move. It's the middle of the night. At dawn, the Dagmari's offer will expire. And the city will wake to the outrage of the Keda.

12.

I don't have to look hard for Naima – she is lurking in the shadows by my house. We both get inside quickly.

"You were gone a while," she says. "I was starting to worry."

I light a lamp, and she takes a step back. "Bloody Camun! What happened to you?"

"We got xer," I say. "Can you let me clean myself up, and I'll tell you about it?"

I put the cleaver on the table, by my crossbow. She helps me light a fire, and I fill a bath. As we work, I tell her about our journey through Val Firuz, the murder of the Blue, and finally the mutilation of Chicken. She gives a low whistle.

"The Crawlers' reaction isn't going to be pretty. Pity xe got to xer *cantu*, you might have been able to hide the bodies."

I grunt.

"So we're safe?" she says. "We're definitely in the clear?"

"Xe can't tell them anything. And the amount xe was bleeding, I imagine xe's dead by now. The only worry I have – I think a Blue saw us. Before we got back into the sewers."

"How far away?"

"Fifty paces?"

"Eh – it's not a disaster. Xe can't tell them much. At that distance, in the dark? We all look the same to them anyway – it tells them two citizens were involved, but that's it."

"I suppose so." I look at her sharply. "What about Darius? The interpreter?"

She looks away. "Yeah. I got him. He came back out over the Bridge of Sorrow, like you said. Looked very nervous. I let him think he was safe. Followed him south, and shot him when he was walking through Ganzić – I've got a contact there, he's taking care of the body for me."

There's a dull throbbing at the base of my skull. This was my fault. Darius didn't need to die. "He didn't deserve this," I say. "He had to do what Chicken told him."

"He had someone in the mines?"

"A daughter."

"Then the order will look out for her. When we free her." She sighs. "It wasn't easy. But you know we had to do it. Too many people are counting on us. He was a loose end."

"I just wish it hadn't been such a rush. If I'd had time, I could've talked to him – could've explained it to him and got him on our side."

She looks uncomfortable, runs a hand through her cropped hair. "We're fighting a war, Razvan. There's going to be some casualties along the way."

To be nineteen again! To have that casual confidence in the rightness of your beliefs! At forty-one, I already I felt too old for this revolution.

"So. Where do we stand, Naima? Onwards with stage two? Now I've killed a councillor, trapping a Justice should be a walk in the park."

"Let me talk to the priest," she says. "My advice will be that we don't do anything hasty. The Crawlers will be on full alert, they'll be trying to find out who's responsible for this. Give it a few days to calm down, and they'll have to forget about it and focus on the Dagmari."

I dip my fingers in the bath. The water is passably warm now. "I really do need to get clean," I say. "Are you all right to...?"

"Sure," she says. "Listen – keep your head down, and try to keep away from Val Firuz. I'll be in touch." She looks dubiously at my blood-spattered tunic. "Do you want me to take that? I'll burn it for you. And I'll take the cleaver too."

"Good idea. Do you want to, ah...?"

"Strangely," she says, turning around, "I have no desire to see your naked, wrinkled body, Grandad. Chuck it over here."

I snort. "I'd hate to give you a heart attack," I say. "Another death on my conscience."

I never thought of myself as old, not until Rico went to the mines. It happens to everyone – you see parents age a decade in the first couple of years after their child's exile to Riona. I take Chicken's hand out of my pocket, pull the tunic over my head, and throw it over her shoulder.

"Be safe," Naima says. "Don't die some damn fool death up on the wall."

"You too, Naima."

She leaves with my tunic and the cleaver. It's silent again. I prise up a loose floorboard and stick the hand in there, already cold and hard. It is a foolish risk, but I trust the instinct I had to take it. I step into the bath and immerse myself in the water. The gash stings, but I ignore it, and stretch my limbs so they are all hanging out the tub. For a moment, I forget about the Keda and the Dagmari, and focus on my aching body. I take some soap and a spherical sponge; I clean the parts of my body, one by one.

My face first, wiping off Chicken's crusted blood. The last piece of evidence linking me to the crime. Then I wash my arms, bloody and sore after the long crawl through the tunnels. I dab at the wound in my gut, as I can see some dirt in it. I push the folds of skin together, feel a delicious stab of pain, and have to resist doing it again, like a nail that needs tearing. Last of all, I clean my legs: coated in filth, and still a murky colour after intensive scrubbing. The sponge is now black and unusable. I give up for now, and luxuriate in the bath. After some time, the water cools, and I allow myself to relive what I just went through.

The twenty year-old me – a naïve, junior interpreter – would never have believed himself capable of this. But twenty-one years later, here I am, a Camonite rebel, leading an incursion into the Keda heartland and mutilating a councillor. And I can tell myself it was all for Rico, that I had to be brave for him. But isn't there a part of me that enjoyed it, that wanted an excuse to hit back? We have a saying in Val Kedić – "The goat, too, bites." Even the most pliant goat, if you mistreat it enough, can surprise you and snap. And this is what the Keda should fear, for they've created a city that is primed to snap – parents pushed beyond their limits and ready to fight back.

I'm woken by a hammering at the door. I lever myself out of bed and hurry to open it, despite the protests of my stiff joints. A messenger is waiting, one of the official city ones.

"What is it?" I say. "Are we under attack?"

"Not that I know of. Get yourself to the meeting-room in Sevanić. Mecunio wants you."

I get dressed, leather armour on underneath, and make my way north. The route takes me through Five Bells and I can't help revisiting where we ran last night, the square Darius walked through, thinking he'd shaken us off. The streets are quiet, apart from groups of soldiers heading for the walls. I find the tavern in Sevanić and climb the stairs to the meeting-room.

Inside, I find Mecunio and Abitha, another elder and one of Mecunio's closest allies. Seated at a table are nine other interpreters – the most senior and trusted, all of us in our forties and fifties. Talia is there, and Silas, worry-lines creased across his forehead. Ozkan, Juraj, and Izem, all of whom I looked up to when I was an apprentice. The one exception is a youngster called Leo, who I realise with a start was always hanging about with Darius. He is sat slightly apart from the others, evidently unsure what he's doing here. Someone has brought grapes, and everyone is picking at them. When I've sat down, Mecunio breaks off his conversation with Abitha.

"Right," he says to the room. "Let's cut to the chase. We're in all sorts of shit. First off, has anyone seen Darius since yesterday evening? Anyone got any idea where he is?"

A few pairs of eyes turn to Leo. "Any ideas, Leo?" Abitha says. "You're his mate, that's why you're here."

"I haven't seen him since yesterday afternoon," he says, startled. "Is he not at home?"

"What's this all about, Mecunio?" Talia says.

"One moment," he says. "Has anyone seen him behaving strangely – any odd conversations, anything out of the ordinary?"

There is a baffled silence.

"All right," he says. "Here's where we are. Last night, I was woken by a Blue. Xe wanted me to come with xer, I could work that out – and xe took me to the High Chamber. A load of Justices were there. I thought the Dagmari must have attacked in the night, maybe even breached the walls. Soon Silas was brought in as well, to translate – one of them began asking me all about Darius, and told me what's going on. They had found two Keda, dead, in their home. A councillor – Chicken, some of you know xer – and a Blue. One of them had managed to blow xer *cantu*, it seems. That was shocking enough. We're all old enough to remember the last time citizens murdered a Keda. And the repercussions. But in their home. In Val Firuz..." He shakes his head. "And then, xe tells me that one of your guild was responsible."

"Hang on," Ozkan says. "Darius? They think Darius killed two Keda?"

Mecunio nods grimly. "Apparently, he had come into Val Firuz after curfew. He had a pass from Chicken. Both Justices remember him clearly, they were able to describe him. It

appears he went to Chicken's home. Something happened
there – an argument, a fight, it's not clear. He killed them both,
with some kind of sword or knife. Then he left over the Bridge
of Sorrow – the Justices remember him leaving, cool as you
like."

"Sorry," Talia says, "but this doesn't make sense. Darius is
as mild-mannered as they come. Are you asking me to believe
that out of nowhere he killed two Keda?"

"It does seem extraordinary," Mecunio says. "I can't pretend
I knew him well, but none of this tallies with what I saw of
him. And yet, he is not in his bed. He has disappeared. If he's
an innocent man, why is he in hiding?"

Leo raises a tentative hand. "I know Chicken had told him
to do a job for xer. He mentioned it yesterday morning. Wasn't
happy about it. Said he was having to give up his evenings."

"Anything else?" Abitha says. "What kind of job?"

"He didn't say. I know Chicken could be tough. Xe was
always giving him extra jobs."

Mecunio frowns. "All the same. That's not reason enough
to murder two Keda. He must know he's a dead man now. We
need to find out what this job was."

I gaze at the wall behind Mecunio, and wonder if I can get
through this meeting without uttering a single word.

"Maybe he committed suicide?" Ozkan suggests. "He might
wash up later today."

"Possible," Mecunio says. "There's more, though. A Blue
apparently saw two citizens running through Val Firuz, around
the time this was happening. One, presumably, was Darius.
The other was in a soldier's uniform." He clenches his fist, and
I realise he's angry, a cold fury that is threatening to bubble
over. "You see my problem," he says. "This is looking less
and less like a freak accident – one man going rogue, having
a breakdown and attacking some Keda. This is starting to
look more like a conspiracy, something that was planned and
executed. A conspiracy, on the eve of when we go to battle with

these bloody savages. And what I want to know is, part of the reason I summoned you all here," and his voice is raised now, a real edge to it, "how is someone from your guild involved in this bastard conspiracy, and could there be anyone else?"

Nobody answers, but a few look at Silas. This is his job. "Mecunio," Silas says, "I don't know what to say. Of course no one else in the guild is involved. If Darius really has done this... I can only imagine this mystery soldier coerced him into it somehow. If the soldier was in Val Firuz too, surely it must be one of the sentries on the river bank?"

"They've all been brought in for questioning," Mecunio says. "As we speak, the Justices are trying to... get the truth from them."

"Surely," Talia puts in, "it can't be a coincidence this has happened just as the Dagmari arrived. Could he have sold us out to them? It might explain why he's missing, if he slipped out along the coast, to go and pick up his reward."

"He's no traitor," Leo says. "He's lived in Val Kedić his whole life. I'm not sure he's even left the city the whole time I've known him. How's he supposed to have met some Dagmari, who randomly promised him gold if he killed some Keda?"

"I had considered it," says Mecunio, massaging his scalp. "But even if, somehow, he turned coat, why commit the murders? It doesn't particularly benefit the Dagmari. What would really be useful is if he stayed in place, feeding them information. Finding them a route in."

"How have the Keda reacted?" I hear myself ask.

"How do you think?" he says. "A thirst for revenge battling with paranoia. They seem to have forgotten about the siege for now – all they can think about is finding the people responsible and punishing them. I was doing my best to convince them this wasn't part of a wider conspiracy, some kind of revolution."

"It's very important," Abitha says, "that if anyone hears where Darius is hiding, they tell us immediately. We need to give him to the Keda. Someone has to be seen to pay."

"They're locking themselves in," says Mecunio. "No citizens are being allowed into Val Firuz right now. Silas and I agreed it would be sensible to move the apprentices out of the compound for a while. And I've got messengers going round the hundred or so citizens who live there – we're suggesting it might be for the best if they move out for a few days. Let the anger die down – we don't want any reprisals. And by the way, this news stays in this room. I don't want the whole city knowing a councillor was murdered."

"So what do we do today?" Juraj asks. "Is there any interpreting to be done?"

"There will still be some Justices circulating round the walls, to supervise," he says. "Everyone should go and join your billeted unit, in case you're needed." He suddenly looks weary, and I see how red his eyes are. "One last thing. Whatever you do, don't bloody die up there. You know how much I value this guild, how much I've supported you over the years. The only way we can coexist with the Keda is if we communicate with them. You all know how thinly we're stretched. I need all of you, alive." He turns to Abitha. "We have to go, Abi."

They sweep out the room, Mecunio adjusting his black sash as he goes. Nobody speaks for a moment. Silas gets to his feet. He looks tired too, and I wonder if he has been up all night, since being woken by the Keda.

"I'd better sort out the apprentices," he says. "If anyone hears anything, please, tell the elders as soon as you can."

He leaves, and Leo mutters something too, before following him out. The rest of us separate into pairs, discussing the news. I'm sat next to Talia.

"I didn't see that coming," she says. "I would have said he's a little mouse. What was he thinking? Hasn't he got a daughter in the mines?"

I nod, and bite my lip so hard I draw blood.

"Kedira knows what's going to happen to her, the poor girl," she says.

"No Justices are going to Riona for a while," I point out. "Let's hope the truth comes out before then."

"You think he didn't do it?"

"I think it doesn't add up. Let's wait and see."

She nods and looks at me curiously. "Chicken – wasn't xe the Keda involved in that nasty business with your old mate? Borzu, wasn't it?"

"That's right," I say. "Xe deserved everything xe got. If I find Darius, I'll shake him by the hand."

Back outside, I'm in no hurry to join Ansić and his men. I go north, plotting a circuitous route, to see Jakub and Ira. Jakub will be first – he should be stationed by the Gate of Triumph. Hundreds of soldiers are by the gate, and captains are shouting commands. I see two boys – must be Street Rats, for they look about fifteen – frantically struggling with armour; one drops his shield with a clatter, and one of the more experienced militia glares at him. I climb up to the walls – one of the benefits of wearing the interpreter's armband is that nobody ever challenges where you're going, not if you walk with enough confidence.

I look out at the Dagmari army. They're in the same position, but there is plenty of action. They're not exactly battle-ready – no formation to speak of – but something is about to happen. It looks like Mecunio's hopes of negotiation are in vain. His message to Shakan has gone unanswered.

A hundred paces along the wall I see Jakub standing in position with some archers. I walk purposefully past the other soldiers. He sees me coming, and detaches himself from the archers.

"All right?" I say.

"Fine," he murmurs. "Are we in the clear?"

"I think so. Naima got the interpreter. And the Crawlers believe he killed Chicken. As long as we keep his body hidden, they'll be chasing shadows for a while."

"Good."

"But a Blue saw us," I tell him. "So keep clear of Val Firuz. They know a soldier was involved."

"Right you are. Now clear off, will you? I'm supposed to be on duty. And Razvan?"

"Yes?"

"Stay alive."

"Why does everyone keep reminding me not to die? I promise, I'll do my best."

To my surprise, he puts an arm around me and squeezes me in a bear hug, then sends me on my way. I go down the next stairs and follow the wall west, all the way to the north-west corner of the city. Even though Ira's quarter is Blackstone, she has been billeted up here. I suspect some of the more senior interpreters arranged to go on the wall in Blackstone – by the coast, and relatively speaking, a safe place to hide. The greenhorns have been shoved onto the northern wall: the most dangerous section, but also where good communication with the Keda is essential. So it goes.

It takes me a bit of time to find Ira, but eventually I catch sight of her, standing in the shade at the base of the wall. No Keda in sight. I see the relief in her eyes as I approach.

"Razvan," she says. "What the hell happened?"

I give her a condensed version of the events of last night, from the moment we left her in the safehouse, to seeing Naima back in Wesson.

"So she killed Darius?"

"Yeah. It doesn't sit that well with me, but... I guess it had to be done."

"I suppose."

"I'm just glad I wasn't the one who had to do it. How about you? How was your night?"

"Not as exciting as yours. I cleared out the safehouse, took the armour and crossbow back to my place. Sat up most the night, half-expecting a Justice to come and break my door down."

"I'm sorry. I should have come to tell you what happened. I was in a state."

"Forget it. Does that mean the safehouse isn't burned?"

"I guess not. We should be able to use it again. But no activity for a while. Naima wants us to keep a low profile while the Crawlers let off some steam."

"Makes sense."

We talk a bit more, but a militia sergeant is scowling at us, so I leave her to it and carry on round the edge of the city, cutting down past the Western Gate, into Val Varin. I find Ansić's men doing drills, in full armour. He points at me, calls out in a bantering tone, "Where were you, interpreter? We had a Justice walk past, wanted to speak to us. Fine time to be oversleeping!"

"I was summoned to a meeting with the elders, captain," I say coldly. "There are only twenty-eight of us covering the whole city." Twenty-seven, a wicked voice whispers. "You'll have to survive without me occasionally."

"Now, now, no need to sulk," he says. "I'm just teasing. Truth be told, it's quite a relief. All they do is interfere, I'm happy to take charge without them shoving their noses in."

He spies someone else to yell at and stalks off. I watch the drills, until Bones comes to me holding two swords.

"You're going to need one of these," he says. "If any Dagmari get over today, you don't want to be caught standing there with your cock in your hands."

"Thanks," I say.

"Do you know how to use it?"

I think of Jakub slashing at the Blue. Third time I've seen someone die in front of me, and at least I didn't vomit on this occasion. And I remember chopping down with the cleaver, my eyes fixed on Chicken's wrist and the knobble of bone that was sticking out. It makes me think I won't have to worry about freezing up when the fighting starts.

"I'll give it a go," I say. "It's heavier than it looks."

"Just swing it, as wild as you can. Should slow them down enough for an archer to finish them off."

I lift it, and take a few practice swings.

"Not bad," Bones says. "We'll make a swordsman out of you yet."

He takes his sword and lunges at me. "Watch my hands," he says. "Keep your feet wider apart."

I parry his gentle swings, and get used to the grip of the sword. We spar for a bit, and I'm just starting to get comfortable when the call comes down from the wall:

"Boss! Here we go!"

Ansić races to the steps, and his squad go streaming up behind him. Part of me wants to stay at the bottom of the wall – I'm no use up there, but I have to see what is happening, and I follow the line of men up. At the top, I peer over someone's shoulders, expecting to see thousands of Dagmari flooding towards us, over the empty plain.

But instead, they are moving aside, making space. The trebuchets are wheeling into position. And the drumbeat starts up – *tum, tum, tumpity-tum...*

13.

All around me, soldiers are muttering as the trebuchet closest to us grinds to a halt. Ansić is shouting above the noise, "Hold! Hold your position!"

The archers are helpless, still too far away to hit anyone. A dozen Dagmari are milling around the trebuchet and up its attached ladders. Suddenly, the drumbeat stops and all conversation dries up too. The counterweight drops, the casting beam is released, with a thwack audible from several hundred paces. A huge lump of rock comes hurtling through the air, describing a perfect parabola; over the heads of soldiers fifty paces to the left of me, and it smacks into someone's home with a splintering crack. Everyone on the wall has turned to stare at the crumbling masonry that remains. And then, a hysterical screaming starts, a woman's voice – short, repeated bursts of horror.

Ansić grabs two conscripts. "Go!" he snaps. "Clear out the buildings close to the wall. Get everyone well away from here."

"Where to?" one asks.

"I don't bloody care! Just move them!"

I turn back to the Dagmari. I can see four trebuchets – a fifth in the distance, as their line curves around to the north. For the first time, I notice the two massive wheels bracketing the counterweight and several men inside them, running round to turn them. They are winching the counterweight back up, pace by pace, agonisingly slow. Once the beam is back in its firing position, the men start to reload the slings.

"Just getting their range," Bones murmurs nearby. "Now let's see how accurate they are."

A few of the conscripts have started to move, towards the steps.

"Where the hell are you going?" Ansić says.

"If we stay on the wall," one of them says, "aren't they're going to smash us?"

"You stay on the bloody wall or you'll be court-martialled for cowardice," he snarls. "We abandon the wall, and when they come at us, there'll be no one left to repel them. What did you think we'd be doing up here today?"

Further to the north, we watch as another boulder goes flying into the city. By the Western Gate, one hurtles right into the lip of the battlements, and there are cries and bodies diving for cover. It has bitten a massive chunk out of the wooden hoarding and the top of the wall, and a cloud of dust fills the air. Three archers lie dead on the ground in front of the walls. My attention switches back to our closest trebuchet.

"Here it comes, boys," says Bones conversationally. Again, the counterweight drops, and I watch the leather sling this time, racing high into the air before releasing the boulder. I watch transfixed as it seems to head straight for me, inexorably seeking me out; there are several shouts and running feet around me. But the height is too low, and it dips down, crashing into the wall below. There's a vibration as it disintegrates, and the ground seems to shudder. Everyone around me is crouching. Behind me, I hear shouting, and I look to see citizens coming out their homes, staring at the destroyed houses, and running.

The men on the trebuchet are resetting it again. I can see a pile of rocks – they can keep this up most of the morning if they want to. The wait between missiles is infuriating – not so short that it would be a relentless attack, but you have time to recover, get to your feet and watch as the next attack is prepared. It's an assault on the nerves. The men controlling the trebuchet opposite the Western Gate have found their range, and another rock goes flying towards the crumbled battlements. In the silence that follows the explosion, I can clearly make out the screaming of a single man: "You... bastards!"

Huge rocks rain down on us. There is a slight wind towards the sea, and a fog of dust and rubble is floating down past us. They are pounding the section by the Western Gate. The trebuchet opposite us is a bit more erratic – some go high, some go low, in a range of directions. I am standing up after another boulder smashes into the wall when I see them carrying several smaller contraptions into position. There are two for every trebuchet, and they each consist of a wooden stand and what appear to be two enormous bow arms, with winches behind them. They look, in short, like giant crossbows.

There's a horrendous, ratcheting screech as operators draw back the slider.

"Get down!" Ansić shouts, and everyone ducks for cover.

Whereas the trebuchet boulders lumber over in a lazy arc, the stones from the giant crossbows whizz towards us in a straight line. They are much smaller, these stones, they look like you could hold one easily in two hands. But they are just as terrifying, and have a longer range. The first one sails above us and carries on into the city. I have no idea where it lands.

The bombardment carries on in a regular rhythm - trebuchets, giant crossbows, trebuchets, giant crossbows. We are all on our knees or crouching, enduring it. Every rock that doesn't kill us is another one gone. Ansić is exhorting his men – shouting, swearing, threatening. I should go back down below the wall, it is stupid my being here – but I can't, the shame would be too great.

The noise is horrific – no human voices, but a relentless stream of rock smashing into rock, and the occasional rumble as some masonry collapses. The events of last night seem a million leagues away, like they happened to a different person. I imagine the Keda right now, farcically hunting through Val Kedić for a dead man and a conspiracy, while the Dagmari bombard their city walls.

I give an involuntary smile, my first of the day. The daydream is interrupted by a shout from an archer.

"Oi! Something's happening!"

There's a clanking of armour and weapons as everyone gets to their feet. Indeed, the Dagmari are starting to form up. Cavalry are riding out into position, and as far as I can see, men are taking up their weapons, getting ready. Some are in lines of ten men, holding scaling ladders. At that moment, a stone hurtles towards us. I don't even have time to react as it slams into the chest of one of Ansić's men, just ten paces from me; he gives a grunt, and it bodily lifts him off his feet, sending him flying over the wall into the street below. The man next to where he stood is hyperventilating, looking at the empty space, and he lets out a strangled, "Oh my shit!"

Then, a long, braying horn sounds. And the massed ranks of Dagmari roar, "Shakan! Shakan!"

And they come pounding up the plains towards us.

Bones and Ansić are yelling, the archers are drawing back their bows. The soldiers in front of me have held up their shields, while some run to towers and bring out baskets of rocks and cauldrons of scalding sand. The Dagmari horse archers lead out, in single file to make a small target, then they peel off, firing on us. Our archers let loose, then kneel to reload. I can see Dagmari archers, carrying small wooden barricades in pairs. They get just within distance and crouch behind the barricades.

"Shoot at the ladders!" Ansić shouts at the archers.

The ladder bearers are holding the ladder with one hand, and a huge circular shield with the other. They run past their archers, accompanied by several other warriors – to the north, I can see a concentration of ladders, headed for the breach made by the trebuchet, and a mass of warriors running towards the Western Gate. I spot a few Keda up on the wall, too – Justices in their green robes, scimitars drawn.

Arrows rain down on the ladder-bearers, but their shields protect them. Some of our archers have lit their arrows, and flames roar up from the fire gullies. The flames and the sharpened stakes slow them down, and we're able to pick off dozens of the ladder-bearers, so that a few go crashing to the ground before even reaching the wall. The rest charge through, pivot at the base of the wall, and spring up over the battlements. One appears fifteen paces to the south of me, another a bit further to the north. Our soldiers roar and run towards them – trying to push them back, but the ladders are supported from below. The movement leaves me exposed, and I drop and crawl south so a Dagmari archer can't pick me off. Men are lifting up rocks, hurling them down; others have got hold of a cauldron, and tip scalding sand over the wall, designed to go through armour joints. There are screams and the hiss of arrows everywhere. I can hardly see anything of the enemy now, I'm stuck behind a mass of bodies. I hold my sword out and wish this day over.

There are cries by the nearest ladder to the north, as a Dagmari shield appears, peppered with arrow shafts. Men crush forward, but he climbs the last steps, and springs over the battlements. He barely looks human, covered in black lamellar armour, head in a barbuta helmet, only a Y-shaped opening revealing any skin. He sweeps his sabre round and the soldiers edge back. Then men on both his flanks attack; one falls under his sabre, but it emboldens the others and the circle of men rush him. He can't wield his weapon at such close quarters, and disappears, buried in a sea of soldiers, just as another Dagmari appears over the battlements. It seems we're having more success with the ladder on my other side, and there's a scramble as the men get some purchase on it, and manage to lift it off the battlements. I see one man collapse, struck by an arrow, but there's a roar as they get momentum and fling the ladder away from the wall.

A stench hits me, and I realise it's a dead man, his bowels loosened. I crouch again and pray I can ride this out. Most of the shouting has stopped now, it's just grunts and pants. I lose all track of time.

I snap into focus as an archer calls out in a surprised voice, "Catapults again!"

"Don't be stupid," someone shouts from behind their shield. "They're not going to fire on their own bloody men."

But I peek through the gaps, and he's right, the Dagmari are preparing their trebuchets. The counterweight drops, and I watch a human body, in rags, come flying towards us. To the north, I can see other bodies too, mid-air, limbs splayed grotesquely. I turn to follow the nearest one and watch as it crashes into a roof, bouncing into the street, followed by a shower of broken tiles. I wonder what it was in aid of – some kind of punishment? A beggar comes running down the street and she starts to rummage through the rags. Ansić appears at my side, glaring at the corpse.

"Archer," he says, grabbing a man by the shoulder. "Shoot that woman."

"What?"

"Do you think they're launching bodies at us for fun? It'll be riddled with plague, you clown! And that woman is about to spread it through the city!"

The archer stares at him, and Ansić loses patience, grabs the bow off him. He lines up the shot, and as the beggar stands an arrow buries itself into her gut. He thrusts the bow back at the archer, and taps a conscript on the shoulder.

"You," he says, then notices me. "And you. Make yourself useful. Go and burn those two bodies. Don't touch them, whatever you do. Then bury the remains."

He ducks as an arrow thuds into a nearby shield, then returns to the fray. The two of us hurry down the steps, away from the fighting. Relief is written all over the other man's face, probably mine too. We walk up the empty street together, glancing up at the occasional destruction. With every step, I can feel the tension dissolving from my body. The soldier grabs an unlit torch from a wall holder.

"Wait here," he says.

He gives a cursory knock on the nearest door, and goes in. The two bodies are twenty paces away, and I have no wish to get any closer. The beggar is slumped over the corpse, as though she's weeping over it. Even from here, I can see Ansić was right. The corpse's neck is bloated, with discoloured patches, and its chest is covered in dried pus and fluid. Whatever it died of, it wasn't natural causes.

The soldier comes out the house, the torch burning now. "Get some shovels, will you?" he says.

I run through Val Varin. It's not far from the safehouse here, and the street where Chicken confronted me and Ira. I spot a group of craftsmen, dragging a pallet of timber. I explain the situation, and one of them takes me to his workshop, to get some shovels.

"What's happening?" he asks. "We saw the rocks, flying over the wall."

"I think we're holding," I say. "They had ladders, but I don't think anybody managed to break through. Not round here, anyway. But they smashed a load of walls down – you boys are going to be busy tomorrow."

He gives me the shovels and I take them back to the bodies. They are aflame when I return, skin crackling and popping while the soldier watches from a safe distance. I pass him a shovel.

"That's playing dirty, that is," he says. "Sending diseased bodies in here. Should be against the rules."

"Think someone forgot to pass the Dagmari the rulebook. Where do we dig?"

We find a patch of earth at the side of the road and start

digging. The noise from the wall has gradually eased, and there is a sense that we have weathered the worst of the first attack. It could be that they are storming over the eastern wall as we speak, or part of the northern wall has crumbled. But it does no good to worry about what might be.

The digging is hard work, but strangely satisfying after the terror on the wall, arrows and rocks flying at you. Halfway through the job, the clouds open, and torrential rain pours down on us, making the earth good and moist. The flames lick and curl and die out. The clothes have burnt up, and all that remains are two blackened bodies. It occurs to me that it will be easy to get rid of Darius' body today, with hundreds of corpses to dispose of after the fighting.

We dig faster now, and I'm building such a sweat that I take off my leather armour. There is another horn blast in the distance, and the two of us stop to see if anything happens. The soldier shrugs, and gets on with the job. Eventually, the pit is deep enough, and we approach the bodies gingerly.

"Do you want to roll them over there?" the soldier asks, holding up a rag to his face as he gets close.

When it comes to plagues, Val Kedić remembers. The Keda brought the Shivering Sickness with them when they first arrived, and it killed off thousands of elderly citizens. In more recent times, it was the Grey Fever, which came when I was a boy, and swept through the slums. It touched young and old alike, Keda and citizens. I remember Queenstown in the east, by Lekaan – it was the worst affected, and they quarantined off the whole quarter. When they opened up the roadblocks, they found bodies piled high at the side of the road. A rumour went round that stray dogs were carrying the disease, and it was a common sight to see militia with crossbows, hunting the mongrels that scavenged in the streets. The Grey Fever's still here, but only killing dozens a year instead of thousands, like my poor Margrethe.

The thought of a new plague is enough to terrify any citizen.

I cover my face with the leather armour, place my shovel under the beggar, and roll her over. And again, and again – the body's surprisingly light once the flames have reduced it. As she rolls onto her back, her eyes stare sightlessly at me. I didn't do this, I protest to the accusations I read there. It was Ansić. He had to do it.

Like Darius, a voice whispers. Another one that had to die, supposedly. And that time it was Naima who had the guts to follow her convictions through.

I would have tried to reason with Darius. I would have run to the beggar and screamed at her to get away. Probably both would have failed: Darius would have told the Keda, and the plague would have decimated the city. But it's what I would have done.

Not for Chicken, though. Seems like hate trumps any moralistic considerations.

"You do the other one," I say to the soldier, suddenly disgusted.

At the other end of the street we can see some men from Ansić's unit descending the steps. A good sign. They look exhausted, and trudge downwards, oblivious to the rain that is soaking them. I help cover the two corpses with earth. Then I head back up to the wall, to find out what happened.

At the top of the steps, I find a clean-up operation taking place. Stretcher-bearers are taking away the injured and there are dead bodies scattered along the wall – the occasional Dagmari ones are already being stripped of weapons and armour. In the distance, I can see the enemy have withdrawn. A messenger is reporting to Ansić. I walk right up to the battlements, and look down at the carnage. The bodies are in clusters, around where the ladders used to be. Some have limbs still twitching. There are a lot of them – though it doesn't seem to have made the slightest dent in their army. Rain is streaming down into the trenches we dug, stained red with blood.

I feel a hand on my shoulder, and turn to face Bones. He has taken his helmet off, and his hair is plastered to his forehead.

"How did you find it? Your first battle?"

"Didn't do much," I say. "Hid at the back, then Ansić sent me to bury some bodies."

"You made it to the end," he says with a laugh. "That's all that matters, ain't it?"

"What happened?" I ask. "They had enough?"

"They pulled back soon after the rain started. No good mounting an assault like this in wet conditions."

"Looks like we killed a lot," I say, nodding at all the bodies below.

"So we should. We're defending, they're throwing men at a fortified wall. If we've lost half the men they have, it'll be a disaster." He wipes his hair out of his eyes, and gestures towards the Western Gate. "They'll be reasonably happy – that breach over there ain't good news for us; and they got a few men over the wall before we kicked them out. But they were just probing. Testing us out to see what we're made of."

"Well, I'm glad we passed the test, anyway."

"Where were your mates, then?" he says abruptly. "The Crawlers? Happy to beat the shit out of innocent kiddies, not so keen when it's a warrior waving a bloody great sabre."

"Don't know," I say. "And they're not my mates."

I look out to the west, to the coastal road. I am facing the wrong direction. I should be at the Queensgate, looking towards Riona. Killing Chicken has released something in me, and I want to go right now, to get Rico and take him out of that place. They are wrenching the city apart between them, the Dagmari from without, the Keda from within, and the citizens are caught in the middle. I'd give anything to escalate the Camonite uprising, to kidnap the Justice this afternoon, and set off tomorrow with our weapons. Because right now, my greatest fear is that when I get there, I'm going to be too late – too late for my son to forgive me.

INTERLUDE (2)

The seven Keda left the previous morning. Whitehair had watched as they saddled their horses. Some fool of a trader had mentioned news of the Dagmari siege, was gossiping about it at the gatehouse. A curious Keda, doubtless hearing the words "Val Kedić", had asked Half Moon what he was saying. Whitehair should have spoken to Half Moon earlier, that was careless of him. If the Keda suspected the hillsmen of keeping them in the dark, they didn't show it. With a minimum of fuss, they had acquired horses, water and provisions, and quit Riona, riding south. No instructions to Half Moon. No indication of when they would be back.

Then this morning, they woke to discover that five of their own number had deserted – including two who were on night patrol, guarding the gatehouse that was the main entrance to the colony. They must have fled north to the hills, taking horses and weapons. There were half-hearted suggestions to give chase, but nobody followed it up.

Whitehair doubts they will be the only ones to desert – stories of the Dagmari have been circulating for the last few years. The mood in the colony is nervy and mutinous.

He is inspecting the stores, checking how much the deserters took, when Half Moon finds him.

"There you are," Half Moon says.

"What's happened now?"

"Nothing. Bearhide wants to meet. We three, and Splitmouth."

"What for?"

"Things are falling apart, Whitehair. We could lose control of the colony."

"And Bearhide wants to exert some authority, is that it?"

Half Moon shrugs. "If not us, who?"

Whitehair grunts, and the two men leave the stores. Whitehair studies Half Moon – a short man with a braided ginger beard and moustache; watchful blue eyes and an infectious grin. He's not a fighter, but the others like him, they know he's crafty – learning some of the touch language gives him kudos as well as indispensability. Whitehair enjoys his company, but can't say he fully trusts him.

"Why me, then?" he says. "Why Splitmouth? What did we do to earn invitation to your little clique?"

"Come on, Whitehair. Between the four of us, we can run this place. Bearhide has the authority. You've got the experience. Splitmouth has the popularity, he'll bring the younger guards with him."

"And you?"

"Ah," Half Moon grins. "I'll be the brains, shall I?"

They pass the armoury, nod at some of the sentries. They come to an abandoned building where Bearhide and Splitmouth are waiting. The four of them stand among the rubble and a pile of timber. The big man, Bearhide, looks impatient. Splitmouth stands the same height, but has a hunched, slender frame, and his eyes dart around, hardly ever staying still. Whitehair can think of three others who have senior status and take a cut of the Roć income, but he decides Half Moon is right – between the four of them, they should be able to handle this.

"What's this all about, Half Moon?" Bearhide says, and Whitehair understands this is in fact Half Moon's idea, not Bearhide's – an imposing man, but lacking imagination.

"This is a delicate situation," says Half Moon. "The Keda are gone. We don't know when, or if, they will return."

"What are you worried about?" says Splitmouth. "We can still handle the kids."

"I'm not just thinking of that. You've all heard the stories of the Dagmari. What if they take the city, then come here? And the rest of our men – what if more desert? Thirty or forty guards aren't enough. I'm more worried about a mass escape than a revolt."

Bearhide nods slowly. "He's right. We need to let everyone know someone is in charge. That it's business as usual."

"How?" asks Splitmouth.

"Yes, how?" Bearhide says, looking at Half Moon.

"For starters, you could talk to the old-timers – give them a speech, tell them to stay calm. You're the boss 'til the Keda get back, that sort of thing. And Splitmouth – you could do the same with the younger crowd. You're popular with them, they'll listen to you. A few words from you would go a long way. And they're the ones I'm worried about deserting."

"Can't understand it, myself," Bearhide rumbles. "Cowards, I call them. Nobody's attacking us yet. They're running from a pack of children."

Whitehair speaks up for the first time. "They're new blood and they've just been paid. They weighed up the risks and benefits: the risk of the Keda not returning, meaning no more silver. The risk of another Camun. The risk of the Dagmari coming here. The benefits of going home, alive."

Bearhide spits. "Sounds like cowardice to me."

Half Moon gives Whitehair an appraising glance. "He's right, though. So as well as sorting out morale, we need to make the colony safe."

"I'm sure you're going to tell us how," Bearhide says.

"Cut the bridges," Half Moon says. "Only one way in, through the gatehouse. Easier to defend if we have to. And makes an escape less likely."

"Do we really care," says Splitmouth, "if a few southern brats break out and starve in the mountains?" Again, Whitehair is reminded why he dislikes this man.

Half Moon shakes his head. "Imagine when the Keda return and find we've lost some of their charges. Think they'll be impressed?"

"Those bridges have been here longer than I have," Bearhide says. "Is this really necessary?"

"If everything gets back to normal, putting the bridges back up will be a day's work. Trust me. You and Splitmouth handle the men, Whitehair and I will handle this."

In the afternoon, Whitehair finds himself supervising a group of guards as they cut down the rope bridges that traverse the mountain ravines. The gatehouse will become a chokepoint, the only way in from the south. They could still be attacked from the north, but only from downhill, through the Riona valley and the mines. There are five bridges, so he takes the two hardest, while Half Moon's group takes the other three. They go to the opposite side of the ravine, to dismantle them at that end. Each side of the bridge is held tight with four different ropes. Two loop round a cypress tree, ending in bulbous hitch knots, two are wrapped round stakes in the ground. The knots are ancient, stiff and coated in pitch. Three men push the stakes out with shovels – back-breaking work in this rocky ground. Two men work on the knots that tie the bridge to the tree, drawing them out with knives. Whitehair has no wish to damage the bridges, so they work patiently through the afternoon. When they finally have the bridge loose, they release it with weary shouts, and it flails across the ravine, hitting the other side with a clatter. A couple of wooden slats break loose on impact, and drop to the bottom in a silent, graceful descent.

When both bridges are down, hanging on the side of the

colony, they walk back – Whitehair a few paces ahead of the rest. They have to climb over some mossy rocks, and round a quarry before they get back to the gatehouse. To the west, they can see Half Moon's group working on their final bridge. Whitehair carries on through the colony, planning to return to the barracks, but he stops when he sees there's some kind of commotion down by the mines. He changes direction and hurries down the valley.

About thirty boys and girls are gathered by one of the adits, and four guards. There is lots of finger-jabbing and raised voices. Whitehair ups his pace, skids on the stony path, uprights, a hand on the rockface as he scrambles down.

He follows the path to the mine entrance. He recognises the kids – all from Blackstone, Wesson and Saalim barrows. Always, it's the slum kids where they have the problems – less to lose, more to fight for. They shouldn't all be working together, he'll have a word with whichever idiot put them in the same mine. There should be some of his good Roć boys with the Blackstone ones, a few North Ash girls to smooth out those from Saalim. These guards don't speak much of the southern tongue – he hears them shouting a few broken phrases – "Naughty!", "No!", "You boys pay!"

Some of the bigger lads are smirking, and the situation is threatening to spill out of control. The guards fall silent as Whitehair arrives, and he pushes through the crowd.

"What's happening?" he asks a guard.

"The little bastards say they lost their shovels down the mine, and all their equipment," the man says, sending a sour glance at them. "And they've broken the minecart wheels. They're saying it was an accident."

"Accident my arse," another chimes in. "This is deliberate sabotage, so they don't have to work. We don't have that many shovels to spare."

He should have anticipated this – the Keda's departure has made them bold. He turns to the teenagers. Most look away with a satisfied sneer, but one, a tall Wesson boy he recognises, holds his gaze.

"This was foolish," he says lightly, in their tongue. "What do you gain by this?"

"Why don't you come in, help us find what we lost?" the boy says, innocent-eyed. There's some stifled laughter.

Whitehair sighs. "You've been here, what – five, six years? You really want to spoil it all now? Waste all that hard work when you're this close to the finish line?"

"What happened to the Crawlers?" the boy says.

"The what?" Whitehair says, frowning.

"The freaks. The green-robed ones. The monsters who pay your wages."

"They've returned to the city, as normal. Some more will be back soon."

Everyone is listening to their exchange. There's palpable tension in the air, and Whitehair is tempted to shut the conversation down.

"Has it got anything to do with the bridges coming down?" the boy says. Whitehair looks at him sharply. All the teenagers glance up at the ravine, where there are now yawning chasms instead of bridges. *No fool, this one,* Whitehair thinks.

"I'm sorry," he says. "Did we forget to consult you on the running of the colony? Next time I'll make sure you're involved in our discussions, so you can do something useful instead of breaking equipment."

His sarcasm falls flat. "Something's going on," says the boy. "You lot look nervy as hell."

The boy is in danger of besting him, making him look foolish in front of the others. Shouting won't work, though. He turns to Fifthson, a younger cousin of his from the hills.

"Put them on half-rations," he says. "Nothing more. Don't turn them into martyrs, it's what they want."

Fifthson frowns. "Don't they deserve more of a punishment,

cousin? All that lost equipment. Others will follow their example, surely?"

Whitehair puts his arm round him. "Right now, Riona is a tinderbox, cousin. We will not be the match that lights the spark, you understand me?"

He leaves them to it, and starts to make his way back up the valley. He has a bad feeling in his belly, and the dawning realisation that, although none of them here have any love for the Keda, they are the glue that keeps the colony together.

14.

The rain lasts for three days. The Dagmari calmly see it out
in their tents. On the first day after the bombardment, news
arrives that a couple of their galleons have arrived in the
Southern Sea and are patrolling the straits. The city of Mura
sends word that they cannot risk their ships, and they have
turned around and returned to Mura. Our last source of
supplies has disappeared. The noose is tightening.

A group of citizens turn up at the harbour, apparently
demanding that our fleet go and attack the Dagmari ships,
but in the end it's decided we can't spare the men from the
city walls. Meanwhile, the masons and carpenters go into
overdrive, and the sound of chisels and saws fills the air as
the city tries to repair its gaping wounds. The only Keda to be
seen outside Val Firuz are Justices. The guard on the Bridge of
Peace and the Bridge of Sorrow is doubled. Wealthy citizens
who were encouraged to leave their homes on the island begin
to trickle out over the bridges, with servants carrying essential
possessions. Rumours start to circulate about the cause of the
Keda's anger.

On the second day, the Justices start to investigate Chicken's
death in earnest. Darius lived in Ganzić, Borzu's old quarter,
and stories go round that over twenty Justices are personally
ransacking the area. They scour every building, accompanied

166

by scores of militia. Dozens of Darius' associates are brought in for questioning, and some do not return. But they do not find him. Naima's associate manages to keep the body hidden.

Despite the Justices' threats, reports of Chicken's murder get round the whole city. Whether an elder let it slip, or an interpreter, or a victim of one of the Justices' interviews, no one can say. The story grows in embellishments – an old sot in the Western Glory confides to me that a masked man killed five Keda before swimming the Firu to escape. At the same time, Camonite cells are having no trouble at all spreading the rumour that Dagmari spies are ensconced in the city, killing citizens and trying to find a way to let the enemy through the gates.

I don't hear from Naima or the priest, but I hear on the streets the proof that the groundwork for stage two is underway. Tension in the city is stretching to breaking point.

On the third day, an announcement goes round that because of the blockade, the grain ration is to be cut dramatically. The grain stores in Val Firuz are, of course, safe. I am strolling through the People's Market when the news filters through, but the atmosphere on the street is febrile, angry, and I return home to keep a low profile. Trouble, however, seeks me out.

Soon after third gong, there is a knocking at my door, an insistent triple-rap. I open the door to find what can only be described as a mob outside. They fill the street, rows and rows of citizens, some holding everyday items that serve as weapons. I recognise the men and women at the front, all Wessonians, a strange mix of rich and old – the citizens who managed to avoid conscription into the army. Katya, the Wesson delegate, is there too, under duress it seems, and addresses me first.

"Razvan," she says. "This matter of the grain ration has caused some, ah, concern."

"Too right it's caused concern," a thickset merchant shouts. "We can't live on that!"

"I sympathise," Katya says quietly, "but we are under siege. We must–"

"And will they go hungry?" a woman in the middle of the crowd interrupts. "The Keda? Of course they won't! They're hoarding it, and we want our fair share!"

"I've promised, I will raise your concerns through appropriate channels," Katya says.

"You're our delegate, and you do what we say," the merchant says, to cheers and cries of approval – he seems to be the mob's spokesman. "And we don't want to be fobbed off, we want them to hear us."

A woman at the front, a mother I know with two children in the mines, puts a firm hand on my arm. "You need to come with us, Razvan," she says. "You're going to put our demands to the Keda."

"They don't react very well to demands," I say.

"If they won't work with us," the merchant says, "they'll be left ruling the ashes of this damn city. We've given them everything – everything! Now we want something back in return."

Hands gently ease me into the street. There are a few ragged shouts and whoops, and we set off down to Six Ways. People are packed close around me, but I manage to shuffle through until I am next to Katya.

"This is not going to end well," I say to her. "Now is not the time to provoke the Keda."

"Don't I know it," she says. "I haven't had any contact with them for four days. What was Darius thinking?"

"Maybe it didn't pan out the way he expected," I say.

The rain is just a trickle as the mob marches up the People's Market, and it's not unpleasant in this heat. The curious and the hungry join us as we go, we must be one hundred-strong by now. At the top of the People's Market, we turn off towards the square with juniper trees; and as we turn the corner, we see it's not just Wessonians who have had this idea. There are well over a thousand people packed into the square, facing the Bridge of Peace. Citizens spread out into the connecting streets;

some stand on benches, others have climbed the trees. It's not a very focussed riot, but it's a riot all the same. The crowd is facing a line of ten Justices, who are protecting the bolted gates of the bridge. A few citizens are chanting, and some are seated on neighbours' shoulders and making speeches.

The merchant who was leading our mini-mob looks rather put out. He and the more vocal protestors start to thread their way through the crowd. The Wessonians seem to have forgotten about Katya and me – any hope of communication with the Keda has vanished. I can't see a single interpreter near the Justices, making the whole protest absurd – like fish shouting at the actions of the fishermen.

For a while I stand there helplessly with Katya, no space to move or any idea what I'm doing there.

Then there's a surge behind me, and we all stagger and try to hold our balance. People are shouting at each other, telling everyone to stop pushing; I am turned around and find myself backpedalling, away from Katya, until I am squashed against the bark of a young juniper tree. A man next to me is holding a mug of chuka – he is glassy-eyed, and stumbles to the ground. A woman's elbow is in my face, and I can't see the bridge, or any further than a few paces away – I am shoulder-to-shoulder with over a thousand citizens, and we are all starting to panic.

There's a screeching wail as the gates open, and everyone cranes their necks to see what is happening. The elbow disappears, and I get a clear view through the junipers. A wooden wagon trundles through the gate, topped with a pyramid of barrels. At the top, five grey ceramic pipes are pointed towards the crowd, sleek and curved, looking like some horribly deformed claw. Either side of the barrels is a black-robed Keda. Most people have probably never seen an alchemist before. The crowd quietens, from the front to the back. Almost as one, everyone starts to edge backwards, like you would on the beach when you spot a scorpion hiding in the rocks. There are a few stumbles and cries. Then the wagon stops. And smoke starts to billow out of the pipes.

One of the women trapped at the front reacts first – she dives straight into the Little Firu. Others just turn and stampede. I am being crushed back against the bark, but there's not yet space to move – and for a moment I think what a stupid, stupid death this would be. Not under a Dagmari sabre or a Justice's scimitar, in the pursuit of something heroic – but trampled in a bloody grain riot. I mean, I'm not a vain man, but really, it's undignified.

Someone falls in front of me, and I pull her to her feet by her tunic. I dare a glance behind. The smoke, glistening with silver, is drifting this way, and a small circle has cleared around the wagon; one man staggers into the empty space, back and forth, like a drunk trying to dance – he puts his hands to his eyes as though trying to scratch them out. He totters, and collapses onto the cobbles. Some citizens are shoving past, trampling over the fallen. Others are turning to look... time seems to stand still as we watch the smoke. None of the Justices have moved a pace.

I feel myself tune out all the noise, and I am gloriously at peace for a moment. The silver – like sunlight breaking through the clouds–

A foot stamps on mine, and it breaks the spell – I realise the smoke has a hypnotic pull to it: the silver specks are dancing through the cloud in eldritch patterns, which seem to move the smoke of their own accord. More citizens are staggering and falling at the fringes of the circle that has formed around the wagon.

I pull my gaze away with an effort, and suddenly I hear the shouting again.

"I can't breathe! I can't breathe!"

"My daughter! Where's my daughter?"

"Let me out! Get off!"

People are still running and shoving all around me, but space is starting to form as the crowd thins out. Everyone is

funnelling off down side streets, and I follow blindly. I feel a
stab of shame, for we're like a herd of goats here, the chaos
and noise in humiliating contrast to the disciplined Keda. I
climb a wall to get more space, into some public gardens. I pass
a man on his knees, rocking and wheezing.

"You need a hand?" I ask, but he bats my arm away, so I
continue on. I exit the gardens and follow the crowd through
Five Bells. The danger of death by stampede is gone now, and
I orientate myself – I'm going north, towards Sevanić. I slip
into a side street, desperate to get away from all the people.
Just four days of proper siege warfare – there's already been a
riot, and the Keda have turned their weapons on us. It's not a
good omen.

I find myself aimlessly wandering in the opposite direction
to the smoke. As I get close to the northern walls, I see the
buildings are in the same state as in the west, destroyed by
the trebuchet bombardment. Some are abandoned now,
rubble filling the rooms where walls have collapsed. In others,
wooden boards cover holes in a patchwork mess. I pass a tavern
I remember frequenting with Borzu – a jagged bar has been
smashed out at the level of the second floor, and floorboards
and bricks stick out like rotting teeth. I spot some steps, and
walk up, hoping to find Jakub. On the wall, all the sentries and
archers have their attention fixed on something outside the
city. I join an archer.

"What's going on?" I ask.

He points east, and I see the Dagmari have set up a white
tent on the Ilić Royal – a warrior standing on either side. It
must be just within range of the archers on the gate, but they
are not firing.

"Not been there long," the archer says. "Some slaves set it
up. Then about ten people went to the tent. Think one of them
must be this Shakan feller they keep banging on about. Big
horse, big sword, big bloke."

"And what have we done?"

"Nothing yet. But looks like they're offering some kind of parlay. They're in there, waiting."

"Shit." I realise the priest would want me there, that the biggest gift I can offer the Camonites is access – a pair of eyes among the elite of the city.

I hurry back down the steps, and head along the base of the wall, towards the Gate of Triumph. It's normally rammed down here, with beggars and merchants unloading stock after their arrival. Now it's nearly empty, apart from the occasional soldier, and walking down the ghostly street is unnerving. As I near the Triumph, an elder spots me – he raises a palm and beckons me over.

"Razvan," he says. "Just the man. We sent someone to find you ages ago, what took you so long? Silas is here, and some greenhorn, but we need our best people on this."

He waves away my explanation, and guides me over to one of the gatehouses. Eleven is seated at a table, fingerspeaking to Silas – it's the first time I've seen a councillor since I chopped off Chicken's hands. Three Justices are with xer – one of them is Beast, accompanied by a young interpreter called Leni. Several of the top militia are standing around them, and Mecunio and Abitha, too. The elder whispers to Leni – she looks at me gratefully and scurries out of the gatehouse.

Eleven finishes xer message and Silas nods.

"We will see what the Dagmari have to say," Silas says. "If they want to negotiate already, perhaps they have less appetite for a fight than we had feared."

"Excellency," Mecunio says, "they will not want an extended siege, you are right. They know now we will not fold easily." He gives Silas some time to translate. "But they also have the upper hand in the negotiation. They know we lost many men in that first attack." He turns to one of the militia captains. "Nearly three hundred, I think?"

"Four fifty," the man replies, "if you count those too badly injured to be any use."

"The longer this goes on," Mecunio says, "the more chance they have of breaking in. They know this. But I have little doubt they'd prefer a quick resolution. That'll mean gold."

"If we give up all the wealth of this city," Silas translates after a pause, "we might as well fling open the gates and welcome them in. Submit too easily, and they will be back, like a buzzard returning to its carcass."

"Forgive me, Excellency, but we cannot win this battle," says Mecunio. "We might be able to hold out a while, but they will wait if they have to. Until we are broken."

"It would help," Silas translates, with a stammer, "if we did not face… treachery from within the city. The Justices inform me there are reports of more traitors, working against us, aiding the enemy. Traitors such as the citizens who dared kill a councillor."

"I – ah–" Mecunio says.

The three Justices and Eleven rise to their feet.

"The Justices did not want me to leave the safety of Val Firuz," says Eleven, through Silas. "But I will meet with this great warrior, this Shakan. We will see what kind of man he is. My ancestors took this city. I will not give it away so cheaply, bowing and scraping to savages."

Xe withdraws his arm from Silas, and we stand aside as the four Keda leave the gatehouse. I follow Mecunio out and he inclines his head to me.

"You see, those early diplomatic approaches are paying off," he says, and turns to Silas. "Now we just need to make sure the Keda say the right thing. You might want to consider giving a *generous* interpretation of their words to the Dagmari."

Silas nods. "I'll stick with Eleven," he says. "You stay close to the Justices, Razvan."

"And listen, observe," Mecunio says to me.

We make our way to the Triumph, where our party is preparing to go. Eleven waits there, dwarfed by the three Justices and four soldiers with crossbows. Mecunio, Silas and I sidle up behind them. Beast is bouncing on the balls of xer feet, fingering a scimitar. Xe's buzzing, like xe's spoiling for a fight. One of the captains calls instructions, and the gates grind open. The Keda walk outside, and we follow.

"There was a riot, outside the Bridge of Peace," I say. "Things are falling apart, Mecunio."

"What do you mean, a riot?"

Beast turns and stares, and we fall silent. We step onto the Ilić Royal. The ground either side is soggy and churned up, littered with splinters of wood and other battle debris. A few Dagmari bodies are still lying by the wall. We follow the Keda, one hundred paces now from the tent.

"It's the grain ration," I say softly. "Citizens aren't happy. Must have been over a thousand people there."

Mecunio has pinched his nose, eyes closed. "How can they be thinking of rioting now? What did the Keda do in response?"

"The Justices just stood there, did nothing. Then the alchemists turned up on some wagon. It started pumping their smoke out at us. There was a stampede to get away."

Mecunio stares at me in horror.

"Oh, this gets better and better," he says. "I'm trying to save the city here. I didn't realise I'd have to contend with traitors and rioters, not to mention the Keda attacking us." He shakes his head. "Did anyone die? You know what – don't answer that. Let me focus on this."

We approach the tent, flanked by two Dagmari and several horses. A Dagmari lifts the flaps and appears in front of us. He is a broad man, lightly armoured, with a good-natured smile, despite the fact that three Justices are a few paces away, their scimitars out. His arms are adorned with bangles, and his left ear has a string of silver studs.

"Welcome," he addresses us, in a passable accent. "My master Shakan is waiting for you inside. My name is Odisse, I speak with his voice." He gestures to the Keda. "Please, enter. Your soldiers, I must ask, remain outside. My master is able to defend himself perfectly well, but the crossbow is a coward's weapon, and we have no wish for any... unpleasantness."

I pass a quick message on to Beast, and xe nods assent. The soldiers wait outside with the two warriors, and we proceed inside the tent behind Odisse. We file in, the four Keda facing the Dagmari warlord. Shakan sits on a couch, an ornate piece with carved legs that end in claws. His limbs are splayed, goblet in one hand. He looks bored. He's as stocky as Odisse, but looks taller, and is covered in lamellar armour, bronze plate over his arms and shins. He is bald, but grey tufts of hair line his temples, framing a broken nose and startlingly blue eyes.

Silas slips down next to Eleven, on one knee so he is not in the way. Behind Shakan is a young woman, also in platelet but rimmed with gold, with her hair tied high in buns. Then there are two more Dagmari warriors beside her, and at either end of their semicircle is a slave – I realise with a start one of them is Jordi, who I last saw being punished in the harbour by the ambassador. He has a black eye, and his face is covered in bruises; but it seems he has otherwise survived his previous trip here, and has since rejoined the main host.

I move to stand by Beast, and Mecunio goes to the other side of the Keda. My eyes meet Jordi's, and he edges nearer to me, closing the circle. It is too small in here – there are fourteen of us, and it is festering in the heat. I listen to the rain, spattering on the roof of the tent at irregular intervals.

Odisse spreads his hands wide and smiles. "Thank you for coming," he says. "I am glad you bought interpreters, it saves us having to use our own." He gestures towards Shakan, while I give Beast a summary of what he is saying. "This is my Lord Shakan, Master of the Wilds, Breaker of Seven Cities. Behind him is his daughter Shakanna." He cocks his head towards Eleven. "Who, pray, am I addressing? It so helps diplomacy, I find, to establish names and build a relationship."

"I can't really, ah, translate Keda names for you properly,"

Silas falters. "The only way would be if I showed you the touches on your arm – that's xer given name."

"Of course!" Odisse says. "Fascinating, fascinating! I would love to spend some time exploring the language – it's a marvel!" He claps his hands. "But, to business. You have witnessed, I think, a taste of our power. If it is Shakan's will, we shall take your city apart, brick by brick. None of your people will live."

Eleven raises xer hooded skull to regard Shakan for the first time and fingerspeaks to Silas. "You, too," says Silas, translating, "lost many men. A long war will be costly for you also."

Odisse flashes a wolfish grin at Eleven, showing all his teeth. "Undoubtedly, my good fellow, undoubtedly. And as you say, if we were to take this to the bitter end, many of our brave warriors would die. But let me be frank." His brow darkens. "What you saw two days ago was a fraction of what we can do. That was just... foreplay, feeling each other up. If you want to be properly fucked–" he grins again "–then by all means extend this war."

I give Beast a diplomatic version of his words, as Silas does for Eleven.

"War?" says Silas. "This is not war, we did not seek it out. You brought it to our doorstep."

"Let us not quibble over semantics, my nameless friend," Odisse says. "The fact is, you have what we want, and we can hurt you if we don't get it; so I hope we can resolve our dispute today, in this tent."

Shakan utters something in Dagmansh, and drains his drink. His daughter raises an eyebrow and Odisse gives him a polite chuckle.

"Our leader is not a patient man, I fear," he says. "And he dislikes talk. War is more to his taste. But luckily for you, I am the dove in his ear, trying to find a... solution that meets with all our approval."

"What kind of solution do you propose?" Silas says as Eleven taps out xer response. "We offered terms to your ambassadors sixteen days ago. But they had no interest in negotiating, and your army was on the march before they left our halls."

This is what it comes down to, then – the sordid thrashing out of how much we're going to pay them to go away and leave us in peace. Odisse starts outlining their terms, but I'm distracted, for Jordi's hand has snaked behind my left arm, and his fingers have clasped the back of my bands. No one else is able to see, we're at the edge of the tent, backs against the white fabric. I nearly turn to look at him in surprise, but manage to keep my poise.

Translating from behind is strange, like reading upside down, but it's doable. His thumb taps my upper section twice, and his middle fingers dance a delicate trill on the lower section.

In coarse pidgin fingerspeak: *Help / Me /*.

15.

Pidgin fingerspeak was generally known as 'Knuckles' by the apprentices who spoke it. It was an attempt to bring Spidertouch in line with the syntax and grammar of our own tongue, to make it easier to translate. The infuriating lack of pronouns in their grammar, for example, was rectified with a series of touches, and most of the modifiers disappeared. One invented touch conferred plurality, the word order was brought closer to ours – and it had a few decent swearwords. No one would dream of using it to talk to Keda, of course. It tended to be used by apprentices when they were struggling with formulating sentences.

It also had other advantages – I remember sitting in arse-clenchingly boring grammar lessons with Borzu, supposedly practising tenses with him, but actually having a meandering conversation in Knuckles. It was a bad habit to get into if you were serious about joining the guild; but it did make your brain hurt less, to say, for example: *You / Want / Go / Seven / Goats / Tomorrow /*, rather than *(Question) / Want / Go / Seven / Goat / (Future) / Night /*.

The last time I heard someone speak Knuckles was Borzu, nearly twenty-six years ago. So it came as some surprise to hear it again in Shakan's tent. I half-listen to Odisse and give the vaguest of summaries to Beast with my right hand. With my left, after bending my elbow, I twist my wrist and reply to Jordi. Speaking left-handed is like writing in a looking-glass, even harder if you're speaking right-handed at the same time. But I give it a good shot and keep it simple.

(Question) / Help /, I say, sticking to standard Spidertouch as my Knuckles is rusty.

I / Want / Return / Val Kedić /, he says. *Keda / Evil / But / Foreigners / Evil / Also /.*

It's a long time since he fingerspoke regularly. Even for Knuckles, his tapping and trilling is sloppy, and I'm reminded of trying to understand a drunk in a tavern. Meanwhile, Odisse is still chuntering on about the tribute they expect, all couched in euphemistic terms. I strain and do my best to understand Jordi's touches.

Allow / Foreigners / In / Val Kedić / Take / Gold /, he says. *They / Leave / And / Kill / Keda /.*

(Question) / Do /, I say.

Odisse has stopped and Eleven is giving his reply to Silas. Jordi thinks about it while Silas replies to Odisse.

Foreigner / Soldier / In / Val Kedić /, he says at last. *Secret /.*

(Question) / SecretSoldier /, I say, checking I've understood him.

He gives the faintest of nods, eyes straight ahead. *Queen / City / Palace / Two / Five / Three / Seven /.*

I think I know what he's trying to say, and memorize the numbers.

(Positive) /, I say, and repeat the numbers back to him.

Yes / Help / Secret / Soldier / He / Talk / Foreigners /. He pauses, then repeats, *Allow / Foreigners / In / Take / Gold / Kill / Keda /.*

I realise I am missing the negotiation that is going back and forth between Eleven and Odisse. I fob Beast off with *Councillor / ChiefForeigner / Negotiate /.*

I / Try /, I say with my left hand, slipping into Knuckles for Jordi.

Eleven, via Silas, keeps posing objections to what Odisse has said, and I can tell Shakan is getting impatient, drumming his fingers on his couch. I pick up that the Dagmari are demanding a number of slaves from the citizens – but that's not the sticking point, it's the annual tribute they are demanding for the future. I can tell from Mecunio's face that he's desperate to get involved, but he can't.

I want to help Jordi. He's no better than a slave for the Dagmari – at least I have semi-freedom. There must be more I can ask him, but I can't think what. I want to know more about this spy that is in Queenstown, but the question needs to be expressed in simple concepts that he will understand in left-handed fingerspeak.

Eventually, we run out of time. Shakan growls something from his couch, and he and Odisse have a rapid conversation in Dagmansh. The conversation is animated – Shakan barks, while Odisse shrugs and makes pacifying noises.

The Dagmari warlord rises to his feet, and makes an impatient gesture at Eleven. Jordi quickly removes his hand from behind my arm.

"I regret," Odisse says, "that we've reached the limit of my master's patience. We have reached an impasse, and the only way forward is to break the impasse."

"Maybe," Silas says, "we could–"

"The time for negotiation is over," Odisse interrupts, smiling coldly. "You had your chance. Now, it is time for a lesson in humility. If we return to the negotiating table, you will perhaps be more... forthcoming. But I cannot promise our terms will be as generous as they were today."

Shakan stalks from the tent, pushing through the back flaps, followed by Odisse and the two warriors – Jordi and the other slave close behind. Shakanna glances back, and I see her catch Mecunio's eye before following her father out. We are left alone in the tent. Mecunio is tight-lipped, Eleven smacks xer hands together in frustration. Xe has a short conversation with one of the Justices. Then the four Keda turn round and head back towards the city. I step in beside Silas, and we collect the soldiers who were waiting outside the tent.

"The daughter," Mecunio mutters. "She's the key to avoiding a massacre. Did you see the look she gave me? We can work with her, we just need to convince the Keda."

The rest of the walk back is silent, Mecunio clearly unwilling to discuss the negotiations in front of the soldiers. The gates open, and as we walk in under the barbican I can't help looking round at the murderholes and slits, and shivering.

Back inside, nobody hangs about. The Keda carry on walking, straight towards Val Firuz, while Mecunio confers with Abitha and the other elders, and they set off together. I'm left with Silas, and we agree to go to Sevanić, where the guild has set up a temporary compound.

"It's the annual tribute that's the problem, right?" I ask.

Silas nods. "Looks that way. Eleven wants a one-off payment and them out of our lives. There was a bit of to and fro on the number of slaves, but xe told me to make our position flexible."

"I can't believe they'll go along with letting the Dagmari take hundreds of citizens as slaves," I say.

Silas looks unhappy. "Not very pleasant, is it?"

"How will they choose the slaves? It could be citizens who fought for them on the wall!"

"I agree. And yet… what other choice is there?"

I feel that powerlessness welling up again, the frustration that we're just fodder to the Keda, for the wall, for the mines, for their haggling.

"Just because there's no other alternative, doesn't mean we have to take it," I say.

Silas raises his eyebrows, says nothing. The streets seem calm now – no sign of any more rioting, though there are still groups of dishevelled citizens sitting together, having urgent discussions. We reach the temporary compound, and Silas is dragged into some administrative drama with the apprentices.

I want to talk to Ira, and my luck is in – she is here, with a group of four other interpreters, sipping mint tea and gossiping about the riot. They have heard about our meeting with Shakan, so I give them an account of what happened, and a description of the Dagmari warlord.

Eventually, I manage to catch Ira's eye, and give her a discreet sign of Camun. She finishes her tea, and the two of us make our excuses. Outside, the rain has eased off and we talk in the shade of the compound wall. We both have until fifth gong, when we're due to return to our units, and I'm keen to tell her about Jordi.

"You wouldn't know him," I say. "He was a few years younger than me. But he left when he was eighteen, never joined the guild. And he managed to pass me a message when we were in the tent together – he spoke in Knuckles."

"What did he want?"

"He was asking for help – he wants to come home. His theory is – we help the Dagmari in, they take the Keda's riches, but at least the city survives."

She looks sceptical. "Not sure how wise a plan that is."

"I know. The Dagmari want slaves. And I'll have no part of that."

"So?"

"He told me they've got a spy, in the Palace of Shadows, who can communicate with them. He wants me to help the spy get them in. Now, I've no intention of doing that – but we do need to open up a dialogue with the Dagmari. The Keda are going to sacrifice us all if they have to, and we need to talk to them ourselves, as Camonites."

"For the march to Riona."

"Exactly. I don't think the priests realised how big their army would be – or that they would hold the mountain road. If – when – our army sets off, the Dagmari might just attack and ask questions later. We need to negotiate first, so they'll let us through."

"You think we should talk to this spy?"

"Yep. I'd discuss it with Naima first, but I've got no way of contacting her."

"Me neither," she says. "Do we ask Jakub for help?"

"I don't think so. He's out there fighting these bastards, I'm not sure he's on board with the whole 'my enemy's enemy is my friend' vibe."

"Especially if they're also our enemy."

"Well, quite."

"Let's do it. It's our only chance. Tonight?"

"After our shift. I'll come and pick you up."

We separate and I hurry straight to the wall before fifth gong sounds. It is a quiet afternoon, and I have little to do, apart from a few messages when a Justice passes. I had wondered if the Dagmari might attack immediately, but there is no sign of preparation for battle. Black clouds still haunt the skies, and the mood is grim among the soldiers as they do their drills. At ninth gong, the night shift relieves us, and, along with the other soldiers, I return home. I raise the loose floorboard, and take out Chicken's hand, rigid and grey, as proof of our credentials.

I meet Ira at her residence in Blackstone. She is wearing a shawl, for the evening has cooled rapidly. The walk to Queenstown is the width of the city, from west to east. Fortunately, since the first attack, the curfew has been quietly dropped. The Keda have locked themselves away, and the militia have neither the will nor the manpower to enforce it any longer. But the streets are still empty. We cross the river Firu as it ends its long journey, via The Stain, emptying into the Southern Sea. As we walk through Ganzić, we see linen everywhere, draped on balconies and washing lines that hang between the tenements. After the rainfall, citizens are finally using the opportunity to dry their dirty sheets and clothes. The Keda favour bright colours for their robes, but the dye is expensive and most citizens have dull greys and browns. The early moonlight falls on the grey linen, glinting to give it a metallic sheen.

The Palace of Shadows looms into view soon after we enter Queenstown. There is something alien about it – with its cold, black marble walls and the towers and domes that dominate all the dwellings around it. Everywhere you look are sleek lines and curves, making the surrounding area look even more of a shantytown. People say it was a mausoleum for the old monarchy, the rulers who preceded the Keda. When the Keda conquered the city, they destroyed most of the royal buildings, but left the Palace intact. Ever since, citizens believed it is cursed; the Shadows of kings and queens were said to haunt it. And so it remained unloved and untouched, while Queenstown reinvented itself as a slum. No feet trod through its vast halls and courtyards, except for stray dogs.

Then, fifty years ago, an enterprising young man called Serkonin decided to ignore the horror stories and find a use for the Palace. With his three brothers, he took over one of the main domes – cleared the place up, kicked out the dogs and rats, made it habitable. He employed carpenters, bought silks; he put beds and partitions in there. He posted a guard at the only entrance to the Palace, while he and each of his brothers went to the four gates, to lure in travellers and sailors. No locals would go there, but he undercut all the taverns and boarding houses, and it quickly established a reputation as an off-beat place to stay for visitors to Val Kedić.

Its success took everyone by surprise, including Serkonin. Within a few years, he found his investment had paid off, and he began taking over the rest of the Palace – more beds, more partitions. Locals got wise to it, and its functions expanded. No longer just a boarding house – one hall became a gambling den, one became the in-house brothel, and he found a hall which had alcoves cut into the marble – perfect for discreet meetings. If you were thrashing out some illicit business, and wanted a safe, neutral venue, it was the place to go. The number of burly gatekeepers increased, as did the prices, and one golden rule developed: you could do whatever you wanted in the Palace, but no weapons, no violence. Serkonin paid off the militia – no doubt the Queenstown Justices, too – and made examples of anyone who broke that rule.

Nobody was allowed in unless you had business there – so of course, stories developed: the merchant who had paid most of his fortune for his teenage daughter to hide there for seven years and avoid the mines; or the hall that was reserved each year for the elders and city elite to enjoy an orgy. But whatever the truth of these rumours, Serkonin and his brothers never said a word, for their success depended on guaranteed discretion.

When the Grey Fever came to Queenstown, the brothers shut the doors and everyone inside rode it out. Eventually when the city-wide quarantine ended, the militia burnt the bodies in massive bonfires, but when the Palace of Shadows opened its doors, they say not one single corpse was brought out. During my childhood, it was commonly agreed that you could not die in the Palace – the Shadows would not accept you because they only allowed royal blood there. But we heard one day that an underworld boss had been stabbed in there by a paid assassin. As a message to the gangs that settling private vendettas in the Palace would not be tolerated, Serkonin dumped the underworld boss's body on the street, along with his killer's head, hands and feet.

By the time I was an apprentice, Serkonin had died, but the business stayed in his family. His son – also called Serkonin – now ran the Palace. I had never been inside – never had reason to – but whenever I passed through Queenstown, I made sure to walk past it. I would place my hands on its walls as I walked, looking for breaks in the black marble. I never found any.

It is the perfect place for a Dagmari spy to be staying. Once we circle round two sides of the walls, we present ourselves at the only entrance, in front of the six armed gatekeepers. Its façade is the only part of the Palace that is new – Serkonin senior bolted it onto the front to beef up the security: it looks like a fortress, with turrets, thick oak doors, a drawbridge and pit before you get to the front door. You would need forty well-drilled men to break in here.

"Good evening," I call across the pit to one of the gatekeepers, a massive brute who should really be defending the city walls right now, not keeping a private business running. He looks at me expectantly.

"We have a meeting with one of your clients," I say. "Number two five three seven."

The anonymous code of the Palace – known only to Serkonin and his staff – is probably unnecessary, but adds to its mystique.

"My name is Raaki," I say. "Please tell him that, it's important." Ira had told me it was the Dagmansh for friend – a bait the spy should not be able to refuse.

The gatekeeper speaks through a grille in the wall, and we wait in silence for some time, ignored by the other gatekeepers. Finally, someone lowers the drawbridge, and we cross over. The gatekeeper checks us thoroughly for weapons, then the oak doors open and a woman appears, dressed all in black.

We follow her through the courtyards. The way is lit by braziers, and their burnished orange flames. In the corners, away from the fires, is a deep, infinite darkness. Up in the towers there are some windows, and I see shadows and movement, eyes watching us as we make our way deep into the mausoleum. They must be short on guests, I imagine – any traveller would surely have made a swift exit when they heard the Dagmari were on their way.

The guide takes us through an opening into a dome. It is not all black marble inside – we climb up limestone steps onto a thick woven carpet. We pass a few partitions, then the guide directs us towards a room. The spy is standing by his bed. He is a short man in a tunic, with bland features and thinning hair – and there are hints at his foreignness: his light skin and almond-shaped face. Something about him seems familiar. He gives our guide a coin, and a dismissal, watching us all the time. When we are alone, he says something in Dagmansh.

"We misled you," Ira says. "We are from this city, but we are friends. I speak your tongue, but my colleague does not."

He looks across at the neighbouring partition, and gestures with his head. "Outside," he says in our tongue, no trace of an accent.

We exit the dome together, and we walk to one of the gardens that encircles a tomb. In profile, I realise where I recognise him from. He is one of the slaves the ambassadors brought on their ship.

"You came here with the ambassadors, didn't you?" I say. "What did you do – slip away when you were processing through the city?"

He ignores my question. "How did you find me?"

"I was at the negotiations with Shakan," I say. "One of your people told me about you – said where we could find you."

"And why would they do that?"

"He thought we could help each other. We're from a secret order called the Camonites. You might have heard of us during your stay."

He makes no comment.

"We have a common enemy," says Ira. "The Keda."

I take out Chicken's withered hand. "We're not messing about," I say. "You probably heard about the dead councillor. That was us."

"I did hear about it," he says, an impassive glance at the hand. "And no end of trouble you caused me. They're all sniffing around now, convinced there are spies and traitors in every corner."

"Well, it would seem they're not entirely wrong..."

"Your countrymen are inconveniencing us," Ira steps in, "by laying siege to our city. So let's start working together."

"How?" he asks.

"At some point, in the near future," she says, "we will ask a favour of your army. Something that will damage the Keda. Can we count on you to deliver a message to your people?"

"What makes you think I have any method of communicating with them?"

"You've been feeding them information about our defences since the siege began, haven't you?" I say.

His silence confirms my theory.

"So do we have a deal?" Ira asks. "You will pass on our message?"

"How do I know this will damage the Keda?"

"It'll be obvious," Ira says. "Look, all we're trying to do is bring an end to this war. Surely that's what you want too?"

"It depends on who runs out of soldiers quicker. How many men have you got left now?"

"How about," Ira says, "we both knock off all the evasive goatshit, answering questions with questions?"

He smirks. "Very well. And – I hate to answer you with a question – but what are you doing for me? In return?"

"How about this," Ira says. "We won't let a load of loyal Val Kedić citizens know who you are, so that they can tear you limb from limb? Will that do?"

"Aha," he says. "How quickly the hand of friendship becomes a fist."

"You can cut out the cute aphorisms, too," I say.

He shrugs. "Come ask me for favours if you wish, *raaki*, it makes no difference to me. But before this season is over, the walls will fall and my countrymen will take your city. I would advise you to have an escape plan ready."

Odisse sounded confident when he was negotiating. I remember his words – *a fraction of what we can do... time for a lesson in humility...*

I'm worried suddenly, for I realise the Dagmari are indifferent to the internal squabbles of the Keda and the Camonites. We need to hold our defences, long enough to get the Camonite army ready and out of the city. I feel a sudden surge of hatred for the supercilious little man in front of me, living among us while he betrays us – and yet, right now, we need all the allies we can find.

16.

The following day sees growing pressure from the Dagmari. Bones tells me about some skirmishes that took place at dawn – a concentrated assault on the Western Gate, and four skiffs that came sailing down the Firu while their archers and catapults bombarded the jetties. Both attacks failed, but at a cost of more lives – and more worryingly, reports come in of a nocturnal attack on the harbour: several hundred warriors sneaked in from the coast, running over the sands to surprise our fleet. They overcame the skeleton guard and scuttled several ships before the alarm was raised, and our archers came down through the Southern Gate to send them fleeing back. The troops on the wall seem on the light side, and I'm sure some of the conscripts are missing.

I slip into Val Varin to get some water, and it's while I'm at the fountain, filling my cup, that Naima kneels down a few paces away and starts filling her own cup.

"Don't look at me," she says in an undertone. "The priest wants to go ahead with stage two of our plan. The other cell is ready, the trap is set."

"Who will it be?" I ask.

"He's approved us to go after Beast. Xe's tough, but xe's also experienced – one of the most important Justices. Xe should know all sorts of information about the mines."

"All right."

"And I've told Ira already. She wanted to be there when we take xer. It seems fair enough, xe killed her parents."

"Where do I find xer?"

"We've been following xer the last few days. Every day, in the afternoon, xe does a tour of the northern wall. Then xe follows the principal street back from the north-west corner to the Bridge of Peace. When we see xer pass the Triumph, a messenger will come and find you – that's your signal to get into position."

"Where?"

"You just have to intercept xer before xe arrives at the bridge. If xe gets that far, there's a risk other Justices will get involved."

"So I get xer to follow me..."

"Take xer to the warehouse in Five Bells we talked about. Right by the Little Firu, nice quiet spot, should be no one around."

"And what do I do when I get there?"

"All you have to do is make sure xe walks in first. Don't come in, stay by the door. Once xe's inside, we'll spring the trap. I'll be there, along with the other cell, and the priest – he's in charge of both our cells. Plus you and Ira – that's eight of us. Should be enough to subdue xer. The key thing is we take xer alive. We've got a cellar all ready – once xe's inside, our part is over, and we leave it to them. Clear?"

I nod.

"You're doing a good job, Razvan. We can't do this without you, you know."

She makes to get up, but I've remembered about the spy. I tell her quickly about our meeting with him, and that we can get a message to the Dagmari through him.

"Good," she says. "That could come in handy. Just don't give him any details until we're ready to go. We might be able to use them, but we can't trust them."

"One more thing," I say. "How do I contact you, Naima? It gets tiresome waiting for you to show yourself."

She pours water over her cropped hair, shakes it off. "Fair enough. I move around – but if you need to talk, leave me a mark." She glances around, and throws me some chalk. "Draw three parallel lines, right here, on the base of the fountain. I pass here every day, I'll see it. If you need me, I'll find you."

She jumps up and disappears into the back streets. I return to the wall. All I can think of is that the Dagmari might attack this afternoon and ruin our plans. But although they are out of their tents and busy, no attack comes.

Ansić looks in a bad way, unshaven with heavy lines under his eyes. He snaps at his men even more than usual, and is always on the wall when I come; day and night, he never seems to take a break. He doesn't strike me as especially patriotic, but he does seem bloody-minded enough that he will fight until he's the last man standing, just to spite the invaders. Other soldiers, however, are starting to mutter about the Keda. There were dozens of serious injuries in the riot, and seven deaths reported, and many soldiers had friends or family there. Some of them have homes that are damaged, and all are asking if more Justices will stand on the wall alongside them when the next attack comes. There's a dirty, disgruntled mood in the air, and I'm beginning to worry how long we can last. If the Keda lose the confidence of the army, we really are finished.

It is nearly sixth gong when the messenger arrives. He comes past at a run, stopping only to deliver his message before carrying on down the wall: "A Justice needs you," he says to me, "at the Five Bells meeting point."

I tell Bones, and set off to find Beast. I rush through Val Varin, though I know I should have plenty of time to intercept him. I don't notice anyone else, I'm so focussed on staying calm. Much like speaking, it's very easy for nerves to betray you when you fingerspeak. At least Beast might just mistake it for a clumsy accent. I cross the boundary into Five Bells, and take up position behind a pair of cypress trees at the side of the road. I have to shoo away two children who come begging, as I don't want Beast to spot me. I wait and wait, and I'm starting to panic, thinking I've blown it.

What if xe took a different route today? What if the Dagmari attacked and xe is on the wall, in the thick of it? What if xe's with another Justice – do I cancel the trap or hope we can handle both of them?

I'm so busy catastrophizing I nearly miss xer, striding down the road in xer distinctive green robes. I move out into the road, do a dumbshow of "aha – perfect, just the Keda I wanted to see", to which xe is probably oblivious, and run up the road towards xer. Xe stops as I approach, and xe must recognise me from yesterday for xe holds out an arm imperiously.

I put my fingers between xer bands, and say in a rush, *(Request) / Help / Justice / (Positive) / Find / Traitor / CouncillorKiller /.*

Xer eyes narrow, and xe grabs my arm with meaty fingers. *(Question) / Place /.*

Building / Near / LittleFiru /, I say. *Soldier / Prevent / Traitor / Run /.*

A brisk double tap on my upper band. *(Exclamation) / Go /.*

The two of us run down the road, and citizens move away with distrustful eyes. Xe keeps slowing for me and making impatient gestures. I am running as hard as I can, pointing out the direction to go – off the main road, downhill towards the moat. It's all timber merchants and boat supplies round here, and as Naima promised there's no one around to see us. We're on a track that runs alongside the moat, no paving, and it's muddy and poorly maintained, with weeds grasping across the path. The buildings are on our left, dilapidated and pitiful, and I slow as we come to the warehouse Naima told me about. I point at it, and nod at Beast – xe breaks into a sprint, and I cough and wheeze as I try to keep up. As xe approaches, I see a movement in the upper window – they've seen us. There's no danger of me entering the warehouse first: I run in ten

paces behind xer, just as the trap is released. Xe has stopped
and looks up reflexively at the roof. I follow xer gaze, to see a
carpet of black sand come crashing down on xer.

Beast dives for cover, but the carpet is too wide, too thick,
and it knocks xer to the ground. Xe half-rises, a hump-
backed shape in the sand; and a twine net is falling now,
weighed down by stones at each corner. Xe crawls on xer
elbows and knees, as two Camonites come running out from
behind a rotting rowing-boat by the wall, scarves round
their faces. The net is slightly off-centre, and xer desperate
crawl means only xer lower half is caught in it. As xe shakes
sand from xer face, the first Camonite rips off xer *cantu*,
and the second plucks a scimitar from xer robes, and hurls
it across the warehouse. I step inside, not wanting to get in
the way but hoping I can help. I spot an open trapdoor and
a cellar, just beyond Beast, and two figures up on a platform
by the roof, climbing down.

Xe wriggles free of the net, which didn't land properly
because of the sand, and the first Camonite comes down
swinging a cosh at xer head. Xe rolls to the side, and despite
xer bulk, xe is as quick as everyone says. Xe bounds to xer feet,
as the second Camonite rushes in, and in one fluid movement,
xe pulls out xer other scimitar and rips open the man's belly. I
hear a curse behind me, and I see Ira has come in.

I turn just in time to see the first Camonite smashing Beast's
hand with his cosh; xe drops the scimitar with a hiss, and I
hear more running footsteps now, from the other end of the
warehouse. The Camonite kicks the scimitar away, and Beast
knocks him over with a vicious right hook. I have frozen,
but Ira is moving towards xer, and I hear Naima shouting,
something about a crossbow.

Ira gets to xer first, and everything happens so fast I struggle
to make sense of it. I see the knife in her hands, I see Naima
crouching and aiming, but the Justice moves fastest. As Ira
thrusts at xer, xe grabs the hilt of the knife and head-butts her.

I run forward, as Ira falls into my arms with a cry – and Beast cuts down, slitting her windpipe.

The crossbow twangs, and the bolt skewers xer leg, pinning xer robe into xer thigh; xe falls to the ground with a puff of air. In the background, Naima and the priest are running over, the two other Camonites have climbed down from the platform, and the first Camonite is rising to his feet.

I cradle Ira as blood pours from her throat and she chokes, and dies, eyeballs rolling back in her skull.

Beast stares over at the cellar, at the approaching Camonites, and comes to a decision. With a baleful glare at me, xe cuts xer own throat, without even pausing. Naima covers the last few paces, but she's too late. And even though I'm holding Ira, for a moment I'm half-appalled, half-in-awe of Beast's implacable resolve.

"Shit," Naima says, kicking at Beast's body. "Shit, shit, shit."

The first Camonite checks over his mate, who is still just about alive, but blood is flowing steadily out of the gash in his belly.

"Bloody Camun," he says, kicking at the net. "What the hell happened?"

I look up at the roof, where two ripped halves of a fishing net are hanging, sand still dripping from them. A girl, who managed the trap, shrugs. "It pretty much worked," she says. "We nearly got xer. I don't know why that girl brought a knife–"

"Don't you blame her," I say. "Don't you fucking dare."

The priest puts his hand on Ira's head, and on the other man, who is fading fast. "We knew this plan entailed risk," he says. "We all knew. They made great sacrifices."

"For nothing," Naima says.

"A dead Crawler," says the girl. "That's something."

"We need to hide xer body," the priest says. "Let's save the post-mortem for later."

Two of the other cell take Beast and carry xer towards the cellar. I lay Ira down gently, and shut her eyes. The priest kneels in the sand, and performs a death rite. I barely listen to the words, tears running down my cheeks. He does the same to the other Camonite, who has stopped breathing.

"You know we have to hide their bodies too?" he says to me gently. "We'll give her a proper burial tonight, I promise."

I nod miserably, as the Camonites move the two bodies. The priest claps me on the back.

"Get home, Razvan, we'll finish up here." He gives me his cloak. "Hide the blood. Clean yourself up."

"What's going to happen?" I say. "To the plan?"

"Nobody said this would be easy," he replies. "I will reflect with my brothers and sisters – we will pray on it." He goes to pick up one of the scimitars, and I fasten the cloak around my shoulders.

"What a mess," Naima says. "I should have taken the shot earlier. I didn't know she had brought a knife."

"Not your fault," I say.

We've just killed another Keda – the most ruthless, most dangerous Justice of them all. Part of me should be elated, but all I feel is the bitterness of loss.

"Just you and me now, Grandad," she says, and her eyes are wet with tears. "Just you and me."

Afterwards, I find Jakub and we go to the Western Glory to get drunk. I haven't been drunk since my twenties, and it's neither as fun nor as easy as I remember. I slur my words a bit more, but despite my best efforts, I can't lose control. Jakub has the constitution of a buffalo, and the alcohol hardly seems to affect him.

"I'm sorry about Ira," he says. "She seemed all right."

"Yeah. She deserved better than that."

"Listen," he says, toying with his mug awkwardly. "I get why you joined the Camonites. I really do. They're not the nutters I thought they were."

"But…?"

"But right now… the city needs you, Razvan. The Dagmari could wipe us out, if we're not careful. You can try to liberate the mines – but it's not much use if there's no city left for you to come back to."

We had been so close. When Naima first told me the plan, I felt like I could reach out and clutch Rico in my arms. I saw it all unfolding ahead of me – the weapons, the kidnap, the march on Riona. In my head, I was planning what I'd say to him, which room he could have, which guild he could join – a dozen future paths, mapped out in my daydreams. But maybe the Camonites weren't quite as competent as I'd thought. Always one step behind the Keda – lacking their iron will, their cynical brutality. Just playing at revolution.

"It's those greedy bastard Crawlers," I say. "I honestly think the Dagmari would leave us be, if we just paid the tax."

"Don't forget the slaves," Jakub says.

"Perhaps. But I bet we could negotiate that."

"Or give them the Keda." He laughs infectiously. "Can you imagine that? A Crawler in chains, clearing out Shakan's shit?"

"I'd keep a few councillors," I say. "They could do interpreting for me."

"Yeah. What? No! That makes no sense! Who would they be interpreting for?"

I consider it. "That," I say, "is a good point. Wait! We'd disband our guild, so none of us knew how to fingerspeak any more. Then they'd have to form their own interpreter's guild, buck up their ideas and learn to tonguespeak."

"Tonguespeak? Is that a thing?"

"That's what Silas calls it sometimes." I wave him away. "Not the point. Then they can pass on my instructions to the remaining Blues in Fal Viruz–"

"Fal Viruz?"

"Val Firuz, that's what I said. And they can make our food, do our laundry, and so on."

"Now that," Jakub says, jabbing his finger, "is a doctrine I can sign up to. Get your holy mates to write that down."

I drain my mug and signal to Igor for two more.

"Promise me, though," he says, serious again, "any more dangerous stuff, you tell me. Even if I don't completely agree with it, I'll back you. Like I did with Chicken. We've all got to stick together right now."

"Sure."

"This business with Beast – an extra pair of hands might have tipped the balance. These Camonites of yours, I've no doubt they're brave, but have they got the experience? You and I, we're the only people alive who have ever..." He gives me a meaningful nod. "You know."

"What, killed a Crawler?" I say, in a mock whisper.

"All right, all right, keep your voice down!" He sips his chuka. "Mind you, we could have done with Beast on the wall tomorrow. Xe's a proper fighter. Seems like the Keda are still sulking over our little accident, but we need all the help we can get. If the Dagmari breach the wall, we're screwed."

At this point, Jakub starts to commandeer all the cutlery and mugs in the tavern, to explain some strategic point of the Dagmari tactics. He builds a wall, starts moving the enemy troops around, positions our defenders. I try to get involved, because he's listened enough times to me droning on about fingerspeak. But it gets very convoluted, and I zone out until he starts throwing dried peas at his wall, at which point I get a fit of the giggles, and he looks at me, nonplussed.

17.

Much like dogs can tell when a thunderstorm is coming, the old hands – the Muranese archers, the professional soldiers – say they can tell when a major attack is brewing. I have been on duty since dawn, nursing a hangover. The speculations of Bones and his comrades, that the Dagmari were going to attack, seemed unlikely, but as first gong approaches I can see they were right.

All the slaves and camp followers have disappeared, and we're faced with a sea of black warriors, fixing armour and mounting horses. The Justices have somehow picked up on the mood on the wall and are out in force – more joining all the time, as the message filters back to Val Firuz that an attack is imminent. They stand spaced along the wall, slightly separate from the soldiers, scimitars drawn. I would guess there are at least thirty on the western wall, and I am sure I recognise one as Scorpion. Since there are one hundred and thirty Justices – less Beast – and a handful who were stranded in Riona, it suggests the majority are out to defend the city today. It seems to boost the men's spirits, even those who profess to hate the Keda.

I also spy an alchemist up in a turret overlooking a section of the wall, near the Western Gate. Xe is holding what looks like a portable version of the smoke device I saw in the riot. It's a bulky contraption with a single ceramic pipe, with a strap over the alchemist's shoulder. The soldiers have given xer a wide berth, and xer section of the wall is completely empty. The Keda, it seems, are taking this attack seriously.

The waiting is the worst. Everyone is willing the Dagmari to get on with it and attack, but they take their time, one long death-knell that sounds for us all.

Finally, the drumming starts up again, and the trebuchets wheel into place.

"Here we go again," the man next to me mutters.

Then there is a horrendous noise, the sound of bones splintering, and tall wooden constructions wheel out in front of the trebuchets. They are towers on wheels, with ladders going up on either side. On the first level of each tower are four archers; on the top level are two men who appear to be kneeling, only their heads visible above a wooden barrier. Around twenty men are pushing each tower, building up some momentum before they come to a halt just outside the range of our archers.

"What are they for?" I ask the man next to me.

He squints. "Not sure. Not big enough to be siege towers. Seems like a lot of effort just to get a better position for a few archers."

The Dagmari fall silent, then there's a wordless scream, and the bombardment begins. The men handling the trebuchet have lit torches, and carry them to the boulders, which are covered in pitch. The arm springs up into the sky, and a flaming boulder comes flying towards the city. Everyone turns and watches as it passes overhead and hits an abandoned building. Part of the wall crumbles, but more seriously, there's a crackling and a sputtering as an exposed beam catches fire.

Val Kedić has managed to avoid serious fire – at least it has in the city's collective memory – but the Keda have always had a fear of it. By law, every street has to have a bucket of sand at its corner; and every quarter has citizens responsible for arranging a chain of water from the Firu, in the event of fire. We watch, helpless, as fire comes sailing over us, all along the walls. Not aiming for us this time, but the buildings. Some Val Varin citizens have come out into the streets, and immediately they jump into action, grabbing the buckets of sand, and putting a human chain in place. Meanwhile, the mobile towers are on the move again, and dozens of extra Dagmari archers move forward to support them as they come within range. We crouch as the archers do their stuff, but through the battlements, I glimpse what is happening on the top level of the tower.

One of the Dagmari stands – he has a sling in his hands – he starts whirling round, spinning like a top with the momentum of the sling. There's some kind of ceramic pot in there, and a flash of green –

He releases the sling, and the pot comes flying towards us. The pot is ringed with caltrops, and as it flies a tail of green liquid trails behind it. It explodes on a tower to the north of us, and a boom reverberates through the air. Green fire lights up the wall. For a few moments, there is anarchy, as men scream and run, abandoning the patch of wall that is alight. Thick smoke is drenching the air. I see some men dropping their weapons and running for the stairs. I see a Justice, xer robes on fire, wildly flapping and twitching like an insect that's been soaked in water, hurling xerself around to try and extinguish the green flames. To the north and south, it's the same – whole sections of the wall ablaze, and chaos.

I edge closer to Bones for safety. "Thunder of Heaven," he says, his face pale, wafting away smoke with his hand.

I look at him expectantly.

"Heard of it, ain't seen it before. Much harder to douse than normal flames. Water's no good, but sand might do the trick."

He calls over two conscripts, who run off to get sand. The second man on the top level of the tower gets to his feet, and starts the same spinning manoeuvre, knees low, leaning back as he swings the pot.

"Get him," someone screams. There is a hail of arrows from their archers, and I see two of ours fall. He releases the pot – and it veers off at a wild angle, before smashing against the wall with the same thundering noise.

The smell is horrendous – a medicinal stench mixed with burning flesh. The smoke is getting in my eyes, and everywhere men are coughing, covering their faces. Without warning, another flaming rock flies over from a trebuchet, just twenty paces above me. On the tower, a fire-swinger has re-loaded. As he stands, and brings round his sling in a wide circle, one of our Muranese archers takes his chance, and releases a tightly-angled shot with his longbow. The arrow takes the Dagmari in the gut as he whirls and he collapses, with his pot smashing into the tower. The structure disappears in a green inferno, and there's a ragged cheer from the wall. It eases the pressure on us, though fires are still raging all around, citizens and conscripts battling them with buckets of sand.

"Boss," one of the soldiers says to Ansić, pointing north. I look over, and the Dagmari are massing, lining up for what looks like an assault on the Western Gate. Squeezing through the warriors, like a ship cutting through the sea, is a ram-tortoise: I can see the battering ram, jutting out, beneath two angled roofs. I can't make out the men underneath the shelter, but there must be space for at least fifteen. The roofs are covered in animal skins, and suddenly the Western Gate looks very small, and very fragile.

And then, close by the ram-tortoise, five sambucae trundle over the ridge. They look like giant weighing scales on wheels: a counterweight on one end, and a covered trestle platform on the other. The counterweights are in the air, and twenty soldiers are pushing each one along, slower than the tortoise. I look closely, and I think I can make out the figure of Shakan's daughter, Shakanna, in her gold-rimmed armour, running alongside one.

"Shit," says Ansić. "Sambucae. Sneaky buggers must have built them while it was raining."

A Justice has seen them too. Xe appears from the south, sees my white armband, and grabs my arm.

Twenty / Soldier /, xe says. *WestGate / Now /.*

"Captain!" I shout, above the din of the fire. "The Justice wants twenty men to accompany him to defend the Western Gate!"

Ansić looks out at the enemy. I can hear the cogs whirring – it will leave our stretch of the wall exposed, but there is no sign of a serious attack brewing here, and the Western Gate will need support. The Justice is already moving to the steps. Ansić shouts some names, taps some shoulders, and we all follow xer – Bones stays behind with a handful of archers and conscripts.

We run along the base of the wall through Val Varin. There is a pile of burning timber blocking the street – the Justice hurdles it, but the rest of us go round the side. I am sweating in the heat, and can't imagine what it is like for those in proper armour. Further in, I see citizens in their doorways, nervously peering our way, watching the blaze and looking like they're preparing to run for it. A pack of goats gallops off as we approach, and I see one of Ansić's men – beardless, he must barely be eighteen – diving into an alley with a guilty look back as he disappears.

As we approach where the Western Gate should be, I am utterly confused, for it seems to have vanished; but then I realise the masons have built a wall behind the gate, sealing us in. Others have had the same idea as the Justice, and there is a scrum of bodies as we all climb the steps. When I get to the top, there are over a hundred soldiers massed above the gatehouse, with rocks, arrows, and all manner of weapons. The Dagmari have descended on us, hundreds and hundreds of them, and they are hacking away at the stakes and debris, clearing a path for the ram-tortoise. It emerges through the crowd, under a storm of arrows, and sets a course for the gate.

The ram crashes into it with a sickening crunch. Some of our archers have sent down fire arrows at the tortoise, but they sink into the wet animal skins and die out immediately. Everyone is hurling rocks and blocks of marble at the angled roofs, but they bounce off and the ram pounds into the door remorselessly.

One swing, two swings, three swings. Each time I can feel the shudder up on the wall. Their archers, meanwhile, are picking our men off as they stand up to throw the rocks.

Four, five, six. From a machiolation in the gatehouse wall, protected by corbels, some of our soldiers are lowering ropes with iron hooks, to try to hoist the ram.

Seven, eight –

On the ninth swing, it breaks through the wood, and there's a cheer from the Dagmari. They retreat, pulling the ram out, and start pounding again, widening the hole. Our iron hooks are getting close now, and one of their warriors jumps towards them, trying to slash the ropes, but is caught in a blizzard of arrows. Three swings later, and the gate collapses; the Dagmari surge forward – only to be confronted by the new wall, right behind it. Our soldiers jeer, and shake their fists with glee. The ram-tortoise, seeming to take it as a personal offence, takes a huge swing back, and charges towards the new wall. A horn sounds, and hundreds more warriors come running forward from their ranks, trailing grappling hooks.

The noise is unbearable.

To the south, meanwhile, the sambucae have nearly arrived. Ansić shouts at his men and we run along the wall, swords out. Thirty paces further down is the turret with the alchemist, and xer empty section of wall. The contraptions come to a halt, and the warriors jump into the boxed trestle platforms. Two men remain to control the mechanism for each, and as the counterweight of the first sambuca drops, the platform rises up to the height of the wall. Soldiers are pushing archers aside on the wall, preparing to meet the enemy as they board. The bridge falls forward from the platform, and lands on top of the crenellations with a thump. The Dagmari come charging down the boarding bridge, wielding their sabres, ululating and screaming. I watch as they crash into our soldiers – the force of the collision causes one warrior to run into the back of his comrade, trip, and go flying off the bridge.

They push us back, and I find myself near where the second sambuca has landed. I am gripping my sword, too tight, turning around all the time, watching my back. The Dagmari have cleared some space here, and start hacking down the defenders. I spy Shakan's daughter at the heart of it, ducking, slashing and feinting. She's a lighter build than everyone else, but makes up for it with her skill. But then the Justices arrive – no less than five of them shove their way through. Many of our soldiers step back, and let them handle the warriors.

Only yesterday, I helped lure one of these Keda to xer doom, now I'm marvelling as I watch them fight two-handed, jabbing and slicing with both scimitars at the same time. I am crushed against the back of the wall – it reminds me of the riot. I look down at the streets below and push the man in front of me. Five paces away, a Justice is taking on two Dagmari at the same time – they are bigger, and must be stronger to wield their massive sabres, but the Justice toys with them. One lumbers forward and lashes out at xer, but xe dodges, and slashes at the man's legs. His greaves protect him, but his knee still buckles, and as the second man stabs at xer, the Justice spins the first around to block the blow. From behind, xe thrusts upwards under the man's armour and he chokes blood before collapsing.

I can make out plumes of silver smoke as the alchemist joins the fray further down the wall. The Dagmari must have spotted the empty wall was some kind of trap, for no sambucae landed there. Small groups of fighting have drifted into the Keda's domain, and xe directs xer smoke at them indiscriminately

– our soldiers and Dagmari alike choke and stumble to the ground.

I am managing to keep a low profile, in a group with four others, who also seem happy to avoid the fighting. But two Dagmari warriors hack their way through to us, back-to-back, a trail of bodies in their wake, including one Justice. The man next to me pokes ineffectually at them, but is cut down with a contemptuous swipe. I stumble backwards, and fall over someone's body – my vision swims as the back of my head hits the flagstones. A second soldier falls dead on top of me, making me the filling in a corpse sandwich. The man's shoulder is in my mouth, and I can taste blood, coppery and slick. His arm is slumped over my eyes, and all I can see is green fire in the background, dancing along the wall.

I am starting to black out, but before I do, I have time to see a metal grappling hook landing on the wall.

Aha, I think. Looks just like one of the Crawlers' claws.

Ash floats across the sky, delicate as snowfall. A man jabs at me with his foot.

"You alive?" he asks.

I blink, groggy, my head worse than any hangover. There's no longer a corpse on top of me, but I'm still lying on one.

"Yes," I say, and hack a cough, for my throat feels raw. "We survived?"

The soldier looks around, rather theatrically. "If you call this survival," he says, and moves on.

I get to my feet. The ground is thick with bodies – soldiers, Dagmari, Keda. Some soldiers are prodding the bodies, checking who is alive.

Fires are still burning; patches of green flames on the wall, and steady blazes in buildings on the edge of the city. The air is acrid. A craftsman is carrying a basket, and I stop him.

"What happened to the Western Gate?" I say.

"The gate's gone," he says. "They broke through. But we'd put up a wall behind it – started it after the first attack. Mortar powder and water, easy. Set in two days – not that solid, but solid enough. They started smashing that too, but our boys got their ram with hooks – lifted it up high and dropped it all the way back down. Ripped it off its ropes. Brilliant."

"So we're sealed in now?"

"You got it – nobody's getting out that way, but at least nobody's getting in either. They did the same with the Queensgate."

I stumble down into the city, wiping the grime and ash from my face. Whole buildings have collapsed in some places; in others, just the walls remain. Where fires still burn, there are chains of citizens passing buckets back and forth, pouring sand or water over them. Some are weeping, and none of them look up as I pass.

I head back the way I came earlier, down towards Wesson. At the base of the steps, some of the soldiers I was with are recovering. I see Ansić, slumped by himself, sword on the ground. His hair is matted with blood. Our eyes meet.

"Thought you were done for, interpreter," he says.

"So did I," I say. "Thought we all were."

"We held them off. This time. A steep price to pay, though." He coughs and looks around at the remains of his unit. "It was the Keda," he says. "They swung the balance. Killed enough of the bastards so we could deal with the climbers."

He looks like he might say more, but instead gives a weary sigh. I nod, and he raises a hand in farewell. I drag my aching body home, and with a stab of guilt, start to run a deep bath.

18.

The guild confronts Mecunio that evening, at the temporary Sevanić compound. Juraj organises it. He is a spiky man, middle-aged; an interpreter of ordinary ability, quick to take offence, always raging at Silas' pusillanimity. He tracks down six of us, the other remaining senior interpreters, and we meet in the upper room, to air our grievances. Silas sits separate from us, tight-lipped.

"You need to take us off the walls," Juraj says to Mecunio, without preamble. "How many are we now? Twenty-two?"

"Four dead," Talia says. "And Darius, Ira and Leni missing."

"So maybe twenty-one," Juraj says. "We were overstretched as it was – how will we cope now?"

"You're absolutely right," says Mecunio, who always knows how to handle Juraj. "The Justices wanted to ensure they were able to pass on strategic instruction. But I'm sure they'll also see the importance of the, ah…"

"Of the survival of the guild?" says Juraj, who won't be denied his moment. "What happens when we get down to ten of us? Five? Even if we endure this siege, it won't be much bloody good if we can't talk to the Keda anymore!"

"Agreed," says Mecunio. "I will discuss with the Justices–"

"*Inform* them," insists Juraj.

"How many Justices did the Dagmari kill, anyway?" asks Ozkan. "I saw a lot of them burn on the eastern wall."

"The Keda suffered," says Mecunio. "They fought bravely and were the first line of defence when the sambucae arrived. We believe thirty Justices perished."

"Under a hundred left," I say.

"Indeed," Mecunio says, looking at me coolly.

"And how about us?" Talia asks. "How bad were our losses?"

Mecunio inclines his head. "They were grievous. We are still counting our dead, but my sources in the militia tell me we now have a standing army of just under two thousand men."

"That doesn't sound... so bad?" says Juraj.

"Two thousand is, at a push, enough to man the walls. But not permanently. They need to eat, they need to sleep. These men are already exhausted."

"The Dagmari are going to break in, aren't they?" says Talia.

"All I know is our army, and the Keda, will fight while there is still breath in their lungs," says Mecunio. "The rest of us must trust in that, and work according to our abilities."

"What do you propose, then, Juraj?" says Silas waspishly. "What are we to do, if we're too precious to spare for the walls?"

Red spots appear on Juraj's cheeks. "I'm no coward," he says. "But I'm not a soldier either, and there's nothing for me to do there. We stand at the back, while they fight, and we wait for a stray arrow or rock to pick us off. I can serve this city better by talking to the Keda."

"How about this," says Talia, so often the peacekeeper between the two men. "We have a morning shift and an afternoon shift, eight interpreters on each. Five to cover any evening and night business. We're based here in the compound, and messengers can tell us where we're needed."

"I'm sure that will be acceptable," says Mecunio. "The Council is reopening communications – in fact, they've asked to meet with me tonight. I'm sure you'll all be back in Val Firuz again on a regular basis."

"Well, that's great," says Juraj, looking mollified.

"Now, if you'll excuse me," says Mecunio, rising to his feet. "Silas – Eleven will want you as usual. Shall we?"

The two of them exit, followed by three of the others. I call out to Talia and Juraj. "Hold on – can I talk to you?"

They settle back down at the trestle table. With Ira gone, I need allies in the guild, and these two are my best hope. I don't especially like Juraj, but Silas has hitched himself to the elders' wagon, and nothing I say will convince him otherwise.

"We need to start thinking long-term," I say. "We all know Mecunio, Abitha and that lot will do whatever is best for the elite. And the Keda will do what's best for the Keda. Even if all that's left is Val Firuz in a sea of ash, the rest of us dead or slaves."

"Probably," says Juraj. "What's your point?"

"We're in an unusual position – we know their secrets, we hear the decisions that are being taken. We should be looking out for the city – making sure someone is doing what's right for the citizens."

I turn to Juraj. "You were a Queenstown boy, weren't you?"

"I was, but–"

"You're from the slums too, aren't you, Talia?"

"Saalim," she admits.

"And I'm from The Stain. I'm just saying, these are our people. We owe the elders nothing – and we should make the most of our position."

"I don't disagree with any of what you say," says Talia, "but what can we do, practically?"

"A time may come," I say, "when we have to choose, between the Keda and the Dagmari. The elders will side with the Keda, every time. Now, I'm not saying we have to actively choose the Dagmari. But we can do whatever it takes to make sure the city survives. And make sure the citizens know what is being decided about their futures."

The two of them look dubious. "I've no love for the Keda," Juraj says, "but all I am, all I can do, is interpret for them. That's what they call me, Razvan. Interpreter. Without them–"

"If it meant I never had to fingerspeak again," I say, "I'd take it like a shot. Become a fisherman, start again. They make out like it's an honour–" I rip the white armband off. "It's a curse, Juraj. A curse."

"It's the system we have," Juraj says. "We've all profited from it. Maybe not in the slums, but show me a system where everyone profits."

"Now you sound like Mecunio," I say. "Don't forget what we are to the Keda. We're fuel, we're a pair of hands, we're a source of food production. If they could replace us with monkeys or automata, they would. All I'm saying, is if we get a chance to change things, I want people with me I can trust."

"This sounds like Camonite talk, Razvan," Juraj says. "Is this something to do with them?"

"No," I say. "It's about doing the right thing."

"I'm not sure," Talia says. "Yes, the Keda look out for themselves, but the elders try to do what's right for the citizens. They're tough decisions to make, that's all."

"Talia, we could be days away from defeat. All of us dead or in chains. So every meeting of the Council, every message you interpret, could be critical. Just promise me that you'll consider it."

"What exactly would you want me to do?"

"Just listen to what is being discussed. If the Keda or the elders want to sacrifice the citizens, I want to know."

"I'll consider it," says Talia. Juraj gives a non-committal grunt. It is a risk, but I am doing what Ira would have done, and following my instinct.

The city receives some much-needed respite. As the fires burn out and the soldiers recover, the Dagmari hold back from any more major assaults. Their masons and carpenters can be seen hard at work, suggesting they have exhausted much of their ammunition, not to mention scaling ladders and sambucae. There are still night raids, which keep our men on their toes, but for five days there are no reported breaches.

Our soldiers are rarely seen in the city. They sleep on the walls, snatching short rests when they can. A bigger problem is the grain supply. After seventeen days of siege, rationing is in full force and citizens are starting to panic. They get a smaller ration than the soldiers, and there is resentment towards extra mouths such as conscripts' families from the farms and homesteads. We are not starving, not yet, but already I have seen citizens hunting stray dogs for meat.

As for me, I am no longer out on the walls with Ansić and his unit. The Keda demurred without any argument to us staying in the compound, and I am part of the afternoon shift. I am needed in Val Firuz most days, not to translate for the Council as often as before, but with Blues and delegates, poring over maps of quarters, and translating about grain distribution, repairs and disease.

Dysentery has swept through the eastern slums, and scores of citizens have fallen sick. The rains have returned, and they carry the disease through the streets. I keep myself busy, for if I stop working I find myself thinking about Ira, and guilt gnaws away at me. I always prided myself on staying cool under pressure – it was Ira who worried about panicking. So how is it that in the warehouse I froze? That it was Ira who reacted first? I should have known what she was planning. Should have held her back. Should have reacted faster when Beast headbutted her and took her knife. Should. Should. Should. Didn't.

My grief and guilt is no use to Ira, wormfood now. So I tell myself to stop wallowing and get the work done.

Meanwhile, the Keda have not forgotten Chicken, and, along with the rest of the guild, a Justice subjects me to a grilling about Darius. But I give them nothing, and the mystery remains unsolved. What Naima has done with his body, I do not know. I let him take the blame. Maybe if I can help free his daughter from Riona and give her some money, it'll pay off, oooh, about a tenth of the guilt I feel over his death. The death of Beast, meanwhile, seems to have gone unnoticed. Whether the Camonites have kept xer body hidden, or whether they dumped it near the walls during the battle, I do not know. I want to know what is going on, and leave a mark for Naima on the fountain, but she does not contact me.

Five days after the Dagmari attack with fire, six days after the deaths of Beast and Ira, I run into the priest. I am walking home along the People's Market after an afternoon translating, when I see him on the other side of the road. He is wearing a cloak and a cowl, but I recognise his distinctive fuzzy beard. I hurry behind him and grab him by the shoulder.

"Hey," I say, and he whirls round, before relaxing when he sees me.

"Razvan," he says. "Some other time, I'm afraid – I'm in a bit of a hurry."

I put a hand on his arm. "Just a moment, priest. I want to know what's going on."

He glances round – citizens are brushing past us, but no Keda or militia are in sight. He draws me back into a doorway. "Let's get off the main road, at least," he says, brushing sand off his cloak. "What do you want to know?"

"I haven't heard from Naima for six days," I say. "What is happening? Are we still planning to march on Riona? Something else?"

"We are... discussing it," he says. "Without a Justice's information, an assault on the mines is a risk – we'd be going in blind. I have instructed Naima to lie low for the moment. Do you know how many of us there are?"

I shake my head.

"One hundred and forty-two," he says. "Thirty-two cells,

and the priesthood. Enough for a small army, certainly. But not so many that we couldn't get wiped out if we're not careful. We're still trying to work out how well defended Riona will be. An unsuccessful attack risks the very existence of the order."

"But the whole point of the order is to hurt the Keda!" I say. "To stop the mines. This is it. We'll never have a better chance!"

A market trader who I recognise has turned to look at us, and I stare him down.

"Keep your voice down," says the priest. "Look, it's wonderful to see the... zeal of a recent convert. But some of us, we've been preparing for this for nineteen years. I was in the mines, I care about this as much as you. It simply requires patience."

"We're running out of time," I say. "Eventually, they'll breach the walls. And who knows what'll happen once they get in?"

He scratches his beard, looks at me appraisingly. "There is a school of thought, Razvan – and I don't subscribe to it, not entirely – that it might not be such a bad thing if the Dagmari break in."

"For who?"

"For us. The Keda are our primary enemy – if the Dagmari destroy them, but leave the city intact, then so much the better for us. So the argument goes."

"I get that. But how could we ensure they don't burn the city down?"

"That is the question. The Dagmari are wild and strong-willed. And getting them to do our bidding is an even bigger challenge than trapping a Justice. How can we ride that tiger?"

I spend a frustrated evening, unable to settle. I can't help feeling that we've let something slip from our grasp, that the city is sliding towards oblivion, and we've lost our chance to stop it. Worse is to come the next morning, when Talia corners me. Neither of us were on shift, but I needed company, so headed over to the compound at second gong. It was nearly empty, so I wandered into the temporary library, and was flicking listlessly through the lexicons. Talia comes in and shuts the door.

"Razvan – there you are. I tried your residence, then guessed you'd be here."

"What is it?"

"What we talked about," she says. "Choosing between the Keda and Dagmari. Doing what's right for the city."

"Yes?"

"I was working in the High Chamber yesterday evening. Big meeting, the Council summoned the elders. They're going to try and restart negotiations."

"That's good, isn't it?"

She shakes her head. "They're going to offer more slaves. A lower tax, but we give them more of our citizens. And they were discussing this with the elders – how to choose which citizens to give up, how to ensure compliance." She is clenching the side of the table, and her knuckles are turning white. "And Mecunio and the rest, they were going along with it, talking logistics like it was a grain shipment! They were discussing the slums: which ones were overpopulated, which ones don't pay their way. I had to sit there and listen to Abitha explain how little revenue Saalim brings in!"

"Are you surprised?" I say.

"I don't know. Maybe not. Maybe they think they're doing the right thing to save the rest of the city. But I can't stand by and be a part of it."

"Good. Okay," I say. "Let me think. When are they going to do this?"

"The plan was to send out an envoy with a parlay flag this afternoon. They're finalising details of the offer right now."

I drum my fingers on the lexicon, tapping out touches

reflexively. With sudden clarity, I know exactly what I have to do, the only way I can cut this knot.

"What?" says Talia. "What are we going to do?"

I give her a grim smile. "It's time to throw the dice. I'm going to speak to the Dagmari myself."

I want Jakub by my side, but he's so busy these days. The captain of his unit was one of the many who died in the fire bombardment, so Jakub was promoted to take his place. I've only seen him once since then. So I make my way alone to the Palace of Shadows. The rain trickles down its domes, creating streaky patterns which make it appear less imposing in the daylight. All over the city, the old and the homeless are being pressed into service – swords put into their hands, training at the barracks. It makes me glad to see there are only three gatekeepers outside the Palace now. Clearly they are doing their bit too.

I call out to one, just as I did before: "I have a meeting with one of your clients. Number two five three seven. My name is Raaki."

After a wait, they let me in, without even bothering to check me for weapons. Standards are slipping everywhere, it seems, as the city limps towards destruction. The guide takes me to a hall this time, near the tower where the spy was staying. I watch the rain, and marvel – the drainage system is hundreds of years old, but still works perfectly, siphoning off the water into gutters as it comes down.

She leads me to a series of recesses cut into the marble. The spy is sitting in one, picking his teeth and watching me with amusement. The black marble curves out from the recess with a flourish, so we can see no one, and no one can see us.

"So," he says. "Here you are, *raaki*. How are we doing? You seem to have mislaid your partner."

"Just me today," I say, aiming for insouciance, but my heart constricts.

"Maybe for the best," he says. "I don't think she liked me."

"Luckily, we don't need to like each other," I say. "I've come here with a proposal for you."

"Ooh," he says, rubbing his hands. "A proposal. I like proposals."

I ignore his mocking tone. "The Keda want to reopen negotiations," I say. "Our envoy will attempt to parlay with you this afternoon. But I've got a better suggestion."

"Go on."

"There's a way into the city. Through the sewers. I could guide you, and several hundred of your finest warriors. I'd take them all the way to the citadel."

The spy has stopped picking his teeth now.

"Everything you want is there. All the riches of the Keda. Your warriors can take it all."

There is no sound except for the pattering of rain on marble. The spy crosses his legs, uncrosses them.

"And why are you offering us this?" he says. "Sheer generosity of spirit?"

"You know why. I'm a Camonite. I want nothing more than the Keda destroyed."

"And afterwards?" he says. "After we've looted Val Firuz and killed the Keda?"

"There's nothing left for you in the rest of the city. You've lived here, you know that's true. We'll give your warriors free passage out, all the way to the Gate of Triumph."

"Free passage? I don't think you would be able to stop us either way. Besides, it seems to me that we can break in ourselves soon enough. With none of your conditions attached."

"We've still got plenty of fight in us. And many more of your men will die before you break in."

"Seems to me–"

"Look," I snap. "With the best will in the world, you're just the messenger-boy. Now, I want a meeting with Odisse – can you get me that or not? If you can't, I'll find another way to contact him. And I'll be sure to tell him how… *helpful* you were to the Dagmari cause. Our envoy is going out this afternoon, so I need to know."

There's a cold glimmer in his eye when I call him "messenger-boy", but it fades, and he says, "All right, calm down. Pays to be suspicious in this business, *raaki*. I'll set up your meeting. But I want to be there too."

"Looking for a share in the glory?"

"Something like that. We have a deal?"

"Deal. How do you communicate with them?"

"Normally I do it at dawn. But there is a protocol for an emergency. I have to go down to The Stain to do it. Come along with me, and you can tell me the message for Odisse. The when and where of this meeting."

I agree, and he goes to his room, returning with a leather satchel, and we leave the Palace of Shadows together.

"We're going out via the Gallows, then?" I say. "You have a pass?"

"Do you?"

I show him my white armband.

"Aha. Well, getting a pass round here is pretty easy. I've never met such bent guards. Mind you, we have a saying in my language: 'Travel south, corruption festers.'"

"Snappy."

"It's not well served by my translation. There's a pun on the word 'south' I had to sacrifice."

The two of us cut down into Lekaan, the bottom corner of the city, and head for the Gallows, the pair of hoist elevators that carry citizens between the city walls and The Stain below. I used to hate them as a boy, and to avoid them I would sometimes go all the way to the harbour and enter via the Southern Gate. In a wooden cage, swaying in the breeze, they managed to make me feel both exposed and enclosed at the same time. Borzu once told me a story he'd heard about a big group of

Street Rats, who were in the bottom cage and apparently in an experimental mood. They picked the cage lock, and all jumped out as they started to rise; the sudden weight shift sent the other cage plummeting, crashing to the ground before the operators could get to the braking mechanism. Net result: a lot of broken bones, but a successful prank. Probably all goatshit, but it didn't help my nerves.

The spy is ambling along and I try to up the pace. It will be a challenge to get to The Stain and back to Sevanić before my afternoon shift starts, but this is too important. Talia will have to cover for me.

"So," he says. "Details. When shall we set this meeting for?"

"Midnight," I say. "Tonight."

"And did you have somewhere in mind? Or am I going to have to smuggle the two of us out of the city?"

"I grew up in The Stain," I tell him. "I think I can get us past the guards, thanks. You get Odisse to come to the beach, south of the mountain road. There's a little cove there, nice and secluded, about a thousand paces from their camp. We can meet there, and agree on a plan."

He concurs, and we continue west along the wall until we reach the Gallows. The cages are hanging from a pulley system, one at the top of the wall, the other on the ground. A handful of fishermen and soldiers are already inside the top cage. Normally anyone can pass through the Gallows, but since the start of the siege security has tightened and everyone entering or exiting the city is checked by the militia. The spy flashes his pass and a guard nods at my white armband, and we climb down into the cage. After a short wait, our cage fills up with ten passengers, and two guards each drag an iron makeweight into opposite corners of the cage. They whistle to the cage at the bottom of the wall, one of them kicks away the struts to release us, and the cage jolts down.

Above me, hemp ropes spool through the pulleys and we lurch down. I squint out between the wooden stakes of the cage. The sea is a dull blue, pockmarked by bitter lashes of rain. The other cage is soon rising past us, and a beggar gurns at me through the stakes as we sway past. Our cage is caught by a gust, and the ten of us stagger into the corner, squashing some poor fisherman. We awkwardly extricate ourselves as the cage slows and bumps onto the ground, and step out into The Stain.

Inside the slum, the spy blends in nicely, but I get a few strange looks for my clothes appear out of place here, too well-cut. It is a couple of years since I was last here. Each time it's a little smaller and grubbier than it appears in my memories. I follow him as we pass the street where I lived. A baby squalls in a dwelling somewhere.

"Bit of a shithole where you grew up, isn't it?" he says.

I don't reply.

He takes me up a hill to a cemetery, surrounded by cypress trees. No houses look down on us here and we are safe from prying eyes. There's a fug of lethargy in the air, the only sound is cicadas buzzing in the heat. The spy points out a Dagmari encampment near the coast.

"There you go. I was pleased when I found this spot." He takes a looking glass from his satchel, a small hole in the middle and a lever on the reverse. "So. Midnight. The beach south of the mountain road." He holds it up, looks through the hole towards the camp, and angles it so it catches the sunlight. He flashes it twice.

I nod at the looking glass. "Clever. You can send messages just with that?"

"Not that different from your fingerspeak," he says. "Let's see if they're paying attention."

Indeed, we don't have to wait long before they send back an answering flash.

"Now," he says. "Here's the tricky bit."

He flashes a long message, angling it with the lever to change the length of the flashes. The linguist in me wants to know more about how it works, but I squash the impulse. Finally, he stops, and after a long pause, a short answer flashes back.

"Explaining the location was tricky," he says. "Had to fudge a few things, but I think I got there. You'd know more than I do about all that."

"But they understood?"

"They confirmed it. And Odisse will come, you can be sure of that. I'm his man – it was his idea to smuggle me in here. You can explain your plan to him there."

He packs away his looking glass and I survey the cemetery. Whole plots are set aside for families going back generations, and some stones have forty or fifty names carved there. They pile in the corpses, deeper and deeper, with little regard for the dignity of the skeletons below. Cypress leaves cover the graves, dry and brittle as parchment. I feel a twist of envy, these sprawling families that have filled up The Stain with their bloodline. We were always just a duo, my father and me. I never knew my mother, and my father was a lone wolf. I had an idea there was some family in the city, but he never spoke of them. For all my talk with Talia and Juraj, these aren't my people, not really. Perhaps that's what drove me to the guild, and always kept me on the fringes – not a citizen, but not a Crawler either.

Despite all that, though, despite what ungrateful, blinkered bastards they are, despite the wrong turns I've taken, I have to do this – for the city of Val Kedić must stand. Even if we have to drag it to its knees first.

INTERLUDE (3)

Pigeons bring further news of the siege. Bombardment, escalades, green fire. Huge losses. The southerners even command the hillsmen to send relief to the city! They laugh grimly at the idea.

Despite the efforts of Bearhide and Splitmouth, men continue to slip away in the night. In twos and threes, they depart north, through the Riona valley. They can see the way the wind is turning – the Keda will not return for some time, if at all. Only thirty-three of them are left, and Whitehair is losing hope. Bearhide does nothing. He holds court in the barracks and ignores the collapse. Half Moon furiously explores ideas and options – he comes to talk about the possibility of keeping the mines going without the Keda; taking on their trade agreements for the coal and marble. But the impracticalities are evident, and Whitehair is not sure if Half Moon's heart is in it. He wonders if he is planning to desert, if he's made his calculations and decided they've reached the end of the line.

Splitmouth, meanwhile, is slowly assuming control. He has developed a swagger which Whitehair does not care for. He has a band of ten close allies, and they have begun to treat the colony as their private fiefdom. They terrorize the kids and work their way through the dwindling supplies. Barrows like Roć and Sevanić continue to work in the mines, but elsewhere work has ground to a halt without equipment or enough guards to enforce it. Some of the barrows continue their passive resistance and antagonise the guards, and Whitehair fears it will end badly – he has heard the mutterings of Splitmouth and his friends.

Whitehair is on one of his nocturnal prowls, on his way back from The Noose, when he hears shouts coming from the colony. He climbs round the rockface and looks down on the barrows. He can make out Splitmouth and his gang, armed with clubs and crossbows; some are waving torches. Eighteen men, he counts – more than half the guards. They are plainly drunk.

In squads of five or six, they storm into a barrow, and pull out two or three of its inhabitants, who struggle and shout. The youngsters are wearing underclothes, shivering in the bitter night. He tries to make out the faces of the children in the torchlight – they are the ringleaders of the passive resistance, he realises, all older children from the slum barrows. Some of the boys are as big as the hillsmen, but they look exposed and vulnerable here. A couple of the guards lash out with their clubs, sending them hurrying away from the barrows. As a group, they all head in the direction of the mines, accompanied by the guards' laughter, shoving, occasional punches and dragging of the teenagers. Whitehair descends into the colony, watching, following. One girl falls, and two guards hit and kick her, but she refuses to get up. They leave her, and the party goes down into the valley.

Whitehair climbs an escarpment and crouches, waiting to see what the guards will do. The hillsmen have taken their prisoners into the valley, and they stop, mine entrances on all sides. There are fourteen teenagers, and the guards with crossbows chivvy them into a corner where they cower. Twelve of the guards with clubs, form a wide circle. They grab a boy and push him into the circle. A guard calls something, and there's a gale of laughter. The boy gets to his feet. Looks around, all the way, three hundred and sixty degrees. One guard moves in and lashes out, and the boy darts back. He sees an opening and makes a break for it, but two guards cover it, and he backs away. The boy probes, turns, twists, as the circle of guards moves across the plain.

This is what a hunted animal looks like, thinks Whitehair, disgusted, but he does not permit himself to look away.

The boy lowers his head and tries to charge through a guard, but the man grabs him round the waist and they fall to the ground. They beat him savagely. He writhes around, protecting his head with his fists. Eventually though, he manages to rise.

The guards shepherd him towards an adit, the mine entrances that loom in the dark like portals to another world. The circle squeezes closer. He sobs and backs away towards the entrance. He gives up the fight and disappears into the mineshaft. Whoops and yells follow him.

Then the guards return to the rest of the group. Another is chosen and Whitehair watches the whole process repeat itself. One by one, the teenagers are dispatched into different mines. They know what is coming now, and each try different tactics, but the result is the same. One girl stands tall, runs directly into a mine entrance, denying them their fun. The guards manage to get some hits in, but she refuses to give them the satisfaction of crying out. Whitehair recognises the Wesson boy, the one he sparred with, who spotted the bridges were down. He's not a big lad, but he doesn't back away from a fight – he gets some punches in before a guard knocks him over with a brutal jab. He too, ends up in a mine, and soon just the guards are left in the valley. They stand in twos and threes, in animated discussions, chuckling. They have even remembered to bring flagons of drink with them. A few start up a tuneless shanty. Splitmouth and some others start to walk back.

This place is finished, Whitehair realises with dismal clarity. It's all over.

You should go, a voice tells him. *Get out of here while you still*

*can. Before things get even nastier. You've done what you can – twenty
years you've given. Now it's time to walk away.*

He looks north, towards the hills. Not much family left there,
but they are his people all the same. He will be a rich man there,
too. All that Roć income. For years, he was sending some back
to support his mother and her smallholding, but she died last
year. It will be just him now. He could find a young wife. Start
a new life. The daydream drifts through his mind, and he fills
it in with more details. For a moment he curses himself for
waiting this long, for the self-indulgence of spending his best
years trekking back and forth on the mountain road.

A noise makes him turn back to the mines. A girl has crawled
out of one of the adits, and the guards have noticed.

"Oh no, you don't!" one shouts. Another drunkenly raises
his crossbow and sends a bolt flying in her direction. It misses
by a long way, but she scampers back in. The men laugh.
"Night-night!" one calls out. "No comfy bed for you tonight!"

Whitehair pulls his cloak tight. How long before those kids
die of exposure? He looks towards the barrows. What will the
rest of them do once the colony is finished? Where will they go?

Night drifts past. The guards filter back to the colony in dribs
and drabs. Whitehair tries to gauge the tipping point between
when they will ignore him and when they will do what he
says. When a trio leaves and just two are left, he strides down
into the valley. They start to greet him amiably. They seem
sober now and are not regulars of Splitmouth's gang.

"Hey, Whitehair, guess what–"

"All right," he says. "You've had your fun. Now piss off, will
you? I'll take it from here."

One looks away, smirks, and heads off. The other stutters
something, but Whitehair waves him away.

"Come out!" he calls out in the southern tongue. "It's over!"

About half crawl out, blinking in the moonlight. He goes to

one girl, and her hands are icy cold. He puts his cloak round her.

"Get yourself back to the barrows," he says roughly.

The teenagers cling to each other for warmth, and stumble away. Two are in better condition than the others and go to look for their missing friends. Whitehair heads to the entrance where he saw the Wesson boy go. Twenty years he has been here, but he's never been inside. Through the entrance he goes, into the hollowed-out mountainside. After a few paces, the cavern narrows into a shaft, and he has to go on his hands and knees.

"Boy!" he calls out. "Come back!"

There is no reply. He must have gone deeper into the shaft than expected to escape the wind – it is the sensible thing to do. Whitehair's shoulders rub against the walls, he is too big for this. There's a reason they use kids. His jerkin tears, and the cold pierces his ribs like an arrow, cutting into his bones. He crawls on, cursing his countrymen, cursing the Keda, cursing the stubborn southerners.

He wonders how they can bear this. How long they must spend, in a cramped position like this, shuffling, or chipping away with a pickaxe. He realises now the reason they are not supposed to go down the mines themselves – not because they are too big, but because of the horrifying reality of what they force these children to do.

He looks up. At one point, the miners here hacked away at a crevice that shoots up from the roof of the shaft. The rocks up there sparkle, even in the darkness – they must have hit a mini-seam of the quartz. The Keda give rewards for anyone who finds these. Despite himself, he pauses, dizzy for a moment, taken aback by the beauty that is concealed in the rock. With an effort, his arms drag the rest of his body on.

He rounds a corner and sees the boy's body, slumped by some wooden struts where the shaft splits in two. Every so often, he gives a harsh cough. He calls again, but the boy does not respond.

Whitehair crawls closer. He is wedged in tight, and suddenly he starts to panic that he cannot go backwards. For a moment, he cannot think of anything except the cage of rock that is surrounding him; the fact his elbows can barely move, and he has lost all feeling in his toes.

Nobody knows I'm down here, he thinks. *It's just me, and this boy.*

A silent scream is building in his throat. He slows his breathing right down. Looks at the boy. He tries to look behind him. Getting himself out will be hard enough but dragging the boy out of here too is going to be a mission. He thinks back to his daydream, starting a new life in the hills. He thinks of the boy's mother, his father, somewhere in the city.

Outside, a girl is weeping raggedly, tears mixed with chattering teeth.

19.

On my way from The Stain to the compound, I leave another chalk mark for Naima on the Val Varin fountain, big and jagged, trying to get across the urgency. I arrive in good time in the end, to see Silas and Ozkan leaving for the Gate of Triumph in order to assist in the parlay. The remaining six of us are stuck in the compound for most of the afternoon, sipping mint tea and playing dice. Calls come in for interpreters, jobs in the citadel and the harbour, but I let the younger ones deal with them, and I end up not moving from the compound.

Dusk arrives, and with it, the return of Silas and Ozkan. Silas looks irritable.

"What happened?" I ask him.

"Nothing," he says. "Spent the whole time at the Triumph. An envoy went out with a parlay flag, we waited for their response – not a peep."

"Looks like Shakan wants to fight."

"That Odisse, though, he seemed to have some influence. I really thought his strategy would be to keep coming back to the table until he gets what he wants."

Or, more likely, he wants to hear what his spy has to say, before taking part in any further negotiation.

Our shift comes to an end and I slip away. Under a pink sky, I make a detour to the barracks, where I find Jakub. He looks harassed and tired – sergeant is a more natural fit for him than captain – but he listens to what I have to say. He seems dubious, but says he will have my back as promised. We settle on our plans for tonight, and I return home.

It is a long wait for midnight. At some point, Naima turns up at my residence. She is edgy and gnawing her lip. She hasn't heard from the priest recently either and is restless – all the action is on the walls of the city, while she sits on her hands and waits for further instructions. Ever since the debacle with Beast and Ira, she's been desperate to hurt the Keda, so she agrees to my plan readily enough. I had worried they might have disposed of Darius' body, but I'm told it's still here, packed in ice in a hidden cellar in Ganzić. The Camonites still have an important role to play tomorrow, and we agree on a time and place to meet. It seems I'm the one moving the pieces into place now – but all depends on Odisse.

I meet the spy again at the Gallows. At this time of night, we're the only passengers – the single guard looks suspiciously at us, but lets us through, and after the ride down we travel silently through the empty streets of The Stain. I'm in a simple tunic now; I removed my armband once I was past the guard, in case anyone should see us and wonder what an interpreter was doing here at this time of night. As we approach the fringes of The Stain, I take the lead. For all my bluster with the spy this morning, it won't be that easy sneaking out. There is a high military presence, all the way down to the shore. Jakub will ease our way through, however. I head to the back of a row of dwellings and climb a drystone wall. The headland spreads out before us, the cliffs and sea to our right. I can see the backs of the sentries, dotted along at regular intervals, from the sea to the city wall. A patrol of six men is also making its way from north to south.

I hold a hand up and wait for Jakub. We're there for some

time, a breeze at our ankles and our feet sinking into the sludgy earth. But he comes, as promised, and I see his bulky figure approaching the nearest sentry from behind. The man salutes, and turns to him, and we hear the murmur of conversation. The patrol is nowhere to be seen. We slip out, beyond the line of sentries, and run, cutting an angle towards the beach. No shouts behind us. We reach a copse and stop for breath – Jakub will have seen us, but not the sentry.

We used to play and fight in this copse – the biggest kids, ten or eleven years old, would meet for pre-arranged scraps and the rest of us would watch and scream support. It's a grove of cypress trees, a narrow oval with a clearing at its centre. I cross it, the spy close behind; at the edge, it lurches down unexpectedly, into a rockface that leads to the shore. We scramble down, and the shore curves inland, so we are hidden from the view of the sentries on the beach. We walk over the rocks, occasionally glancing back, but we are safe. Around a corner is the cove. There is no sign of Odisse yet, and we squat on the rocks, facing out to sea.

"You sure you know what you're doing?" the spy says. "It's my neck on the line as well as yours, you know. I'm vouching for you."

"What's the matter, you getting nervy now your boss is on his way?"

"I'm just saying, you cock this up, you'll have the Keda *and* the Dagmari after your skin. The only thing worse than a traitor is a failed traitor."

"I prefer 'revolutionary' to traitor."

"I'm sure you do. I'd like to see you explaining it to your fellow-citizens though. Anyway, here comes the big man now."

There are giant sand dunes at the other end of the cove, and Odisse appears between them, accompanied by Shakanna. A couple of warriors are behind him but they stop at the dunes.

We skirt round the edge of the cove and meet them halfway. Odisse is out of his armour, dressed in a long strip of cloth that is pulled to the front and tucked into a leather belt. Shakanna is in a long silk orange dress with a high collar, and a matching cloth tied turban-style round her head.

Odisse looks at me curiously and addresses the spy in Dagmansh. The spy talks for a while, and Odisse replies. There's quite a few approving noises there, making me suspect the spy has rather inflated his own role in all this. Shakanna interjects with a few questions, then Odisse turns to me.

"So. I understand you're the first person from this delightful city to see sense. You want to bring this war to a swift conclusion, am I right?"

"That's correct. It benefits us all."

He cocks his head like a bird. "Do I know you? Your face is familiar."

"I was in the tent when we had the first parlay. I'm an interpreter for the Keda."

"Aha! I knew it. Curious that someone so close to the seat of power is turning coat."

I say nothing.

Shakanna utters something in Dagmansh, and Odisse raises his eyebrows.

"My lady says she saw you when she scaled the walls. She thought you had died."

I pause, unsure how to respond. "I suppose I'm not an easy man to kill."

Shakanna does not respond.

"How about you?" I ask her. "How did you escape?"

Odisse and Shakanna confer for a moment.

"She had to retreat, your defence was too great. A few warriors dragged her back to the sambuca: their lives wouldn't be worth living if Shakan discovered they had left his daughter behind."

There's a pause. It is pleasing to consider that our defence was stouter than the Dagmari had expected. "So," I say, nodding towards the spy, "has he explained my proposal to you?"

"He has in brief. Tell me, though: twice we've had collaborators let us into their city, partly to avoid bloodshed, but mainly for… financial recompense. I've never met someone willing to betray their entire city for no reward. Explain."

"I'm part of an order called the Camonites," I say. "We're committed to removing the Keda from power. It's personal – they have my son and thousands of others in bondage in the mines of Riona. I want to take him out of there. So if I let you in, if you can guarantee you won't destroy the city, there will more than enough loot to satisfy you."

"All right," Odisse says. "It's original, but I'll buy it. Now give me the details of your plan. I've heard a précis."

"First, I want a guarantee. When you've got what you came for, you leave us in peace. No rape and pillage. There is nothing for you outside the city centre."

Odisse shrugs. "We are not barbarians, despite what you think of us. Once we have the riches of the city, we have no other interest in it. I give you my word."

"Very well."

"Come, now – the plan."

"There's an extensive sewer system that runs beneath the city," I say. "Most of the exits around the city walls were boarded up when the siege began, but not those that flow into the sea. There's a perfect one up the coast from here. If you give me five, six hundred of your finest warriors, I can guide them into the city in the middle of the night."

"And where would we pop up, after crawling through leagues of your people's shit?"

"I will take you into Val Firuz, the island at the heart of the city. The home of the Keda. The only opposition you would face would be less than a hundred Keda warriors – most of whom would be asleep. Bring some bowmen, and you'd take care of them with no trouble. The city militia won't get involved. Your men can loot Val Firuz and pick it clean, it's where they keep all the riches of the city."

"And when we've killed off all the opposition and looted all we can find?"

"Your warriors march straight out the front gate, back to your army. Siege over, bye-bye."

"Interesting," says Odisse. "Very interesting."

"You'll get more gold than if you went through with the negotiations," I say. "And far fewer of your warriors will die than if you persist with the siege, until a breakthrough."

"These are two very valid points. And yet, it's my job to probe for holes in propositions like these," says Odisse, clapping his hands and grinning broadly. "So! Here's one – why do I need you? Why not send my men to find the sewer exit and break in by ourselves?"

"You may not find it as easily as you think. The sewer system is a maze. Five hundred warriors blundering around, trying to find the route into the city, is going to cause a lot of disturbance. And if you lose the element of surprise, you'll be butchered as you climb out."

"Very well. And how can we trust each other once we're inside? How do I know your soldiers will not interfere?"

"Our militia is not loyal to the Keda. I have contacts there, and they know of the plan. They will stay out the way, but if you break the agreement, we'll unleash our archers. Maybe some of your men would make it to the gates, to let your army in. But then again, maybe they wouldn't. No one needs to get greedy. We can all get what we want."

Odisse turns to Shakanna, and they have a conversation in Dagmansh, with occasional comments from the spy.

"In principle," he continues, "we like your proposal. Shakan will grumble, of course – he likes the blood and thunder of an escalade. He gets terribly cranky when we break in by stealth. But I will make him see reason, I assure you. The only thing he hates more than stealth is a drawn-out siege. Our last adventure took nearly a year. Eventually we managed to poison their wells, and they surrendered in a matter of days." He tuts. "But he'll do anything to avoid that again."

"Will Shakan lead your warriors?" I ask.

Odisse confers with Shakanna. "I suspect he will, yes," he says. "Shakan generally likes to be there at the moment of triumph, and he is still a formidable hand-to-hand fighter."

Shakanna utters something with a smirk, and he nods.

"My lady is right – her father is occasionally impetuous, and has little patience for fools. Without her or myself by his side, you would be wise to practise *caution*."

"You won't be there?"

"I fear not. One of my vices is that I am a… fastidious man. I don't think I could stomach crawling through sewage with you."

"One last thing," I say. "I want one favour from you. Your fingerspeak interpreter, called Jordi. He's a native of our city. You'll have no further need of him. I want him to come with your forces. He can remain in Val Kedić afterwards."

"An interpreter?" says Odisse, "I don't think I know him."

"He had a black eye, bruises all over," I say. "He was with your ambassadors' party."

"I regret, I don't pay much attention to the staff," Odisse says, with a wave. "But I will find the man you speak of, and he will accompany our warriors, and can translate for Shakan. Deal?"

"Deal."

"The only question, therefore, is when and where. I don't see any reason to delay. Tomorrow night?"

"Fine by me."

"Very good. And where?"

"The entrance is the other side of the city – close to Blackstone, the south-western corner. There's an olive grove a few hundred paces from where you're camped. Meet me there, and I'll take you down to the rocks where we enter."

"Shakan and six hundred warriors will meet you there at midnight tomorrow."

"I'll be waiting. Farewell, then."

He nods and turns to leave. He pauses, facing me once more. "Don't let me down," he says, putting a finger on my chest. "I don't take kindly to people making a fool of me. It's said you southerners know how to hold a grudge, but you don't have a monopoly on petty vengeance, I assure you."

"Understood. As long as your people stick to their word, I'll stick to mine."

He smiles, but there's no warmth there, and for a moment I see the menace behind the smile. Shakanna wheels around and the two of them leave the cove.

The spy and I set off back to the city. We climb the rocks together, back into the cypress grove. It's hard work in the darkness, and several times I scrape my skin. We finally stop in the clearing.

"What about me?" the spy asks. "I don't particularly want to go through these sewers, but I should be involved somehow."

"Do as you please," I say. "Come with me or don't. You won't get into Val Firuz any other way."

"Perhaps I'll leave you to it," he says, considering. "One last night in the Palace – I'm sure I can find some distractions."

"Indeed," I say, not in the mood for his chatter. We creep to the edge of the copse and look for the sentries. Jakub has used his authority and done his job – there's a gaping space where a guard used to be, and we are able to slip back into The Stain unnoticed. We cross the slum, back to the Gallows. My body is tired, waves of exhaustion flooding through me. But my night has only just started.

Back in the city, I accompany the spy along the roads that lead to Queenstown and the Palace of Shadows. We have just passed an alley when a bulky shape steps out. As the spy turns at the movement, Jakub draws his longsword and drives it straight through him. The spy splutters, gives me an outraged look, and slides to the ground as Jakub withdraws his sword.

"Little spying bastard," Jakub says. "Everything go to plan?"

"Yeah," I say, turning away from the body, bile rising in my throat. After my time on the walls, seeing a man die like that doesn't horrify me like it once did. But having been in his company all night, it's still a shock to see him drop dead so suddenly. I never even knew his name. But he had to die. Like Darius, a loose end that could spoil everything unless we swallowed our scruples.

I take his feet and we carry his body into the alley. A cart is waiting there. I lift the hessian covering on it, and find Darius, tongue lolling. I drop the cover immediately.

"Naima came up with the goods," Jakub says.

We lift the spy's body onto the cart and cover it with the hessian. The two of us push it into the road and head back towards the west of the city. It's a long journey, with a few uphill stretches. The spy's blood is dripping through the cracks of the wood, and stains the pavestones. Jakub's rank is a comfort – the only danger would be if a Justice wandered past in the middle of the night. When we hit a bump in the road in Goathorns, Darius' body nearly falls off, and I have to scrabble to the side to lift it back on.

Forgive me, Darius, I ask again. In death, you can at least help us. Even if it wasn't your choice.

We push the cart through the narrow streets of Val Varin. Finally, we reach the butcher. Jakub drags the bodies upstairs, while I dispose of the cart. We prepare our candlelit tableau. I dress the spy in the militia colours, supplied by Jakub – he lays out Darius' body. Then he stabs both bodies, and wipes the blood around a bit. Chicken's hand goes on the floor by Darius – I had given it to Naima earlier in the evening. I put weapons in both their hands, and kick over the chairs. We daub a bit of blood over Jakub and I cut his cheek.

We stand back and survey the scene with a critical eye.

Jakub adjusts the bodies, and I put my white armband back on. I flex my fingers. I've got a hell of a fingerspeaking job ahead of me.

"Ready?" he says.

"Ready."

And I leave the safehouse to search for a Justice.

20.

The quickest way to find a Justice is to go to the Bridge of Peace, so that is where I go, via Five Bells. As I hurry across the square, the Justice on guard stands and raises xer poleaxe. I hold up my right arm, and slowly, xe shifts xer poleaxe to one side and offers me xer left.

(Request) / *Justice* / *Come* /, I say. *(Exclamation)* / *Treachery* /.

Xe stiffens, and gestures for me to go on.

Traitor / *TranslateMan* / *And* / *TraitorSoldier* /, I say. *(Past)* / *Kill* / *Councillor* / *Now* / *Help* / *Foreigner* / *Enter* / *Val Kedić* /.

(Question) / *Place* /, the Justice says.

House / *Val Varin* /, I say. *GoodSoldier* / *Prevent* / *Escape* /.

The Justice looks round at xer comrade on the other side of the bridge. Xe hesitates, then comes to a decision. Xe drops xer poleaxe, points towards Val Varin, and starts running. There are unpleasant echoes of my encounter with Beast, as I run beside xer, occasionally gesturing towards side streets. This time, however, I'm aware that I'm the one putting myself into danger.

We reach the butcher, and I call to get xer attention. Xe takes out a scimitar and follows me in, through the abattoir. We climb the stairs, to find Jakub – sword out, next to the two bodies. He holds his hands up.

"Easy," he says, "Take it easy."

The Justice is crouching in a fighting pose, and I put my hand gently on xer bands, to say, *GoodSoldier /*.

Xe relaxes, but does not put the scimitar down.

(Question) / Happen /, xe says.

"What happened?" I say.

"They tried to escape," Jakub says stiffly. "They had their swords out. I had no choice."

I start to tell the Justice – but xe waves it away, and pads closer to the bodies. Jakub retreats. I point out Chicken's hand to xer.

Councillor / Hand /, I say, *Traitor / Possess /*.

The Justice picks it up with xer cadaverous fingers. Xe looks disgusted, but pockets it. Xe pokes at the spy and Darius with xer scimitar, then turns to me.

Xe speaks, and as far as I can pick up tone in Spidertouch, I can sense the coolness in what xe says.

(Question) / Here / TranslateMan /, xe asks, *With / Two / Traitor /*.

I put my fingers on xer bands and formulate a carefully-touched reply. I take my time tapping it out.

Traitor / Ask / GoodTranslateMan /, I say, *Because / Know / Tunnel / Under / Val Kedić /*.

The Justice scowls. *(Question) / Tunnel / Under / Val Kedić /*.

I can't remember the touch for */Sewer/* in fingerspeak, I'm not even sure there is one.

Tunnel /, I say helplessly, *Send / Waste / Sea /*.

(Question) / (Consequence) / xe taps back.

(Disgust) / Traitor / (Request) / GoodTranslateMan / Lead / Foreigner / In / Val Kedić / Through / Tunnel /.

Xe raises a scimitar to my throat, and I see Jakub twitching his sword arm.

(Question) / Reply /, xe says.

(Negative) / (Negative) /, I squeeze frantically, while xe studies me. *(Question) / Tell / Justice / (Conditional) / TranslateMan / Traitor /*.

It seems to appease xer. Xe steps back, looks at the bodies again. Xe seems unsure how to proceed.

I say, *Six / Hundred / Foreigner / (Future) / Night / Enter / Tunnel / (Question) / (Conditional) / Trap /*.

(Question) / Trap /.

Kill / Six / Hundred / Strong / Foreigner /, I say. *(Possibility) / End / CityWar /*.

TranslateMan / (Negative) / ChiefSoldier /, xe says dismissively.

Know / Tunnel /, I insist. *Possess / Plan*. But xe still looks sceptical.

(Request) / Talk / Councillor /, I say, and attempt Eleven's name.

I'm fortunate xe seems like a fairly junior Justice – xe must be to have the night shift – who seems like xe wants to wash xer hands of the whole business. And the fact I know Eleven's name appears to make xer edgy.

(Positive) /, xe says, *Come /*.

Xe exits the room. Jakub raises his eyebrows, and I shrug as I follow xer. The two of us retrace our steps, back through Five Bells to the Bridge of Peace. Xe leads me over the moat, and stops to confer with the Justice on the other side. I stand awkwardly while the two Keda stare and discuss me. Eventually the first Justice gestures, and marches towards the centre of Val Firuz. Xe spots another Justice on patrol, and they stop to talk. The other Justice heads off in the direction of the Keda's residential area. I, meanwhile, continue to the High Chamber. The Justice lights some lamps, and points me towards the grand trestle tables. I take a seat, while xe waits in silence.

I've never been here at night – nor have I paid much attention to the architecture of the place – but in the darkness, the sculptures seem to rise up in my imagination and come to life. Eight enormous pillars run from the front to the back of the hall, and at the top of each pillar are spikes and flourishes that slip in and out of shadow. This has been my place of work for the last two decades, but I mustn't forget I'm among the enemy here.

By the time Eleven comes, I can see dawn inching closer out the windows. The sky has deepened to a sapphire hue. Xe talks to the Justice for some time, then seats xerself next to me. Xe has dressed in xer crimson robes, and seems alert, unaffected by the nocturnal interruption. Xe asks me for details of what happened, and I repeat my story – traitor Darius and the mysterious soldier asking for my help, to guide the Dagmari in through the sewers; honest Jakub stopping them from escaping while I ran for help.

Xe surveys me for a while, then taps, *(Question) / Plan /*.

It would be unthinkable to hear this from a councillor earlier in the year, but it's clear the siege has altered the dynamic between the Keda and citizens.

Kill / Foreigner /, I urge xer. *(Request) / Allow / TranslateMan / Lead / Foreigner / In / Tunnel / Prepare / Trap /*.

(Question) / Trap /, Eleven says. *(Conditional) / Fight / In / Tunnel / Strong / Foreigner / Kill / Soldier / (Danger) / Val Kedić /*.

A cautious, systematic Keda, this one. I've heard Silas describing xer as the cleverest of the councillors, the least likely to behave irrationally.

Alchemist /, I say. It's not a familiar touch; I had to check it in the lexicon earlier today. Eleven's beady black eyes, meanwhile, flash with a sudden fire.

Smoke / In / Tunnel /, I say, enunciating each touch. *(Possibility) / Justice / Kill / Weak / Foreigner /*.

Eleven leans back and xer curved nails tap a beat on the table. I lean over, and offer my last fillip.

Traitor / Say / ChiefForeigner / (Future) / Lead / Six / Hundred / (Future) / (Possibility) / Kill / ChiefForeigner /.

Eleven nods, and snuffles a little. *(Conditional) / Body / Lose / Head /*, xe says. *(Consequence) / Weak / Body /*.

Xer sallow fingers stroke my arm, and I have to fight the urge to pull back.

(Approval) / Plan /, xe says. *(Future) / Morning / Talk / Alchemist / Justice / Elder / Prepare / Trap /*.

I look xer square in the eyes. *(Request) / Excellency / (Negative) / Elder /*. I allow myself a hammy fraction of a pause. *(Possibility) /*

Traitor /. The last thing I want is Mecunio getting his hands on my plan, taking over and steering it away from its goal.

Xe cocks xer head. *(Question)* / *(Possibility)* / *Traitor* /.

Believe / *Elder* / *(Consequence)* / *Riot* /, I say – another touch that needed research and practice. It's easy to feed Keda paranoia right now, they're so out of touch with what is going on in the city. *(Negative)* / *Believe* / *Weak* / *TranslateMan* / *ChiefTraitor* /.

Eleven is very still. I know I'm gambling here.

(Request) / *TranslateMan* / *Lead* /, I say, tapping myself on the chest for emphasis. *(Future)* / *Morning* / *Talk* / *Alchemist* / *Justice* / *Soldier* / *(Negative)* / *Elder* /.

Xe stands, talks with the Justice awhile and a Blue who accompanied xer. Eleven is watching me the whole time, and I feel sure those black eyes can see inside me. The nightmare of Chicken's soundless screams, the memories of the Blue who died in front of me. Finally, xe returns, and gives me a small square of fabric – a special pass with his mark.

Do /, xe says to me. *Kill* / *Foreigner* / *Defend* / *Val Kedić* /.

The first gong wakes me. I could happily sleep until fourth or fifth, but I drag myself out of bed. Just one more day, I tell myself, then you sleep.

My first stop has to be Talia's residence – close to the centre, but the other side of Val Firuz, by the Bridge of Sorrow. She is the only interpreter I know who has experience of fingerspeaking with an alchemist – xe had come to the High Chamber, to demand some materials. The alchemists rarely fingerspeak, and in a strong accent, so she told me. I want her there with me, since I've already got enough to focus on. After a brisk walk over the Firu, I find myself in her quarter, Roć. It is one of the richest quarters of the city, and seems largely untouched by the siege – buildings clean, vegetation under control, no sign of the starvation and dysentery that is creeping through the slums.

It is a bright, crisp morning, and I know there will be no attack today. I find the interpreter's residence set back from a secluded street and knock on her door.

She looks relieved to see me. "Razvan," she says. "What's going on? I heard the attempts at parlay failed?"

"They did. You were right to tell me about the elders' plans. We may be able to put an end to this."

"How?"

"We're going to ambush the Dagmari. The Council has given me permission to talk to the alchemists. That's where I need you."

"The alchemists?" she says, and I read a spark of surprise there – a suspicion that perhaps I represent something more than a humble interpreter.

"We can use their help to take out the Dagmari. Will you translate for me? I remember you saying what hard work they are."

She shudders. "I'd rather not. Horrible bunch. But if you say it's important, if it will help end this siege…"

She grabs her armband and the two of us make the short walk to the Bridge of Sorrow. We show the Justices our pass, and when they see we are going to the alchemical institute they summon another Justice. Xe accompanies us to the building, close to Victory Avenue. Marble steps the colour of putty lead up to the double doors. On the doors is a gnarled knocker, and the Justice beats it three times. After a pause, a black-robed Keda opens it, and the two of them fingerspeak. The alchemist turns to us, and I get a glimpse of xer face, leathery and lined. I can't be sure, but I could swear xe is one of the alchemists who accompanied the wagon at the riot. Xe beckons us, and we follow xer in, the Justice close behind.

Inside, the institute looks nothing like I expected. I imagined bubbling flasks, perhaps. Piles of parchment, fluids, metal instruments, flames, forceps – all filling the rooms in a ramshackle fashion, while the alchemists worked among the chaos, dust motes dancing in the firelight. It's nothing like that, though. The institute is sterile. Unsullied. The antechamber is empty; in the next room, barrels are lined against the wall, but apart from that, the walls and floor are bare. After that is a long, grey corridor, which connects to several windowless rooms. We pass one, and Talia and I stop, for through an open door we see a woman in a foetal position in the corner. The Justice slams the door shut. I feel sick.

"They do tests in there, don't they?" I whisper. "That's how they try out their new concoctions, isn't it?"

"Stay focussed. Remember what we're here for," Talia says.

The alchemist has walked on; the Justice gestures with xer scimitar. They bring us into an atrium which has a table and chairs. The alchemist takes a seat, and we join xer. Talia presents her arm, and the Keda begins to fingerspeak.

"Eleven asked me to speak with you," Talia translates. "Xe requested that I... make every effort to help you."

"That's right," I say, "we would like to employ your skills on the Dagmari, in the city sewers. This will help us to victory against them."

"Your efforts against the foreigners have been pitiful," Talia says in a neutral voice. "You should be able to beat them without our help. But I owe Eleven a favour. And it would be interesting to see the effects of our art in a different environment, against a different... breed of man."

"Right," I say. "Okay then. So, the plan is to cram as many Dagmari warriors as possible into the sewers, below Val Firuz. Then, when you get the signal, you pump your smoke in, and disable them. The Justices can then finish them off."

It takes Talia a while to get all that across. The alchemist blinks and taps xer reply impatiently on her arm. "This is possible," Talia says. "We can pump it in through the... grilles, I think... above the sewer. We will need a lot of smoke. We will employ a basic mixture. A compound adjective, I suppose we would say 'sleep-inducing'. When will this take place?"

"Tonight."

"Tonight! You people are no different to the Council. Rush, rush. Our art cannot be rushed." Xe gives a hissing *tsk* sound. "However, we can be ready."

We talk a bit further about technicalities – the location of the grilles, the length of the pipes that need to convey the smoke, but I can tell the Keda is bored and I wind it up. I thank xer, and the Justice leads us out of the room. I want to get out of here as soon as I can, for the sterility of the place scares me, more than if there had been smoke brewing and drifting through crowded laboratories.

"What a horrible place," Talia says, as we follow the Justice.

"I owe you one," I say. "Thanks for coming."

I realise xe has taken us a different route – for we're not in a room I recognise. Xe marches into a windowless hall – no torches, either – so we're having to squint to see our way.

"Hold on," I say, "where are we going?"

Talia looks confused too, and turns around. "We're going deeper into the institute. This is the wrong way."

The Justice has not stopped, and I hurry after xer, into the gloom. But the darkness is spreading, rising like a living thing, its maw closing round me – and I realise the Justice has disappeared. How can xe see xer way in here? I turn, and see light from the doorway behind us, but it seems many, many leagues away.

"Talia?" I say. But there is no reply.

The darkness is thick, almost tangible – I hold my hand up close, just so I can make out something in front of me. On the air is the faint scent of smoke.

Slowly, very slowly, I put one foot in front of the other and go in the direction of the Justice. I wave my hands in front of me, groping for a wall, a door, anything. I stop and turn, and I can't see behind me now, no sign of Talia, no sign of a door.

"Oi!" I say, but my voice sounds muffled, like I'm listening to it from underwater. "This isn't funny! Where am I, you bastards? What are you doing?"

They can't understand me, not the Justice nor the alchemist, but I need to get their attention, and even a Keda's robes would be a welcome sight now. I wish I had something to throw, just so I could hear it hit the wall. I carry on, arms outstretched, convinced I'm going to drop into a pit at any moment. There is no way the hall can be this big. I keep going, dragging my legs. All I know is I have to get out of this unspeakable darkness.

How long I walk for, I lose track. But the air is different here, and there is a cool breeze. Under my feet is not the tiled floor of the institute any more, but rock – irregular and jagged. I sniff, and it's the sea I can smell. Somehow, impossibly, there's a tunnel all the way from the institute to a cave on the coast, dug underneath the city.

The gloom has subsided, I can see glints of light on the rocks below my feet. The smell of the sea is getting stronger, and the squawk of gulls – it's making me dizzy. I can see my body now – and I watch, horrified, as cracks appear all over the skin of my palms. I touch my hand with my finger, and it is papery, like feeling dry husks. I try to speak, to shriek, even, but all that comes out is a Keda's rasp.

From far away, I watch as my body crumbles, into dead cypress leaves that coalesce in a pile on the floor of the cave. With no body to hold me, I drift into the blackness, shooting off as fast as I dare, and I'm travelling up to the roof of the cave now, I can see a chink of sunlight above me, and I can feel the sounds and smells of Val Kedić rushing back to me–

And with a stab of relief, I feel my fingers again, a chalky taste in my mouth, and the rough texture of brick against my arm and my cheek. I blink twice, and I know I'm dying, life is ebbing away from me. I can see a Justice standing above me, xer scimitar by xer side, its edge rusty red. I can hear a woman's screams, and with mild surprise, I hear my own voice, Razvan's, shouting, "Borzu!"

My head lolls to the other side, as I try to see where my voice is coming from, but my eyelids are drooping, and I drift away–

And this time, when I wake, I'm in Margrethe's body, on a cot, sweat running down my forehead, and it's hot, so hot I can't concentrate on the strange sight of my own body, sat on a chair by the cot, its hands clasping mine. I vomit weakly into a pail, and all that comes out is a little sputum, mixed with strings of saliva. The last thing I see is the silver threads of saliva, and it's like they're forming a web–

The visions are speeding up, and I wake in instant pain, blood gushing from my wrists, and the arms of my crimson cloak are drenched in blood. I can't scream, all I can do is wheeze so hard it's like my throat will explode, while above me, Keda rush into the room, surveying me with mingled horror and disgust–

Walking through the streets of Ganzić, my heart is pumping normally again, but I'm nervous. I'm not dying this time – but a crossbow bolt hits me with the force of a horse's kick, knocks me sprawling to the ground. It's Naima, I see her in the background, as I twitch, and die–

Head stinging from Beast's headbutt, the sudden shock as xe slits my windpipe and blood gurgles out, gushing all over my chest – oh, Ira! My eyelids flutter–

With dawning horror, I realise I'm in Rico's body now, and I'm stuck in some mineshaft, my head by the struts. And I'm coughing, hacking away and shivering wretchedly. In the corner of my eye, I can see the shadow of a man, crawling towards me. He is calling out to me. The dust of the Riona mines insinuates itself through my lungs, like tendrils of silver smoke–

I wake with a start, shouting. The alchemist is standing by the door, snuffling. Xe puts xer hand on Talia's arm – her face is wan and drawn. The Justice is there too, standing behind them in the corridor. I look around wildly, not sure if I'm in another vision, but this is the institute, one of the bare rooms we saw earlier. I'm still breathing hard – it felt so real, and I remember my son, and have to fight the urge to run straight out, and not stop until I reach Riona. In the distance, Talia is talking, but my ears are ringing.

"What is this shit?" I ask.

"No citizen who enters the institute can leave, without experiencing our art first-hand," she says.

"You too, Talia?"

She nods mutely.

"How long have I been here?" I ask.

"Not long. It's not yet third gong."

The alchemist fingerspeaks again.

"Want to tell me what you felt?" Talia says. "What you saw?"

"Maybe some other time," I mutter.

"Very well. Never forget your place in this city," Talia translates, her voice bitter. "We own you, little man."

This is a bit rich since I tower above xer. Xe has released Talia and is making notes in a sheaf of papers.

"Well, if this prick has quite finished xer fun and games, can we get out of here? I've got the small matter of a city to save."

Talia fingerspeaks to the alchemist, and xe glances over at me, an amused look in xer eyes.

"We've been free to go this whole time, apparently. Something something something, honestly, I've no idea, this twat's accent is so strong."

I get to my feet – my limbs are weak, but my mind is clear, like waking after a long sickness. The Justice strides off, and I follow xer out the room. I stop, just to give a false smile at the alchemist.

"I'll remember you, shithead," I say. "We've got unfinished business."

Talia and I walk into the antechamber, and out of the

institute. The Justice is waiting impatiently, ready to escort us to the Bridge of Sorrow. Xer green robes are already sodden. Rain is pounding down, great drops exploding on the paving stones in front of us.

"Perfect," I say, looking up gratefully at the sky.

21.

After all the drama of the morning, it's a relief to get down to some uncomplicated physical work in the afternoon. Jakub helps me assemble a team to prepare the ambush. He calls on thirty of his unit, as well as asking favours from other captains he knows, who spare us some men. I send a messenger to Ansić, and am pleasantly surprised when he sends us ten soldiers. In total, we have close to a hundred ready to work in the sewers, as well as assorted carpenters that we enlist.

Jakub and I, and a couple of his beefiest men, turn up at the sanitation guild to politely require their cooperation. In the event, the guild engineers are delighted to help. Most of the time the city ignores them – Keda and elders alike prefer not to deal with such insalubrious issues – and they jump at the chance to play a key role in the defence of the city. They bring out and unfold enormous maps of the sewer system on thin parchment, nearly translucent in places. What Borzu and I would have given for these maps thirty years ago! They show all the access points, and we are able to plan a route I can take to funnel all the Dagmari into the sewers, winding them round like a thread. We take notes of which side tunnels need closing off, and then we get to work.

A human chain transports the rubble and wood down the ladders, into the tunnels. Some side tunnels the carpenters board up, for others we dump rubble into the opening and block it off. Jakub is in his element – directing men here and there, patting them on the back, bantering and getting his hands mucky. This isn't my natural habitat, but for one afternoon, I can forget about intrigues and imminent doom, and lift some rocks.

After a while, I leave them to it, and trace out in reverse the route I'm going to take tonight. Once we are under the city walls, in Blackstone, we will head north in a zig-zag fashion, before we reach Sevanić, and spiral round into Val Firuz. As I go, I extinguish torches. It must be as gloomy as possible, this tomb for the Dagmari warriors. The less they see, the less they will suspect anything is amiss – and I want them stuck like rats in a trap, with no escape.

I go all the way to the beach – the same entrance that Borzu and I found all those years ago. I loosen the grille, and sit on the rocks for a while, watching the swells of the Southern Sea. I retrace my steps, wading through the sewage, immune to the smell now. I must be somewhere under Five Bells when I encounter soldiers again, dumping rubble into the openings and packing it in tight. One of the carpenters spots me, and calls me over.

"An elder's getting involved," he says, and points up to the access point.

I climb the grooves in the wall and find Abitha there, talking to a soldier. She turns to me.

"What's going on here?" she says, and wrinkles her nose as my smell wafts over to her.

"Work in the sewers," I say, unnecessarily.

"Yes, I can see that. And what are you doing down there, Razvan?"

"Blocking up tunnels," I say. "It's a Keda operation. I'm down there in case they need to tell us anything."

"I didn't know anything about this," she says. "Mecunio hasn't said anything."

I shrug. "This comes from the top. Eleven spoke to me xerself."

"All right," she says, like she's giving me permission to carry on. "But I think I'll check with Mecunio about it."

She backs out, and I return to the sewers. I'm not worried – seventh gong has rung, and they have run out of time to interfere. By tomorrow, I'll either be dead or vindicated – either way, Mecunio's opinion is the least of my worries.

It's gruelling work, but the team of soldiers and craftsmen finishes the job of sealing off the tunnels. We are all caked in filth, and our arms are aching. Most of the men don't know why we've done it – just the captains and guild engineers are privy to that. But there's genuine camaraderie at the end, from the pleasure of a job well done. It beats being up on the walls, anyway. Most of the soldiers go to get themselves cleaned up and Jakub suggests a last drink at the Glory. It is sorely tempting, but I promised I would see Naima.

I meet her at ninth gong at my residence. Our conversation is brief. She has one small but vital role to play in this – and she will rope in some of the other Camonite cells, too. When we are done, we clasp hands, and I believe it is the first time she has touched my skin since putting a knife to my throat.

"For Ira," she says.

"Ira."

Once she has left, I have nothing to do until the midnight rendezvous. I don't want to be alone with my thoughts – I can still see the images of the morning's daymares. If I drop my concentration, that vision of Rico flashes into my brain, or the sensation of being Chicken and trying to scream.

I set off along the People's Market, for the night market is still running. Buildings have burned to their foundations a hundred paces away, hunger and disease are creeping across the city – but dogs still fight, and citizens still gather to share a mug of chuka. There are no braziers or fires tonight, people preferring to gather in the safety of darkness. But the atmosphere is loud, over the top – people trying too hard to laugh in the face of ruin, and show the world they don't care. The Dagmari are cursed, arguments and fights start. It's just what I need. I'm reminded why I'm doing this – they're like me, these people: not perfect, but none of them deserve to be led out their city in chains, to serve Shakan and his horde.

It's a lonely vigil, in the olive grove outside Blackstone. Jakub had spoken to the sentries, so I passed them without any trouble. It's just drizzling now, so I shelter beneath the olive trees, ducking away from their thorny branches. It's the worst feeling in the world waiting for something, half-willing it to get a move on, half-hoping it never arrives.

I am starting to get cold when Shakan arrives, at the head of his troops. Six hundred warriors file into the grove, filtering through the trees, in an unsettling silence. They look to have removed most of their heavy armour – certainly, there's no clanking of metal. By our estimates, six hundred is a tenth of their remaining force, but it still feels like a hell of a lot of soldiers in this small space. Shakan himself has eschewed his lamellar and bronze plate, and is in all-black light armour and a barbuta helmet. The figure of Jordi appears at Shakan's shoulder, puny and unarmed. Shakan comes to a halt and speaks to Jordi in Dagmansh.

"Everything is ready?" he says.

"It is."

"Take us to the sewers, then. We will follow you into the city."

"Be warned – it is a long journey, and it will be unpleasant. I am taking you to the heart of Val Kedić."

"We have travelled a long way to come here. My people are not afraid of a little unpleasantness." Jordi pauses as Shakan speaks again. "When we hold the citadel and have killed the mutants, I will need to speak to the commander of your army. You will find him for me, interpreter."

I bow, and put a warning finger to my lips. I lead them down to the rocky beach. The Dagmari crouch low, and we clamber over the rocks until we come to the sewer grille. Our sentries are no more than two hundred paces away, though they have been instructed to hear nothing tonight. I prise the grille open. I crawl through, hold it open, and Jordi and Shakan follow. Along the tunnel I go, drawing a line of warriors behind me. I can't help but think of the nooses used by Muranese assassins, that tighten and tighten the more you struggle, as the silk is pulled in through the knot. With the torches extinguished, I struggle to see the way, and more than once I slip as I pass through the slime and shit. Shakan is a head taller than me, and I hear his grunts as he brushes against the roof of the tunnel. I turn to Jordi, who is beside me and breathing hard.

"You all right?" I say to him quietly.

"Fine," he says. "You sure you know what you're doing?"

Shakan speaks up on my other shoulder. "Why are you talking to the slave?" Jordi says with a sigh. "If you have anything to say, it is for me."

Once we're under the walls, we join the major tunnel headed north, and it is easier now. We walk along the pathway beside the sewage. At some point, we must be under Five Bells, or even Sevanić, I stop at a juncture, and do a dumbshow of "Which way now?" The snaking queue behind me comes to a halt, and I take the opportunity to put my hand on Jordi's arm. Still looking in the opposite direction, I say to him in Knuckles, *Be / Ready / Run /.*

Shakan barks a question. "Is everything okay?" Jordi asks, his voice strained.

"Ah," I say. "I know where we are. Not far to go now."

They should all be inside now. In Blackstone, Jakub and a squad of five men will be moving into position. They will have brought baskets of rubble to the access point there. When the last Dagmari warrior has passed, and they hear the signal, they will trigger an avalanche of rubble, blocking off the tunnel at a bottleneck. There will be no way back for the stragglers.

We veer east, close to the Little Firu now. A dozen memories pull me in every time I make a turn into a new tunnel. Racing Borzu across the city; that mad scavenger, rooting through the sewage; with Jakub, chasing Darius into Val Firuz. As we spiral round underneath the Keda's citadel, I start looking for the grilles, where the alchemists' smoke will surge in. And finally, we reach the point I mentally marked as the time to ditch the Dagmari. It is awkward here, the roof hanging low and several chambers twisting off in different directions. Jordi has been hanging close to me since I fingerspoke to him. I stop for a moment and grope for his arm.

After / Corner / Run /, I say in Knuckles, and I squeeze the touch */Run/* twice, just to be sure. I walk briskly to the corner, turn it, and start sprinting before Shakan can react.

I chose the spot deliberately. There's a chicane followed by a higgledy-piggledy mess of tunnels – the sewer system is impressive in places, but it is ancient. I splash over to the other side of the tunnel, and take the chicane, Jordi on my heels. Shakan roars like a wounded bull, and I hear him ten paces behind, cursing in Dagmansh.

"He's not very happy!" Jordi calls out.

"Shut up and run!" I call back.

I dart into a side-tunnel, scraping my back, sewage splashing into my face. I scramble through and cut a right turn – drawing them in, tighter and tighter. Jordi follows me into a wide tunnel that connects to the alchemical institute and the High Chamber, we are running hard and I think we have lost Shakan. Their line must be stretching apart like a concertina, and he will not want to be separated from the rest. I turn into a final tunnel, which has the access point I'm looking for. Behind me, I can hear bellows heaving into action, as the alchemical smoke comes belching down into the sewers.

"Cover your mouth!" I say to Jordi as we round the corner.

As we do, a group of Justices come charging towards us, scimitars drawn. Jordi shouts in alarm, but I grab him and we back up against the wall. They rush past, ignoring us. Six groups of ten are surprising the invaders, from six different points along the route. Sixty Justices, for six hundred semi-conscious, hallucinating Dagmari. I hold my tunic up to my nose, and hurry towards the exit. There's a proper ladder here, rising up twenty paces to an opening. We climb out, onto the cracked tiles of some latrines in Val Firuz. A Blue is standing there, by the door. I nod to xer, but xe ignores me.

"What the hell is going on?" Jordi says, panting and shaking himself dry.

"Change of plan," I say. "Welcome home, by the way."

"Those Justices," he says, "they can't beat six hundred Dagmari."

"Not on a battlefield," I agree. "That's why we're cheating."

"Cheating?"

"Alchemical smoke," I say. "Listen–"

And if you prick your ears up, you can make out the sounds of the massacre. Muffled cries and the thud of metal sliding into flesh.

"But I never wanted to come back to the city," says Jordi, "not while the Crawlers still rule."

"The Dagmari aren't the only ones in for a surprise," I say.

There is a roar from the west, a thousand paces away. The sound of crashing, foaming water, desperately seeking lower ground, as it comes rushing down the tunnels. The Blue hears it too, and comes over to the ladder. The gushing is getting louder, as xe peers into the darkness, looking for the source. It's too late for any qualms now. I give xer a jab in the back with my foot, and xe goes tumbling into the sewers, just as black waves come hurtling past below us.

The sanitation guild has played its part well. It was their job to open the sluice gates of the stormwater tanks at the right moment – filled to the brim, after the rainy season. Naima coordinated it, watching through a grille until the time was right, and giving the signal for release. I can't hear anything down there now, but I can imagine it – a deluge of water, cleansing the tunnels, purifying the filth. The Justices will be wading through bodies, stabbing them with their scimitars – perhaps some of the Dagmari, half-conscious, will be trying to escape. They will hear the water, turn, and the force of millions of gallons will knock them from their feet. The blockages don't just stop the Dagmari from escaping – they stop the water, too.

"What just happened here?" asks Jordi.

"A declaration of war," I say. "You're watching the liberation of Val Kedić. Stage one."

Sixty Justices should drown down there, along with Shakan and the Dagmari troops. Naima met with the priest, and they have put out a call to the cells at short notice: seventeen Camonite hit squads will be moving into action right now, on the hunt for the remaining Justices – on the walls, in the harbour, by the bridges. The torrent of water has slowed down now. It is still flowing, but not filling the tunnel as it used to.

"So... without wishing to sound ungrateful," Jordi says, "you've smuggled me into a city under siege, that's about to erupt into civil war?"

"All in good time," I say.

Faintly, in the distance, is the splash of someone paddling. Somehow, a Justice has managed to avoid being swept away, perhaps finding a recess in the walls. Jordi and I lean over the edge to watch as xe comes into view. Xe has pulled off xer thick outer robes, and is wading through the water, against the flow. Xe is gripping the brickwork to pull xerself along. Xe grabs the ladder.

Step by step, xe pulls xerself up. It is painfully slow progress, and several times, xe stops to catch xer breath. To see xer like this is to see something twisted and deformed – a broken shadow of a Keda. I look into xer eyes, and I think I recognise xer. By a delicious twist of irony, it is Scorpion. How many times has xe administered punishment to Rico? Did xe ever bring xer studded belt swinging down on him? Xe pulls xerself up the last few rungs, and looks at me, pleading in xer eyes. Xe holds up xer arm and I lower mine.

(Request), xe says, and fumbles the next touch.

We swap arms. Double tap on the upper band, squeeze and a tap on the middle, trill from middle to upper, two-fingered triple tap on the lower.

(Imperative) / Give / Regard / Hell /, I say. Xer eyes widen. And I give xer a shove in the chest.

22.

After a hundred and thirty years of Keda rule, it took just a night to wrest back control of the city. They had grown plump and lazy, and without the Justices they were helpless as kittens. Sixty of them drowned in the sewers, and the Camonite cells managed to assassinate thirteen more. Alone, without their comrades, it turned out they were not invincible. They bled, just like us. The massacre left fewer than twenty Justices remaining to defend Val Firuz. There were, of course, the alchemists to consider as well. But for them, we had another surprise planned.

Earlier in the day, Jakub had left a pile of oil-soaked rags behind the latrines for me. While the Justices drowned in the sewers, and Blues ran to raise the alarm, I recovered the rags. A bewildered Jordi followed me as I left the latrines, and headed for the alchemical institute. We kept to the shadows, past the statue of Kedira, looming malignantly in the moonlight. We reached the institute without seeing anyone. The building was in darkness. I found a spot at the rear where the timbers were exposed, and lay out some rags underneath. Jordi was watching, frozen. I think he was starting to realise the magnitude of what we were trying to pull off. I took out a tinderbox, and lit the rags. The flames roared up and attacked the timber greedily. I stepped back and found another suitable

259

spot. Jordi was keeping an eye on the road – but although some Keda ran past, none saw the flames that licked at the institute. We moved around, fanning the fire. We were stranded in Val Firuz now, until the water levels in the sewers lowered or the army attacked. Jordi seemed to realise that it was all or nothing now, and his best chance of survival was to throw his lot in with me.

Eventually, the blaze was so hot all we could do was step back and watch. There was a constant popping sound, and groans as the timbers started to stretch and buckle. A concerted effort by the Keda could still put it out, but I was banking on them being occupied elsewhere. We explored the nearby streets, found three buckets of sand, and emptied them in the gardens. We crouched in an alley and waited. When a timber fell in a shower of sparks, it woke the alchemists up. They came running out of the institute in ones and twos, in their black robes, blowing their *cantus* as they saw the fire. Somewhere, some barrels exploded in the heat. I smiled as I watched their frantic, futile efforts with bowls of water. The institute was beyond saving. Their hold over us was slipping. And then I heard the shouts of the militia, and I knew my plan was working.

Outside Val Firuz, the revolution was well underway. Most of what happened that night, I pieced together from Jakub and other sources. It appears that word spread quickly to the walls and the barracks what had happened to the Justices – some saw them fall in front of their eyes, to Camonite swords. A junta of the militia captains held an emergency meeting. With prompting from Jakub and other captains he had recruited, the militia decided it had to act quickly to seize control – if only to avoid the shitstorm that would come our way and engulf Val Kedić. They launched a coup, led by a captain called Hamza, universally respected among the militia. He was a grizzled veteran, who had served in the militia for thirty years, and through unfussy competence and dedication to his men, had managed to inspire the loyalty of his peers. Under his command, they roused the entire army, and nearly half their forces – nine hundred men – attempted a nocturnal invasion of Val Firuz. By this point, dozens of Blues and the remaining Justices had barricaded the bridges – but squads of soldiers crossed the Little Firu in skiffs and rowboats.

How I would have loved to watch them cross! Our great-grandparents had dug the Little Firu, compelled by the Keda to create their island-citadel. For over a hundred years, they had controlled the city from the centre, protected by the moat and the bridges. In normal circumstances, they would have picked off our soldiers with ease. But with the walls undefended, we were able to storm the citadel. Soon the defending Keda were surrounded, and we were able to pick them off, one by one. I watched as the alchemists died, refusing to abandon the burning institute. Crossbow bolts took them all, and their secrets died with them.

I don't think I'll ever forget that night. Jordi and I had no weapons, so we stayed hidden in the alley, watching the chaos as Blues and the occasional Justice fought pitched battles in the streets with our soldiers. Only a few days earlier, they had fought side-by-side against the Dagmari invaders. It was eerie, for the Keda made no sound as they fought – and our men seemed to feed on that, shouting warnings to each other, but otherwise in silence. It was a very different type of battle to what I'd seen with the Dagmari, filled with yelling and insults and incoherent screams. The Justices killed some of our men, but they had no chance. We had the numbers, and the Muranese archers lurked in the background, able to take their time as they picked off their targets.

With all the commotion, the rest of the city began to wake. Hamza declared martial law, and squads of soldiers moved to place the elders under house arrest. I wish I had been there, too, just to see Mecunio's reaction. Citizens started to congregate on the banks of the river, and near the bridges, waiting to see what was going to happen. A few Keda managed to retreat to their mansions, most of the Blues armed now, but overwhelmed by sheer numbers. The military junta took control of all the key structures – the High Chamber, the armoury, the grain stores, the treasury. The Keda were left holding the residential area, their backs to the river. Soldiers formed a cordon around their remaining territory, and as dawn rose, we knew Val Kedić was ours again.

It felt absurd to just go home, so we crossed the Bridge of Peace, past the abandoned barricades, and I took Jordi to the interpreters' compound. It was there we heard the rumours that mobs of citizens were gathering, and invading the residences of quislings such as the delegates and interpreters. There were only apprentices at the compound, so I advised them to keep a low profile and return to their families. I took off my white armband and suggested to Jordi that we get a drink, to celebrate our freedom.

The Dagmari were a problem that had not gone anywhere. Once Hamza had tightened his grip over the city, he turned his attention to them. Hundreds of their waterlogged bodies were dumped on the beach (though not Shakan's), and a request for parlay went out later that day. Their response was swift – Odisse's corpse, hurled over the walls by a trebuchet. It was a clear indication of who was being held responsible for the fiasco in the sewers. Bound to his broken body was a message, scrawled on parchment. Shakanna, it appeared, had assumed control of her father's army. She agreed to a parlay, and, clearly unaware of the coup that had taken place, invited the Keda to the talks. They put up their white tent, on the Ilić Royal, ready for the negotiations. Jakub wanted me to be involved, to talk to Hamza, but I demurred. For one thing, if Shakanna had any sense I was still alive, she might be less inclined to act rationally. And for another, I was tired. I had played my part, and it was time for others to take the reins and clear up the mess.

Jakub found sleeping quarters for Jordi and me in the barracks – my residence had been looted and wrecked. The junta had restored order, but the troops were thinly spread. Some patrolled the walls, others held Val Firuz, others kept order in the city. If Shakanna had realised how tenuous our hold was, she would have surely sent all her warriors forward in one final assault.

I saw Jakub the following day, after a long, dreamless sleep. He told me about the parlay between Shakanna and Hamza. It quickly became clear Shakanna had no wish to prolong the siege. Mecunio had been correct in his estimation of her as more diplomatic than Shakan. She wanted to return home and bury her father. The city had not fallen like the sweet plum their ambassadors had promised, and the loss of six hundred elite warriors was a blow. Hamza was a bluff, military man with whom Shakanna could do business – and free from the politicians, they did indeed do business. In return for an end to the siege, Hamza promised to pay a tribute, and the return of Shakan's body, undamaged. The tribute was considerable, though no more than the initial negotiations with the Keda. Crucially, however, none of our citizens would be enslaved. Hamza would have to empty most of the treasury to close the deal, but he shook hands with Shakanna, and the siege was over.

It took all day to put together the tribute. They closed the bridges, while citizens gathered in the streets and rumours spread through the city like wildfire. To save face, the junta transported the crates of gold and precious metals at night. There was no need for the citizenry to see the indignity of our paying the Dagmari to go away. They cleaned up Shakan's body as best they could, and wrapped it in white linen. His body, and the tribute, were left outside the Gate of Triumph, for the Dagmari to collect. There were some who still objected to the size of the tribute, but sense ultimately prevailed. All those riches, they were the Keda's, not ours. They were earned on the back of our blood, our sweat, for sure – but they were worth nothing compared to the feeling of the city being ours.

The following morning, the junta ended the ban on civilians on the walls, so they could watch the retreat of our enemy. Along with thousands of others, I climbed the walls to see them depart.

It took them most of the morning, packing their tents, dismantling the bigger siege engines such as the trebuchets, and burying their dead. They abandoned some of the smaller wooden constructs, and without any ceremony, the warriors turned north and left mounted or in pairs, up the Ilić Royal. It was a steady stream of men filtering away, the ranks thinning all the time. The slaves and camp followers were last to go, packing as much as they could into wagons. I had expected the mood on the walls to be more triumphalist, citizens jeering and waving them off. But it was guarded and sombre – people quietly muttering with their neighbours, like they expected the warriors to turn and mount one last attack.

Finally, the plains in front of the city were empty once more. We had survived the Dagmari – the first known city to do so. And Val Kedić was ours, all ours. And although some celebrated in the streets, it felt a touch hollow. Thousands had died, and disease and hunger had a cut a swathe through the poorest quarters. Many had lost their homes, whether ravaged by bombardment or fire, or the ruined farms outside the city walls. It would take years to recover and rebuild. And the Dagmari would return one day, we could be sure.

Besides all that, however, one thought crept into the minds of every parent in the city: with the Keda powerless, they no longer held a knife to our children's throats. The Riona mines were ours for the taking. I remember my son as I saw him last: an eleven year-old boy, the back of his head bobbing as he began his trek up the mountain road. It looked like he had started chatting to the girl next to him – two innocent children, wittering away like they were setting off on an adventure. Those children have vanished now, and it will be a man I hug close when I see him next.

I can only guess how he will react when he sees me. But I will return to Val Kedić with him, or not at all.

EPILOGUE

Citizens have been gathering at the Queensgate since dawn. It was supposed to be an army of a hundred or so Camonites, all armed revolutionaries, setting off on our crusade. Instead, our ranks have swelled to nearly a thousand. The Camonites are scattered through the crowd – I see Naima fifty paces away, and she raises a shy hand in greeting; nearby is the priest, too, with some of the cell who helped trap Beast. But also joining the trip to Riona are hundreds of citizens – rich and poor, young and old. Some soldiers, some merchants, some beggars. Mothers everywhere. Most are carrying a weapon of some sort, even if it's just a big stick or a garden hoe. There's a small herd of goats and a few wagons. There's a giddy, carnival atmosphere in the air, and a sound I haven't heard for a while – genuine laughter. The gathering is completely organic – who started it, I have no idea. Perhaps Jakub let something slip, perhaps some Camonites got chatting with citizens, and it spiralled out of control. Regardless, on the street corners and in the taverns last night, word passed round. In the heady atmosphere since the fall of the Keda, it was the spark these people have been waiting for.

Some soldiers appear with a crudely fashioned battering ram, and they smash through the makeshift wall put up by the masons fourteen days earlier. The Queensgate grinds open,

and for the first time in over twenty days, we can look out
to the mountain road, climbing its way through the plains
towards Riona. The crowd balloons outwards like a puff of
smoke, onto the land outside, pockmarked by trenches and
splintered wood. I am in the midst of it all, shuffling forward,
under the gate. I feel a hand on my shoulder, and turn to find
the familiar figure of Jakub, in full militia garb.

"Razvan," he says. "There you are."

"Are you coming with us?"

"I reckon so. No point doing a job half-arsed, is there? Got
to finish it off."

"Don't they need you here?"

"Things have calmed down now. We're talking to the Crawlers
– thanks to your interpreter mates. Hamza's negotiating the
terms of their surrender. What the future will look like for them.
They'll be put on trial, but there'll be no more bloodletting."

"Hamza sounds like a reasonable man," I say.

"He just wants to restore order. He doesn't want to rule – the
junta will only last as long as it takes to install new leaders.
A council drawn from the guilds and militia, perhaps. There's
even talk of quietly bringing in Mecunio and some of the
elders, people with experience."

I tut. "Too much history. Make it a clean break."

Outside, as the crowd fans out, Jakub and I find some space.

"Are you nervous?" he says. "About seeing Rico?"

"Yeah," I say, and there's not really much else to add.

A few hundred paces outside the city, beyond an abandoned
Dagmari encampment, we find seven dead Justices. Their skin
has started to bleach, and there is a sour, rotting smell. We
realise they are the Justices who were in Riona during the
siege, and our spirits are lifted, as we realise they returned and
died at the hands of the Dagmari. The crowd begins marching
in earnest, nobody leading, all of us proud citizens of Val Kedić.

The plains are flat and vast, and we can see for leagues in all directions, from the sea to the mountain peaks. After the claustrophobia of the siege, it is welcome. We pass through farms along the way, and the farmers are eager to help us. They let us sleep in their barns, and though they are poor they offer what food they can. Granted, it is difficult to refuse help to a giant crowd like ours – but there is also an element of guilt at play. They escaped the attention of the Dagmari, not suffering like the farmers to the west, by the Ilić Royal. And for decades, they have watched while children from the city process past their farms.

For most of the first two days, I walk with Jakub. On the third day, he drifts off to join some other militia. I am by myself for a while, then Naima and the priest appear at my shoulder, and we walk together.

"Razvan," the priest says, patting me on the back, "you're a deep one, aren't you?"

"How so?"

"Didn't think you had it in you. You did for those Justices, didn't you? More than we managed in nineteen years."

"Nah, I just jumped on your shoulders," I say. "We wouldn't be doing this now if it wasn't for Camun, or the Twenty, or all the Camonites over the years." I grin at Naima. "You never doubted we'd pull it off, did you?"

Naima snorts. "Are you serious? When I wanted to join the order, I had visions of jumping across roofs at night, doing covert missions. What was the reality? 'Linguistic subterfuge', wasn't that what you called it? When I found myself in a cell with two interpreters... I thought it was going to be a disaster."

We fall silent for a moment.

"Here's to Ira," I say. "She should be here."

"She was like a big sister to me," says Naima. "Couldn't handle a knife, was always forgetting passwords – but she was the strong one. I miss her."

"Me too."

"It was a mistake, that Beast mission. She didn't need to die."

"I keep replaying it in my head," I say. "If I'd only been a bit quicker…"

"You can't think that way," the priest says gently. "It'll send you crazy. She gave her life for the city – that should be enough."

"So what's next for the order?" I ask the priest. "Once we've taken the mines?"

"Next?"

"Well, we've done it. We prised power from the Keda's fingers. The city is ours. The revolution is almost over. Where does that leave the Camonites?"

"Ah," the priest says. "Well, the city still needs a moral compass. We still need to check that those in power lead us in the right direction."

I'm not sure what I expected him to say – that they would be disbanding, that the priesthood would want to walk away at the moment of their greatest triumph? But it nagged at me, this reminder that we may have removed the Keda, but the city was still split, and divisions could yet derail the peace.

"I hope you won't mind if I call it a day, once we're back," I say. "I feel like I've done what I set out to do."

The priest shrugs. "This is no deathcult, Razvan. You can come and go as you please. Your place in the revolution will not be forgotten."

"And what about you?" Naima asks. "You won't go back to being an interpreter, will you?"

"I doubt it. I managed to make my whole career pretty redundant."

"What, then?"

"I'll worry about that when I get Rico home. Something tells me the city will be a very different place to how it used to be."

* * *

On the fourth day of the journey, we reach Stoneacre, the small trading town halfway to Riona. The town coalesces around the mountain road, which becomes a market street for a few hundred paces. They must see our approach, and a small crowd is gathered at the fringes of the town by the time we arrive. Some look like they're armed, but none draw their weapons. An elderly man comes to the front, looking warily at our flanks, as more and more of our people arrive.

"I'm in charge here," he says. "What's going on?"

"We're from Val Kedić," says the priest, who seems to have assumed spokesman duties for our group. "And we're on our way to Riona."

"Long time since we've seen anyone from the city. What happened to the siege?"

"As you can see, we survived," the priest says. "And now, we're going to right a few wrongs. You'll have to forgive me, it's been a while: does Stoneacre still support the slavers in Riona?"

The man snorts. "We don't support them, we trade, we survive – much like you do in the city. We let them pass through. We hold our noses. Should we refuse them entry to make a point?"

"Things are changing round here," the priest says. "And we have long memories."

"Save your threats. I can see how many you are – very impressive. But a lot of you don't look like fighters. And I reckon your fight is not with us."

A militia captain pushes to the front – Dimas, an ally of Jakub's, who has a daughter in Riona. "Let's cut out the cockwaving, shall we?" he tells the two men. He brings out a bulging bag. "This is silver," he says. "Plenty of it. From the Keda's treasury – ours now. We need somewhere for our people to sleep tonight. We need water, we need supplies, our goats need to graze. Can you sort us out?"

He chucks the bag, and the man catches it. He inspects the coins, gives us an oily smile.

"Welcome to Stoneacre," he says.

I bed down with Jakub, Dimas and some other soldiers. We're in a half-finished house, lying on mattresses stuffed with straw. I drift off for short snatches of sleep, and when Jakub shakes me awake at dawn, I feel exhausted, ready for bed. We gather in the square. Some citizens are staying behind – they don't feel able to manage another four days on the road. It is for the best. The rest of us make our way through the empty town. We have stocked up on provisions and the mood is bullish. The path will be harder now, steeper and less forgiving on the feet, but the Camonites get some chants going, anti-Crawler anthems that everyone had known, but none had dared sing until now. It is possibly my imagination but the wind suddenly feels more biting today, a world away from the warm breezes that caress the city from the Southern Sea.

I walk with Jakub and Dimas, wanting to be among the militia when the fighting starts. I'm not sure what the Camonites will be like – this is their holy war now, and I wonder whether they will be as calm and clinical as the situation requires. My own record in warfare, ever since my quick thinking with Chicken, has been pathetic: no kills, one corpse buried, one corpse tripped over, and one moment of paralysis during a crucial moment in an operation. So I plan to stick with Jakub, and hope I'll have the guts to use my crossbow when I need to. That's when he gives it back to me, of course – I am apparently "too much of a bloody liability", so I have to endure him carrying it around for me, as if I'm a small child.

Jakub and Dimas actually sound confident, more so than the Camonites. I ask them why.

"When those northern pricks see us, they will shit themselves," says Jakub. "They've spent how many years, beating up unarmed teenagers? You think any of them fancy a proper battle?"

"What you've got to remember, Razvan," Dimas says, "is what people fight for. Look at the fire in their belly – where's it coming from?" I like him, he accepted me straightaway as a mate of Jakub's, and talks to me like he's known me all his life. "When you saw our citizens on the walls, they were fighting for survival. That's why Boris the pig farmer fought halfway like a soldier, his life depended on it. Or the Dagmari – that's their livelihood. They weren't doing it for honour or glory. The ones that broke through the wall or killed the most men – they were the ones who got the biggest share of the booty.

"Now – take these pale, hairy pillocks. What are they fighting for? Where's their fire coming from?"

"I guess, the Ke–" I say, and stop.

"Exactly. The Keda. And they're gone. We think. So, as I see it, they're left with nobody in charge, guarding a load of kids. And when the kids' parents arrive, armed to the teeth, and very, very angry – what are the hillsmen going to do? Fight, because some Justices told them to, however many days ago? Or run?"

"I hope you're right," I say.

"Look, I remember the hillsmen. Twenty-five years ago, I was in Riona. They've no love for the Keda, not really. They pay their wages, but they don't talk to each other. They're mercenaries – the mines will drop into our laps, no trouble."

The days pass, and our rations start to run thin. We see no more merchants and farmers. We kill some of the goats, saving as many as we can for the return journey. The road is ragged now, poorly maintained and only a few paces wide as it enters the rocky outcrops of the mountains. Conversation and singing has died down now, and we trudge up the road in silence. On our eighth day on the road, most of the parents drop to the back of the procession, and the Camonites and militia take the lead. Weapons are out, and Jakub even gives me my crossbow. They fan out, with a few scouting ahead to look for the hillsmen. The atmosphere is tense, and, as we peer round crags and climb through the bitter mountain air, I'm reminded of standing on the walls, waiting for the Dagmari trebuchets. The hillsmen can't fail to see us coming, so what kind of defence will they prepare?

No attack comes, however. Everyone is crouching, ready to fight, and I guess we must be close now. One of the Camonites puts up a hand and we all halt. A scout returns, whispers to some of the priests. The message is passed back.

"What's up?" I ask Dimas.

"It's the rope bridges, over the ravines," he says. "They've all been cut down. We planned to attack from three sides, but now the only way into Riona is past the gatehouse. They're funnelling us in." He gnaws at a fingernail.

"Can we go round the back?" says Jakub.

"You can approach from the Riona valley, but I don't know how long it would take to get round there. You'd have to cross the mountains first – we couldn't do it with this crowd."

There is no alternative. If that is the only way in, that is the way we must go. Shoulder to shoulder with Jakub, right behind some Camonites, I reach the top of a slope; and without warning, the gatehouse is two hundred paces ahead of us. A squat, ugly building, feeble compared to the Gate of Triumph, but with a few skilled archers they could do all sorts of damage. The Camonites break into a jog and start to spread out. Mists are lying low, but through a break I can see some other buildings. For a moment, I am distracted, and wonder if Rico is right there, a few hundred paces away. And then a shout interrupts my thinking, and I am back in the moment. A hillsman emerges from the gatehouse. Alone. He spreads his hands, showing he is unarmed. Camonites surround him in a wide semicircle, still watching for an attack. The priest strides forward and takes the lead.

"Where is everyone?" he calls out.

The hillsman is bald, with an ugly scar running down his cheek. "The other guards all left," he says in a thick accent. "Just me."

"And the children?" the priest says, raising his voice over the wind.

"In the barrows," he says. A dozen crossbows are pointed at him, but he doesn't flinch. "Except about two hundred. They broke out about ten days ago."

"Two *hundred*?"

The hillsman shrugs. "They set fire to the dovecote. Stormed the gatehouse while we put it out. We were down to twenty or so guards by then... more could have escaped if they'd tried."

Muttering breaks out as the news travels backwards.

"Which ones?" someone shouts from behind me. "Who escaped?"

"Slum kids," he says. "Older ones. Little ones were too scared."

I clench my fingers and toes. Through the mists, some small figures appear, staring out at us. Some of the soldiers brush past the hillsman, and there are cries from behind me too, and citizens start to run forward. I can't move, I'm too scared what I will find there.

"They left all these kids to fend for themselves?" a Camonite asks, disgusted.

"I don't think they fancied seeing the Keda's reaction to two hundred escapees," the hillsman says.

"But you stayed?"

Another shrug. "Someone needs to keep an eye on them. We keep out each other's way. I deal with the traders."

"I remember this one," Naima says. "He's all right."

The priest nods. "I think I remember him too. You were here in Camun's time, yes?"

The hillsman touches his scar. "I remember it well."

I take a deep breath and step forward, following the other

citizens into the colony. Some of the Camonites are edging forward too, inspecting the buildings. Past the gatehouse, and the children are pouring out of the barrows now – parents are filtering through, looking for familiar faces; everywhere is the sound of children's tears and men and women shouting names. For a while, it's as though we've come to the wrong colony – nobody can find their son or daughter, everyone is at cross-purposes. And then, it's like a key turning in a lock, and suddenly parents are clutching their children, and they're weeping together, an echo of the farewells at the Queensgate. I see some parents hugging two children, and one father who has been engulfed by his three daughters, and is shaking with silent joy. There are also plenty of children by themselves, forlorn and bewildered – eyes hunting for an adult they know. One boy looks familiar to me. I know his father, and I know he died on the walls, when the Dagmari bombarded us with fire.

I am one of the dozens of parents still looking – I recognise many of them, we are all from the western slums like Wesson, Goathorns and Blackstone. A sense of dread is building in my gut. A girl catches my eye, she looks thirteen or fourteen. I know her, she is from Wesson – Serapi. Her mother was part of the mob that accosted me and rioted at the Bridge of Peace. And I know she survived the siege, I remember seeing her in the days afterwards. She wasn't on the march to Riona, presumably because she has younger children.

"Serapi?" I say.

She nods nervously.

"Your mother is fine. She couldn't come all the way here, but she's waiting for you, back in the city. You're going home."

She puts a hand to her mouth, and her shoulders shudder as she cries. I give her a few moments, let her collect herself.

"Do you know my son, Serapi? Rico, he's seventeen. From your barrow."

She dries her eyes, won't look at me. "Yeah, I know him."

"Where is he, Serapi?"

"Half the barrow escaped. Most of the big boys and girls, he was one of them. They ran off with the Goathorns lot, and some others I think."

I'm numb. I was half-expecting it, but it's still like a punch in the solar plexus.

"Why?" I say, more to myself than to Serapi. "Why would he go? He just had to wait a bit longer. We were coming!"

"The guards were picking on them," she says. "The older ones had had enough. They asked everyone if we wanted to break out, but I couldn't. I hoped someone would come and rescue us and... you came."

"Did they say where they were going?" I ask her. "Was it back home?"

I feel a sudden surge of hope – was it not possible, if they had taken a cross-country route back from Stoneacre, that we had passed each other without realising? That they were battering on the gates of Val Kedić while we climbed through the mountains?

"I don't think so," she says. "They said the Keda would kill them if they were caught. One of the big girls told me they were travelling west, until they reached the Ilić. There's lots of big towns there."

Ah, Rico. You sweet, bloody, wonderful fool. You can feel both proud and infuriated with your kids at the same time – and that's me now: proud that he stood up to the men that bullied him, and got the better of them by himself. But infuriated that he had to do it now, when we were carrying out a revolution for him, trekking all the way to Riona to liberate two hundred empty bunks.

And then, a flash of terror that makes my stomach lurch. For while Rico travels west with two hundred other teenagers, the Dagmari horde marches north up the Ilić Royal, returning to their home.

I mutter something trite to Serapi, trying to put her at ease. I walk back in the direction of the gatehouse. All around me, emotional family reunions are taking place. But I don't hear them, I don't see them. Beyond the gatehouse, the hillsman stands by himself, ignored, unsure what to do. Some of the Camonites have started to hunt through the perimeter buildings. Others, like Naima, stand outside. They look robbed – Riona is theirs, but they've not had the battle they wanted, the chance to crush the guards who ruled their lives for seven years. The priest is watching the reunions and smiling.

I approach the hillsman. "They say the escapees went west. Headed for the Ilić Royal. Is that possible?"

The hillsman looks me dead in the eye. "It's possible, yes," he says. "Not an easy route, along the foothills. Lot of bandits. They'd have to wise up quickly, learn how to catch their food. They'd probably be hungry, but they'd get there."

"You know the way?"

"Many years since I've gone that way, but… yes, I know it."

"You can guide us, then. Those of us that want to follow our children. They've got a ten-day head start, but we'll move faster than them."

He looks dubious.

"It's the least you can do for us," I say. "If we had got here earlier, there would have been a battle, you'd be a dead man now."

He sighs. "I want… to go home."

"You and me both, pal. The mines are closing, and you've given most your life to them, right? So finish your responsibilities to these kids, and help us find them."

Jakub wanders over. "Rico?" he says.

"Ran. Went west with the others."

He winces. "Sorry, Razvan, mate. Anything I can do?"

"There's got to be about a hundred parents who can't find their kids," I say. "Maybe less, some will have found younger siblings. Round them up for me, will you? Tell them they've gone west, and we're following."

He heads in the direction of the colony. The sound of tears

is ebbing away, instead there's a low thrum of conversation. Overhead, I see a pigeon beating its wings against the wind – round it goes in circles, above the blackened dovecote. Whatever message it had, it's not going to deliver it. Some of the family groups have started to drift out of the colony. Parents on their own, too, looking dazed. The Riona mines – such a bastion of oppression, a symbol of the Keda's stranglehold over us – suddenly look rather desolate, and pathetic. By this time tomorrow, it will be abandoned to the elements. And, despite Rico's escape, that is something to savour: a victory we will remember, and pass down to our grandchildren.

The relief hits me that Rico's alive, he survived the mines. And I'm so proud of him, so damn proud of my boy. And I will follow him and find him and bring him home.

In general, fingerspeak is not a poetic language – functional, logical, yes, but its touches rarely transport you to the emotional heights and depths in the way speech does. Or maybe it does for native touchers like the Keda, I don't know. But there's one compound touch I've always loved: /(Always)Hope/, a series of finger trills, running from the lower to the upper band, like a musical scale. You could translate it roughly as "Optimism", I suppose, though that doesn't quite catch it. There's a certain grim satisfaction in the /Hope/ touch, which we don't have in our word – a Keda concept that says others may grind you down, but that's what drives you and keeps the hope alive. That is how I feel now as I look west, down through the mountain pass, and towards the Ilić Royal where my son awaits: /(Always)Hope/.

ACKNOWLEDGEMENTS

I was lucky to have such a great team of people working on this book, thanks to all the Angry Robot gang: Gemma Creffield for a cracking edit, Kieryn Tyler for the fabulous cover design, Caroline Lambe and Ailsa Stuart in Publicity/Marketing, and Chioma Ovuworie in Production.

Huge thanks also to my agent Jennie Goloboy, who made some crucial suggestions after reading the first draft; to Lynanne Schravemade for the moody author pics; to Ange Smith and all her students at Russell Sage College; and to my wife Nicki for all her support.

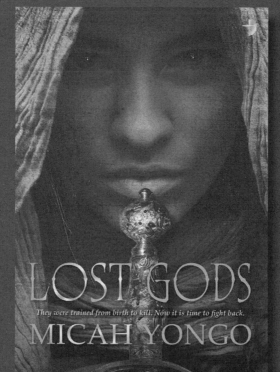

ONE
BROTHERHOOD

"Look," Josef whispered. "There."

Neythan looked to where he pointed. The camp was less than a mile away. He could see the evening fires winking through the trees of the forested valley beneath them like light through a basket.

"I see it," Neythan said.

"Good. Good… I'll circle round for a way down. You stay here. Patience is the way."

"Patience is the way."

Neythan watched Josef go, the mist rolling up ghostlike from the basin below. It was still warm, quiet but for the croaking of insects and the murmur of the stream. A night like any other, save that he was to kill a man. The price of Brotherhood.

In truth, it had been just as Master Johann had said – no chance to plan, barely time to get ready, scrambling from their beds at news from Arianna and tumbling the same hour into the forest's knotted dark to find her. Should be grateful, Neythan supposed. They could be skulking about a cave by night, or down a canyon with only the moon for help. He'd heard tales of such from Tutor Hamir and Yulaan back at Ilysia, of boys his age on their first outing not making it back. But then with Hamir you never knew when he was telling the truth. The only thing he'd said before they left that Neythan knew he meant was, "The first time is always hardest."

"There's a way down."

Neythan looked up as Josef came trotting back toward him along the ridge. "Where?"

"Along the cliff, a half-mile. Steep though."

"How steep?"

"It'll do."

"You're certain?"

"It'll do, Neythan."

Neythan looked back along the ridge. There wouldn't be much time. The others were probably already in place. "Alright." He looked back to Josef, saw the calmness there, and nodded to himself. "Alright... Let's go."

By the time they made their way down the escarpment the campfires were dampening. The sounds of the camp itself – the ribald laughing, the chatter, the faint noise of bells and strings – continued to roll on as Neythan and Josef worked their way through the forest.

By the third watch they'd reached the settlement's edge and sat watching the camp from the long grass, Neythan fingering his crossbow nervously, two quarrels lodged taut against the whipcord. He glanced up at the half moon peeping from the clouds. Sweat prickled along his hooded brow, trailing down the groove of his spine. He felt Josef's hand on his shoulder.

"It's time, Neythan."

Neythan breathed deep and slid the crossbow up against his armpit beneath his smock. He removed his hood and stood, leaving Josef in the bushes, and began to walk, alone, toward the camp's clearing.

The space was a brief and grassless glade as wide as a tanner's yard. Gatherers had set a shelter on either side by the trees, no more than a shack's wood-roofing propped on log poles roughly a man's height, and between the two a sort of platform, overlaid with wool and what looked like bearskin and cowhides. Probably the altar. Neythan came slowly alongside the shelter nearest and leant against the beam, peering in at the crowd. One or two peered back.

"You have lingerweed?" a young woman called to him, slurring. "You have more wine?"

Neythan shook his head.

The woman frowned and waved him off.

Neythan scanned the gathering. There'd likely be guardsmen among them, armed soldiers, perhaps even a prince or two from the crown city, all for Governor Zaqeem, a king by any other name, or so it was said. Since there were no true kings save those in scribes' tales Neythan had never much liked the saying, but here, now, with the clamour of flesh and wine and finery, he was beginning to see its meaning.

Men and women wore armlets of brass and held silver goblets, dancing and laughing. The tart smell of wine filled the air like incense, mingling with the smoke of damp logs. There were no servants here, only rich men without their aides, just as Master Johann had said.

Neythan continued to watch the crowd and saw two young girls, neither one above seven years old, by the altar, studying the women as they danced. He finally spotted Arianna standing as part of the throng, dressed in fine linen, and began to walk toward her. He approached the altar where a turbaned old woman in scarlet was chanting with arms lifted to the sky. He saw Arianna's eyes meet his, saw her acknowledge him with her stillness. Then he saw her reach up, cupping the jaw of a silver-haired man beside her and drawing his lips onto her own.

He was the one.

Neythan let the crossbow slide from the crook of his armpit until he could feel the axel touch his fingertips, its coiled length against his forearm. He could hear himself breathing now, could hear the steady dull underwater chug of his own heart. The man Arianna had kissed – and thereby revealed as the governor of Qadesh, Zaqeem son of Tishbi – was gesturing behind to one of the young girls. The scarlet-clad priestess brought her forward, then made signs over her as others came to lift her, limp and without struggle, onto the altar, laying her on the cowhides like an upended doll.

The gatherers were shouting now, all of them on their feet. The governor smiled as the drumbeat doubled. The dancers and crowd whipped into a frenzy, staring at the child on the altar as the scarlet priestess approached with a flaming stave in her hand.

The crossbow fell fully into Neythan's hand. He lifted it level with the governor as the axel rolled and snapped into place, the whipcord flexing, the arrow ready. The sharp flinthead peeped above the sightline like a curious onlooker as he squinted along the quarrel's shaft. There was a slight tremor to his elbow, but that was alright – the first time's always hardest. *Just breathe through it. Be still, the way you've been taught.*

He heard the splash of oil as the priestess doused the child on the altar. Around him, the congregants were shouting and screaming even louder. *Be still. Breathe. Patience is the way.* The priestess was coming forward, ready to light the sacrifice, the din of the crowd growing louder, deafening, wordless. *Be still. Be still.*

And then… Arianna.

Neythan watched as she stepped in front to obstruct his view. She turned again to the governor, reaching up slowly, gently, as though to touch him – and then, as he dipped his head toward her, she drew her hand across his throat from side to front with a thumb-blade.

The man's head lolled violently as his blood leapt over the heads of those nearby. He went down gagging, pulling at the cloaks of those closest. The screams were immediate, distracting even the priestess, who paused with stave raised above the child on the altar. Neythan saw Josef's arrow thud into the meat of her breast as she turned toward the commotion, snapping her shoulder back as she fell into the mob.

And then everyone was running. Pot-bellied men scampering half-naked into the bushes, others rushing back from the altar to the shelter's corners for refuge, women squealing, bodies bumping, feet trampling as the gathering scattered. Cinders gusted upwards, luminous dust glinting red-gold against the night as a beefy man tumbled headlong into the campfire. Neythan went wading in, shoving his way through the fleeing crowd to find the girl. By the time he reached the altar the camp was almost empty, abandoned, the gatherers now scattered into the forest. A middle-aged man squatted in the corner of the far shelter, trembling in a thin cloak. The rest were gone, running through the moonlit undergrowth where Daneel and Yannick would be waiting.

He found the girl sitting behind the altar, rocking on her seat and humming tunelessly to herself whilst Arianna stroked her hair. The girl's eyes were still and empty, her expression as slack as a corpse. She wouldn't stop rocking.

"No need to thank me," Arianna said, looking up at him. "Had you waited any longer she'd be no more than roasted beef."

"I was about to do it."

Arianna rose to her feet, feigning a frown, before stepping toward him and smiling sourly. "Of course you were." She patted Neythan twice on the cheek and winked before walking away.

It was probably the thing Neythan found most annoying about her, how smug and dismissive she could be. As though the world owed her a kiss on the toes. Neythan was about to tell her that when out of the corner of his eye he saw the trembling man under the shelter rise to his feet, swaying and staggering as he did so. Maybe it was the anger from Arianna's barb, maybe it was something else, but by the time Neythan turned to see what the man was holding, he had, with barely a thought, levelled and loosed his crossbow, and in almost that same instant, watched the quarrel split the man's neck and lodge in his throat.

A perfect mark.

The dagger the man had been readying to hurl in Arianna's direction slid from his hand and clanked in the dust. The man took a step, pawed impotently at the shaft in his throat, and then collapsed.

Arianna turned and looked at Neythan.

Neythan stared at the man he'd felled.

No one spoke.

When Neythan eventually went to stand over him the man was already gone, his blood a dark puddle to one side of his slackened face. The eyes were half-open, everything they'd ever known or hoped now irrevocably expunged. Null. Forgotten. Although that wasn't really what unsettled Neythan. It was like the time he'd feared crane flies as a child, something about the way they'd fly, their legs dangling, like tiny drunken ghouls – until one night Yulaan had taken one, put it down the back of his smock and held him down. He'd screamed and kicked and wriggled until slowly realizing he couldn't feel it, not its dangly legs scrambling against his skin, nor its wings fluttering, nor any pain. Nothing. And that was what puzzled him now, this absence of feeling he'd expected to feel. His first time killing a man and he felt nothing. No fear. No joy. Nothing.

When Daneel and Yannick came wandering out from the forest's shadows an hour later the numbness was still there. Daneel, breathing hard, glanced at Neythan and then studied the slumped body of the governor first.

"So, this is him…" He then looked over at the dead priestess by the altar. "This one… I saw another just like her in the forest." He craned his neck for a better look. "No… Slightly younger maybe. Sister perhaps. Ran like a gazelle."

"So says the slug of the snail," Josef said, wiping his sword on the oil-drenched cowhides whilst Yannick stood off to the side, watching Neythan. Yannick flicked his hand and frowned, signing to him. Neythan nodded and shrugged back. He was fine.

"I mean it," Daneel said. "The woman was as quick as the wind. I had to use my sling to slow her." He turned to Neythan, glanced again at the governor's body, and smiled. "But what does it matter now? What matters is you got him, eh, Neythan? Your first. Governor Zaqeem."

"Actually, Arianna did that," Josef said as he came and stood next to Neythan.

Daneel's smile flattened. "Oh."

"Yes. Oh."

"But he did kill another," Arianna said. She gestured to the body slumped by the corner of the shelter, her gaze still on Neythan.

"That so?" Daneel put his hand on Neythan's shoulder. "So then you *have* done your first. Good. Finally. Well done. The first is always hardest."

For more great title recommendations,
check out the Angry Robot website and
social channels

www.angryrobotbooks.com
@angryrobotbooks